THE PRISONERS *of* ONERS ALLRED

LIFE AND DEATH UNDER THE TEXAS SYSTEM OF CRIMINAL JUSTICE

FINBAR MANGHAN, S.T.D.

CONTENTS

DEDICATION

_FOR THE MEN WHOSE SUFFERING AND IMPERILED LIVES
MADE THIS STORY NECESSARY_

A PRAYER

Lord, I pray that those who read these stories
May be led to perceive what is true, discern what
Is false, and then do what needs to be done.

AWAKE! Sleeping Souls

Awake sleeping Souls, as your rights are taken one by one;
And from that mansion foul, where tyranny sets her throne:
Like undisturbed dragons in their den, the world they plot
To enslave and destroy,
Forgetting they too are men, seeing our miseries with
Insidious joy.
They have made the world their prey,
while the instruments of cruelty they support
Are more murderous still than they:
Law enforcement and the Courts.
Awake ere you see your freedom and gains forever lost,
And you in prison, shackled in chains!

Carlos Ismael Rojas

WELCOME TO HELL!

Thirteen years old. On your way home from school in Costa Rica you are snatched from the street. Taken by plane with some other boys you find yourself somewhere outside of a town near Houston, Texas. A friendly guard who wants to use you as a "sex friend" warns you about taking drugs secretly placed in the food or drink of the other kids to erase their memories. Your group is taken to an office building in downtown Houston where you are used for sex orgies. One of the club members, an important Judge, finds out you have not been drugged and orders two men to take you to be executed and disposed of. Can this Hell really be happening?

FOREWORD

In 2002, I retired and engaged in prison ministry, where eventually I became a "CVAC", Certified Volunteer Assistant Chaplain. Over a period of about eight years I became acquainted with a number of men the Texas Department of Criminal Justice, "TDCJ", designates "Offenders." This book, in the main, tells the stories of four of these men, with a brief episode about a fifth.

I began work on the book in 2010. The men were unusually at risk, in one way or another, and I had the notion that if I could share their situation with the public, someone might take up their cause and try to help. The book was finished and self-published in 2014. I did not even attempt to submit the manuscript to a standard publisher because I knew, even if I did obtain a publisher, by the time the book came out it would be too late.

Since the book was published, other significant events occurred that complete the stories. The present work abridges much of the original version, while also adding vital details about each of the Offenders.

CHAPTER ONE

GUILTY UNTIL PROVEN INNOCENT

The Prelude

Our journey begins with the story of Carlos Rojas, imprisoned in the state of Texas in 2000. When we first met around 2004 he was fifty years old and had been locked up for five years. He was stocky and short, with a broad forehead descending to a pointed jaw, coal black hair (usually a bit disheveled) and a weathered, craggy, though not homely, face. It betrayed the stress of a hard life and the effects of his years of incarceration. He was born in Mexico, but became a world traveler. When he first came to the United States, he knew very little English. In his letter from the spring of 2011 Rojas recalled:

April 27, 2011:
"In 1972 I finished my high school in Mexico and I couldn't afford to go to College. I started working for a fishing company. That was a good job. I kept the accounts for the product. They had fishing boats to catch sharks. That company belonged to the government of Mexico.

"Then I heard of a College in Eagle Pass, Texas. Its name is 'Colegio Biblico'. I would have been happy if they would have taught at least one thing useful. Despite all of the religious nonsense, at least the English language would have been great to learn. With the exception of the choir, that was the only thing worth remembering."

In 1976 Carlos left the U.S. to volunteer to help people devastated by an earthquake in Guatemala. There he met some men who had come from Columbia to help. After a year he began working for IDES, International Disaster Emergency Service. Then he quit and worked for himself, building concrete houses. For almost two years he worked with artisans, learning the secrets of constructing beautiful furniture.

After venturing to Columbia, Venezuela, and all of Central America he found that in Cuba he could study for a career subsidized by the Cuban government in exchange for military service. Eventually he was selected to travel to the USSR to serve as a craftsman.

"We arrived in Moscow the day before Christmas, 1983," he writes, "and on January 2nd we flew to Vladivostok, Kamchatka. None of us knew why they had taken us so far, we thought we would be working in Moscow.

"The reality was that with the deployment of 120 thousand soldiers in Afghanistan, they were short-handed. The jobs they had for us were dangerous and top secret. We would not be allowed to leave the Soviet Union at any time, once we entered the Pacific Fleet of Vladivostok. I was making furniture for the nuclear submarines. Others were welders and painters and electricians. There were 150 in all, all Cubans. I was Mexican, but they counted me as Cuban.

"I left the Soviet Union in February, 1993, through Poland. I visited Auschwitz on June 27, a week after the Memorial Day of the Holocaust. My whole life I have been intrigued by the mere idea of the Holocaust. What evil instinct in human hearts could be capable of such barbarity? I arrived in Auschwitz on a cold day. Its sky was a steel gray, gray as the hearts of those who triggered the most heinous infamy in human history. I saw the hair, shoes, and the luggage of the victims who were transported to that place, not knowing the terrible fate that was waiting for them.

"I can never forget the date I saw written on one of the suitcases: November 25, 1943. I saw the gas chambers and the furnaces where the cadavers were disposed of. It's uncertain how many millions of children, Christian and Jewish children, perished in the Holocaust."

After traveling through Spain, Belgium and France, he arrived in Havana, Cuba, "…in time to start the 1994 school cycle of four years.…It wasn't history that I wanted to study, but [the course in] modern languages was not available and I had to be content with history."

Carlos ultimately made it to a major city near the Gulf Coast in Texas, where he was brought to work as an auto mechanic. When I asked how he came to learn this type of work, he wrote:

June 12, 2011:

"I started working on cars in Cuba, firstly on weekends while I studied in Santiago. They still keep running the old American models from the fifty's and sixty's, the only models that can be sold from one person to another are from 1959 and back. Yet they still import new models (Lada) from Russia, but only the elite possess the right to buy a new car."

"In Spain was where I worked full time on cars. They make a little car named Sea—similar to the German cars. In 1998 when I came back to Mexico [from Cuba], I worked in Laredo [Nuevo Laredo] as a mechanic. It was there I met that man who invited me to Texas to come to work for him. He paid the smuggler for me. I lived in Laredo about seven months **until I crossed and came to Texas in 1999**."

The Crime

In early August of 2000, Carlos was arrested. With no money for bail and no legal assistance, he was taken to the local county jail. A formal complaint, with an illegible Assistant District Attorney's signature, was filed on January 16, 2001, the same day a form in both English and

Spanish that waived the right of the accused to notify consular officials of the arrest was apparently signed by Carlos. He denies ever signing such a form.

Carlos remained in the county jail with virtually no visitation until he was brought to trial February 5, 2002. (The actual date of indictment was March 2, 2001). He had a sister in New York and a half-sister (daughter of his father) in Texas. The sister in New York supposedly sent $3,000 to the half-sister in Texas to obtain an attorney. She gave the money to a lawyer and he disappeared, having given no legal help.

Pre-Trial Motions

On February 5 the trial process began with a motion brought by Carlos to dismiss his court-appointed lawyer, Fernando Somoza.. Carlos argued that Mr. Somoza had rarely visited him and was doing little to protect his rights. Mr. Somoza replied that Carlos had already dismissed his first court-appointed lawyer, intimating that he was a troublesome client. Carlos also stated that the attorney had told him that persons Carlos had asked to be contacted to come to his support had said they were not interested. In contradiction to this Carlos had received a letter from one of these individuals stating she did want to help:

> "One of the persons they contacted wrote me and tells me, say the opposite to what Mr. Castro [assistant to Carlos's attorney, Fernando Somoza] told me. I have the letter here. And she (a Maria Nueces) says that she wants to help me. And he told me that she didn't want to do anything."

Mr. Somoza added that this person had not been subpoenaed because "Mr. Castro has informed me that the witnesses he had contacted were not interested in coming or were not able to come." Later it turned out that one of the possible witnesses was available at court, but was not called by Mr. Somoza, and Ms. Nueces did testify during the punishment phase as a character witness. The interesting thing about this exchange (not in front of the jury) is that Mr. Somoza is making out his own client to be a liar in front of the Judge.

The request for appointment of a new attorney was denied by the Judge, June Carlson, and the trial proceeded.

Somoza then recounted that Carlos had been made several offers (forty-five years, then thirty-five years, then twenty years). Carlos admitted that he had rejected the twenty year offer because he wished to go to trial to demonstrate his innocence. Somoza then asked Carlos to confirm that he had been instructed[1] that later he could decide whether or not he wished to testify in his own defense, but was warned that if he did, all kinds of accusations, true or false, could be entered against him[2] (Carlos is of a strong, fiery temperament with a keen sense of what is just. There is no way he would plead guilty to sexually assaulting two boys whom he had never seen. Also, at this point it seems he had the belief that surely in an American Court he would receive justice.)

There followed some confusion about the cases filed against Carlos. The prosecutor, a Jenny Ware (first licensed to practice law after her graduation from law school in 1998), explained that an original complaint had come from an Antonio Luzan. However, the trial was about another victim who came forward later, a Jose Lunes. (Luzan was introduced as a second victim in the punishment phase of the trial.)

Mr. Somoza then asked Carlos if he had explained to him that there were three cases against him, to which Carlos replied "No." It was repeated that there were three cases, and two of them involved the child [Lunes]. The pretrial motions ended here.

From this session it is evident that Carlos mistrusted his attorney, who continually presented his client in a bad light and was anything but diligent in attempting to secure witnesses who would help in his defense. Carlos's English was such that he had difficulty in understanding some of the process, and instructions were given that might later intimidate

---

[1]   Vol. II, 15:11. The trial transcript consisted of eight volumes. The present reference is to Volume II, page 15, line 11. Other documents included the Clerk's Record, the Reporter's Record, the Appellant's Brief and the Appellee Brief. Footnotes through number 137 refer to these Trial Transcript Volumes and follow this format.

[2]   Vol. II, 14:7.

him with regard to testifying in his own defense. While an interpreter was provided, it is clear from the trial record that she was not helpful.

Voir Dire (Jury Selection)

The procedure, also on February 5, opened in a rather peculiar way as the Judge noted one potential juror was missing. It was clear that the court and attorneys want this affair to move along quickly, so everyone could get on with other business.

A jury panel of sixty-five individuals was assembled. After the usual questioning period, the jury of twelve was selected. Only one had an apparently Hispanic name, a Carmela Gerontes. Ultimately even Ms. Gerontes was excused from the jury because she felt she could not be fair. Thus it appears there were no members of the jury with Latino ethnicity.

In the midst of the Voir Dire, Ms. Ware instructed the panel about the date of the offense "on or about July 12, 1997." She explained that "on or about" is very general. Anything within five years of that date would be sufficient. Why she belabored this point is rather mysterious, since in the course of the trial it is made clear that the assault occurred when the victim was in the third grade (1997). Perhaps if an alibi for 1997 somehow happened to surface during the trial, she would be prepared for a rebuttal.

An extremely significant element in the Voir Dire is the fact that **immediately after introducing himself to the panel**, Mr. Somoza stated "I know you're tired. I know it's cold and raining. I need your attention. I need your honesty. This man's life is at stake here. Please be up front with me. Ladies and gentlemen, **this is not a sexual assault case. It's a case of mistaken identity. To have...**" (emphasis added). Ms. Ware: "Objection, improper argument." The Court: "Sustained."[3] **The possibility of mistaken identity or an alibi for Mr. Rojas is never again mentioned at any point of the trial process.**

The overall impression left by the way the Voir Dire was conducted was to seat a jury that would be disposed to convict on the basis of the

---

[3]   Vol. III,130:16.

testimony of one witness alone, with **no physical evidence**, and to assess the maximum sentence of life.

The Trial (Volume IV of Transcript)

Jury selection was completed in one day and the trial began on February 6, 2002. A child victim services worker who had been working closely with the victim was to be allowed to stand next to him when he testified. Carlos's attorney entered a feeble objection, but it was overruled.

The trial continues before the jury with Ms. Ware charging that on or about July 12, 1997, Carlos "did then and there intentionally and knowingly…[the alleged sexual offense is described in detail but all graphic portrayals will be omitted]… Jose Lunes, a person younger than fourteen years of age and not the spouse of the defendant to []… of Carlos." (It is well known that vivid description of sexual assault on the part of prosecutors is quite successful in biasing the jury against defendants. This fact was not lost on Ms. Ware.)

Ware notes that the victim, Jose Lunes, is now fourteen, but was nine when he was assaulted. The family met Carlos because he was a mechanic, who offered to train Jose to work as a mechanic. Ware says the witness will testify that he was taken to the Carlos home, a one room house near downtown, with a jail gate on the front of the house. Ware goes on to describe many details of what will be Jose's testimony.

Mr. Somoza's opening statement informs the jury that he will ask them to acquit Mr. Rojas. He claims the victim will speak only in generalities (although he knows quite well the testimony, as already summarized by Ware, will be quite specific). He mentions there is no physical evidence, which is not in dispute, and brings his opening statement to an end. **There is no mention of a problem of mistaken identity or of an alibi.**

In his testimony[4] Jose states that he is now in the eighth grade and his family is from El Salvador. He is asked how old he was in 1997, but says he does not remember. He said he met Carlos through his

---

[4]   Vol. IV, 9 ff.

dad's friend, a **Jorge Santano.** Jose said he was supposed to be learning "mechanics" with Carlos, to work on car parts. He then said he was alone with Carlos "all the time." He went to the defendant's house on various Saturdays. He testifies this happened in the summer **after he had finished the Third Grade**. Although he says he was alone with the defendant "all the time" and went to the house on "Saturday, separate weeks, weekends"[5], he alleges the first rape took place at the time of the first visit to Mr. Rojas' house.

He was asked how big the house was, but did not remember. He was asked how many rooms it had, but did not remember. When asked what he first saw when he got to the house, he said "Saw a white door and it had like one of those jail door looking kind of doors." Asked "Was that on the inside or outside of the house?" he answered "Inside." (One wonders why a door with bars would be inside the front door?)

Jose stated Carlos locked the door and he immediately became afraid, thinking Carlos might kill him or do "stuff" to him. He said Carlos said he was going to rape him and was told not to be afraid, rape was a good thing. Asked what furniture was in the room, he said only a table and chair. Ms. Ware then prompted him: "Was there any sort of bed or sofa or anything like that?" He replied "He had a sofa—I mean, a bed on the corner."

Asked to describe what happened, Jose says Carlos made him []. After this, he told Jose he was going to rape him. (Only a few statements earlier Jose said that Carlos had told him this as soon as they entered the room and he locked the door.)

Noting the inconsistency, Ware asked "Was that the first time he told you that or the only time he told you that?" Jose seems to have picked up the clue that he had not answered quite correctly and said "He told me like three times that…when I was in his lap." This did not quite manage to correct the original statement, but who would notice?

The questioning continues "After he had you lay down on the bed [sexual assault]…

---

[5]   Vol. IV,23.

When asked why he didn't tell anyone later about what had happened,[6] he said Carlos had threatened him. He thought Carlos meant he would be killed. Ware asks: "were you afraid just for yourself or were you afraid for other people?" Somoza: "I object, that's leading, Your Honor." Ware: "Doesn't imply the answer, just trying to clarify what his feelings were." The Court: "Overruled on that particular question." (This was the only time Somoza objected during the testimony of the boy.) Ware: "When he told you that, were you scared for yourself or for other people?" Jose: "For my mom, my dad."

Jose says he saw the defendant at least two more times and was alone with him one more time.[7] Nothing is said here about a second sexual assault. He claimed he finally told someone about these assaults before New Year's on 2001 because some "guy" was talking about the coming of the end of the world. He went to the bedroom with his mom, and told her everything.

He then talked to the police and the officer took him to identify the house. Ware: "Were you ever able to show where the house was that this defendant had hurt you in?" Jose: "Yes. But, like it wasn't there no more. It was some other bigger house."[8]1

He was asked if he was ever shown any photographs. Jose: "His photo. The guy's photo. She talked—she talked to me and she told me I'm going to show you a photo and tell me who it is." Amazingly, Jose, who can't remember how old he was when the crime happened remembers the name of this officer "some lady called Drummond."[9] Ware prompts: " Was there one photo or a lot of photos?" Jose: "There were a lot of photos. They were like in manila folders." Ware: "Do you remember how many folders there were of photos?" Jose: "She showed me three, like—there were three folders but the first one, he was in there." Jose then identifies Carlos as the man in the photo he picked out.

The witness is passed and the cross-examination begins. Somoza asks Jose if he ever lies. Ware objects that the line of questioning is

---

6   Vol. IV, 35:22.

7   Vol. IV, 38:19.

8   Vol. IV, 40:25.

9   Vol. IV, 41:19.

irrelevant. The Judge sustains her objection. Somoza then gets Jose to agree that there is no physical evidence of the violation. Then Somoza: "Now, I want you to understand, Mr. Rojas is not taking a position whether you were violated or not, he is simply..." Ware: "Objection." Somoza: "He is saying he didn't do..." Ware: "Objection. That is not a question, Judge." The Court: "Sustained." Whatever line of questioning Somoza was attempting, he was again cut off and drops it.

> Question by Somoza[10]: **"How much time passed from the last time you're saying that you were violated and you saw Mr. Rojas again, more or less?** [emphasis is in transcript]"….A: Later. A year later. Q: During this one year, more or less, did you see any therapists? A: Huh-uh (negative). No sir. Q: Did you see any school counselor? A: Yes. Q: When you saw the counselor, what would you talk about? A: Like school and what's happening in my house, my home. Q: You're saying that you liked history. Correct?" A: Yes, sir. Q: After this incident, were your grades still good in history? A: They were average. Q: Were they average before this incident? A: Yes. Q: So in history, nothing changed, correct? A: A little bit."

[The time sequence is significant here. According to the foregoing testimony, we are more than a year past the time of the incident. Since it was alleged to have happened in the summer after Jose completed the third grade, this places us around the summer after the fourth grade. At this point Jose says he has seen a school counselor, but does not mention a serious deterioration of his grades. Later his mother will testify that his grades fell sharply during the third grade, **which would be before the incident.**][11]

In subsequent cross-examination, Somoza helps the alleged victim explain how he was able to pick out the photo of Carlos, why the house of Carlos was no longer there, and how he wanted someone to pay for

---

[10]   Vol. IV, 47:10.

[11]   Vol. IV, 68:22.

the guilt he felt because of Carlos, all of which helped strengthen the case of the prosecution.

Questioned about the date of the incident, Jose states "I remember what grade was it like after—like what grade I finished when this happened. I just remember that. I don't know what year was it. I don't know the year and the month and the date, exactly, I just remember what year, what grade I finished, what—I just know I finished third grade when this happened, in the summer."

Mr. Somoza passes the witness.

Ms. Ware conducts a re-direct in order to clean up the testimony about the photos, to make sure no one thinks Jose was led to pick a particular photo.

Mr. Somoza in his re-cross:

> "Mr. Lunes, while ago [sic] when I asked you when you were looking at the photo spreads, didn't you tell me you were led to believe the bad guy was in there? ...While ago [sic] when I asked you this, you said you were led to believe that. Are you changing your story now? Jose: No. Somoza: Okay. So you were not led to believe ... Jose: I just recognized him."

Somoza has thus helped to establish in the mind of the jury that the victim was not led, and passes the witness.

Flora Rodriguez, the mother of Jose Lunes, is called to the stand.

> Q: "Was there ever a period of time where Jose was having problems in school? A: Yes. Q: Do you remember when that was? A: He started from '97 forward. Q: When did Jose first meet the defendant in this case? A: It was at the beginning of '97."[12]

...Mrs. Rodriguez explained that they had met Carlos through Jorge Santano, a friend of the family. She said she told Mr. Rojas he could teach Jose because he was on vacation.

---

[12]   Vol. IV, 60ff.

Q: "Why did you agree to let Jose learn the trade of mechanics? A: Well, for starters, I said it was okay because to begin with, he was from our country. Q: What country is that? A: From El Salvador. Q: What about that made you trust him? A: Precisely because we come from the place I felt—I trusted him."

[In point of fact, Rojas was a citizen of Mexico. Mrs. Rodriguez has supposedly known Carlos for months, trusts him to be alone with her son, but does not know his last name or that he is a native of Mexico. Subsequently we shall see an affidavit from Mr. Santano stating clearly that Carlos is from Mexico and **never laid eyes on Jose until the day of the trial!**]

...Q: "What year did the defendant start to teach your son mechanics? A: In that year, '97. Q: Do you remember what month it was they started to spend time together away from your house? A: From July forward. Q: How many times do you remember Jose going off alone with the defendant? A: About four or five times.

...Q: When did the defendant stop seeing Jose alone? A: Until some point my husband heard at a parts shop that this man was a raper or rapist. Q: When did you hear that? A: I didn't hear that, my husband heard that."

[Since this testimony reflects very negatively on the defendant, one might expect an objection of "Hearsay," but no such objection was raised.]

...Q: "After Jose stopped seeing the defendant, how did Jose's behavior change?" [The question should have been: "Did Jose's behavior change?", and an objection could have been raised here, as many other places, "Leading question," but there was no objection] A: "Very rebellious, very aggressive. Q: Did he ever get in trouble after that time, that summer? A: He gave me a lot of trouble at school. ...**Q: How was Jose doing in school in third grade? A: Very badly. His grades were dropping.**"

> Mrs. Rodriguez is asked when Jose began to see the school counselor. A: "He began to see the counselor at the beginning of '94. Q: Was that before or after he met the defendant? A: Afterwards. Q: So when you say '94, are you sure that was before or after '97? A: After." [In 1994 Jose would have been in kindergarten or the first grade!]

In his cross-examination, Somoza asks Mrs. Rodriguez about the process of identifying Rojas at the police station.

> Q: "When you went to the police station and looked at photos, isn't the reason you picked out Mr. Rojas is because you already knew him? A: No." Mrs. Rodriguez has already testified that she knew Carlos during 1997, so Mr. Somoza has to correct her testimony: Q: "But you knew Mr. Rojas already? A: Yes. Q: So it would have been easy to identify him; isn't that true? A: Yes. Somoza: **Pass the witness, Your Honor.**" [Once again the defense attorney has helped clarify a witness' testimony and reinforce the prosecution.]

At the conclusion of this testimony the trial recessed for lunch. During the break the Judge met with juror Carmela Gerontes. She had become so upset she asked to be released from the jury. Her request was granted and she was replaced by an alternate juror. When the trial resumed, Officer Sylvia Drummond was called to the stand and questioned about how she got Jose to identify Rojas as the perpetrator from a set of photos.

> Ms. Ware, the prosecutor, asks her "Why had you presented him [Jose] this group of photos? What were you investigating? A: Okay. What I was investigating is the fact that the family knew the defendant as an acquaintance and didn't know him by his true name. Q: What name did they know him by? A: Just the first name of Carlos and they also knew him by the term 'the mechanic.'"[13]

---

[13]   Vol. IV, 101:16.

[So, again we hear that the family had known Carlos for more than a year, said they trusted him because he, like them, was from El Salvador, let him go alone with their nine year-old boy a number of times, but did not know his common last name of Rojas.]

Somoza passes the witness, followed by Ms. Ware's statement that the State rests. Then THE COURT: "**Thank you. Mr. Somoza?**" To which Somoza replies "**The defense rests, Your Honor.**"[14] Mr. Somoza does not utter one word or submit any evidence or call even a single witness on behalf of Carlos Rojas. He could have called Carlos to the stand to speak in his own defense, to tell the jury that in 1997 he was teaching in Cuba, but he did not do so. We saw earlier—in the pre-trial phase—that Carlos was told he would have a chance later to decide whether or not he wanted to testify. There is nothing in the trial record to indicate this opportunity was ever given. (Later we shall see how Carlos was persuaded by his attorney not to testify, so that an independent witness could testify that he did not come to the United States until 1999. This witness came to Court, but was put in a waiting room and never called.)

In his closing argument Somoza rambles rather incoherently. He states "I don't have any evidence to present to you."[15] He notes that Jose became very specific in his testimony. He asks "How did that happen? How did that change? How did a metaphorist [sic] happen? That's reasonable doubt."[16] Somoza knows very well that the testimony of the alleged crime was going to be very specific and there was no change on the stand. Thus, his vacuous argument for "reasonable doubt" will have no credibility with the jury.

He then submits a modestly more persuasive argument: "Maybe the house was never there. Maybe this young man is just plain wrong. Mr. Lunes [Jose] himself said his favorite class is history. His grades stayed the same. Yet, other people are saying his grades changed. What is the truth? We don't know. He says it had no impact on him. What

---

14   Vol. IV, 114;13.
15   Vol. IV, 116:7.
16   Vol. IV, 116:19.

is the truth? That's reasonable doubt."[17] "Before, he stated it was only contact [sexually graphic comment deleted; Somoza does not deny the offense here, but attempts to mitigate it slightly] …What is the truth? We don't know."[18]

Later Somoza observes about Mrs. Rodriguez "She claimed that Rojas was from El Salvador. He is not." To which Ms. Ware intervenes **"Objection, Your Honor, going into evidence that's not been introduced in the trial.** THE COURT: **"Thank you. The jury will remember the evidence that's been introduced in the trial."**[19]

The fact that Rojas was from Mexico and not El Salvador and the possibility that he was in Cuba and not Texas in 1997 are vital elements to his defense. Why were they not brought into the trial? It is also significant that in his closing defense, Somoza does not argue that Carlos did not and could not have committed the offense, but directs his argument to secondary factors such as the impact of the crime on Jose—or touch rather than penetration—all of which seem to concede that a crime was committed by Carlos.

In her closing argument, Ms. Ware remarks "And we talked about how a child might change. They might be shy, as you saw Jose on the stand. They might misbehave. His behavior changed after he started seeing this defendant. He started acting out. He hurt himself. He did those things. Is he going to—" Somoza: **Objection, Your Honor, he never claimed that."** THE COURT: **Overruled. Overruled.**

After trying to dismiss in the jury's mind some of the inconsistencies in the testimony of Jose and his mother, Ware goes on to try to rescue uncertainty about the date: "The date is not an issue. It could have happened in '96. It could have happened in '98. Under the law it doesn't matter. Although you heard testimony from both Jose and his mother they believed it happened in the summer after third grade, which by his mother's calculations, and the calculations that Jose gave you here

---

[17]   Vol. IV, 118:1.
[18]   Vol. IV, 118:11.
[19]   Vol. IV, 119:8.

in Court that he is now in eighth grade, would put it at least four years ago, approximately back in 1997."[20]

If one recalls the testimony, the witnesses were quite clear that the first incident occurred during the summer after the third grade. Not one year earlier, or one year later. In any case, if Carlos did not enter the country until 1999, he could not have assaulted Jose during the broad time-frame claimed by Ware.

Ware finishes her remarks, which the Court's minutes say began on Feb. 6, 2002 at 2:52 p.m. The jury then "returned into open Court at 3:26 p.m. with a Verdict of 'Guilty' as charged in the indictment." That is, it took the jury only about twenty-five minutes to reach its verdict.[21]

According to the minutes, the trial began on Feb. 5, 2002. At 11:19 a.m., a jury panel of sixty-five "good men and women" was seated. After lunch, the state Voir Dire began at 1:45 p.m. Defense began at 2:43 p.m. At 5:25 p.m. a jury panel of twelve, plus one alternate, was seated, and instructed to return at 10:00 a.m. on Feb. 6.

This phase of the trial began at 10:20 a.m. After being released for lunch, ninety minutes later (11:50 a.m.) the jury resumed at 1:50 p.m., with juror Carmela Gerontes being excused in the meantime. The state rested at 2:09 p.m. The defense immediately rested and the jury retired to the jury room to review the charge. Thus, the core of the trial (testimony and closing statements) lasted a total of one hour and fifty-four minutes. In contrast, it took three hours and twenty minutes just to select the jury. Again, the jury was able to reach its verdict in twenty-five minutes! The transcript of the trial runs 129 pages, compared with 261 pages for the jury selection. In the old days, a lynching might have required more time and effort.

Questions Not Asked, Thus Never Answered (Part I)

Why didn't Somoza, after asserting the possibility of "mistaken identity" and being cut off during the Voir Dire, bring this up during the guilt

---

[20]   Vol. IV, 126:6.
[21]   Vol. I, Clerks's Record 99.

phase of the trial or mention the possibility of an alibi (Carlos' being in Cuba)?

When Jose testified that he went with Carlos "all the time" or on many weekends, but the rape occurred the first time, why didn't Somoza ask Jose why he kept going with Carlos after the first time?

When Jose testified that the house had a white door but also had a jail-like door, which was on the **inside** of the house, why didn't Somoza ask him how he could see this jail-like door from outside the house when he first approached it?

Why didn't Somoza question Jose again about what was in the room? Why didn't Jose immediately mention the bed? Was he sure there was only one bed in the room? Since Carlos had always been kind to him, taking him to Go-Karts, buying him food, teaching him how to work on cars, why did he **immediately** think Carlos might kill him when he said he locked the door?

Jose said Carlos told him he was going to rape him almost as soon as they entered the room. Later he said that Carlos told him this after he was sitting on his lap. Why didn't Somoza ask him which was it?

Somoza could have asked Jose why he used the term []… Where did he learn that legally precise sexual term?

Somoza might also be asked, why during the entire testimony of Jose—in spite of many leading questions on the part of the prosecution— he objected only one time.

Jose testified that the home of Carlos was no longer there when they went with the police to find it in 2001.[22] Somoza had from May of 2001 to the time of the trial, February, 2002, to use discovery to identify the location of the alleged offense and verify it. He would simply need to check the specific address of the house (which was never given in the trial) and determine the date of construction of the home existing on the property in 2001. County records would also show any formerly existing home at that location. This was never done, so naturally Somoza could not challenge Jose's testimony about the house.

---

[22] Vol. IV, 54.

Why is Somoza the first one to emphasize that the rape supposedly happened **twice**?

Why didn't Somoza question Jose's mother about why she let him go so often with Carlos, when they didn't even know his last name. Why did she say he was from El Salvador, when in fact he was a citizen of Mexico? Why didn't Somoza probe Carlos' country of origin at this time?

Mrs. Rodriguez testified that Jose was only with Carlos on four or five Saturdays, but Jose had said it was most weekends. Why didn't Somoza challenge her on how frequently they supposedly met?

Why didn't Somoza point out that when Mrs. Rodriguez said Jose's grades were dropping in the **third** grade, this was **before** the alleged crime? Jose testified that even **after** the incident his grades (at least in history) remained "average." Only after more prompting did he add that he did not do well on the TASP test.[23] This inconsistency of testimony was ultimately only lightly mentioned by Somoza in his closing statement.

When Somoza, in his closing statement, tries to point out that Carlos is not from El Salvador, he is silenced by Ms. Ware and the Judge on the basis that this was not "in evidence". Why didn't Somoza make sure it was part of the trial evidence?

Punishment Phase

On the 6th of February, 2002, the same day as the trial, punishment proceedings began. In her opening statement, Ms. Ware tells the jury they will hear about things they could not hear about during the trial. They will be told that Carlos assaulted Jose a second time, within one week of the first offense. They are also going to hear about an assault on a second child, Antonio Luzan. Ms. Ware says he was eleven years old in February, 2002, but was nine years old when abused. She says this offense occurred "about a year after the incident with Jose."[24] [If so, this would have been in 1998 and Antonio would have been seven years old.]

---

23   Vol. IV, 48.
24   Vol. V, 6:23.

She adds that Antonio waited about two years before he told anyone. Clearly, the numbers used by Ms. Ware don't jibe. If the crime happened when Jose was nine years old, it would have been in the year 2000, three years after the alleged assault of Jose. If it happened in 1998, one year after the Jose assault/s, and Antonio was nine years old, then in 2002, the time of the trial, he would be thirteen. The point of this observation is that the District Attorney was extremely casual about her dates, and no one objected.

The opening statement of Mr. Somoza is extremely brief and subtly implies that he believes the jury was justified in its decision: "Ladies and gentlemen, *Mr. Rojas and I are disappointed but we understand* [italics added by Court reporter] and respect your decision. Perhaps this is an even harder part is determining the punishment [sic]. Like the first part of the trial, there is going to be little or no physical evidence. And we're going to be asking in your deliberations when you go back there, to temper punishment with mercy and compassion and consider the fact as previously stated, there is no hard evidence here. I thank you for your time."[25]

The state called Jose Lunes, the trial victim. Before his examination begins, the Judge asked the jury where it went to lunch and complimented it on its choice.[26] To some, this type of chatting on the part of the Judge might seem out of place when the fate of a man's life hangs in the balance.

Jose testifies now (not in the trial) that the defendant took him to his house on a separate weekend, **one week after the first time**. Jose says it was at the house. He said that the same thing was done to him as before and he could not get out of the house because Carlos locked the steel gate. [Recall that this house with its gate was never found. During the guilt/innocence phase of the trial, under direct examination Jose says he met with the defendant alone one time after the first incident, but does not say he was raped. Then, in the cross-examination the defense attorney mentions a "fact" not yet in evidence that there was a second assault,[27] to which the victim agrees.

---

25   Vol. V, 7:21 to 8:6.
26   Vol. V, 8:15.
27   Vol. V, 47:16.

Jose testified that the defendant took some cream and [sexually graphic material]…"[28] [Once again, the legal preciseness of this term in the mouth of a fourteen year-old boy makes one wonder. He seems to be repeating words that Ms. Ware uses first.]

During his direct testimony in the first part of the trial, Jose stated that on the very first occasion he was "scared" to go into the house with Carlos, because he might do some stuff to him or even kill him.[29] . Yet one week later, without protest, he goes to Go Karts and the house with Carlos, only to be raped again? **No one questions Jose as to why he was willing to do this.**

> Jose is asked what happened after the act, and he says "He went to take a shower." Q: "Where was the bathroom in relation to the bed?" A: "It was separate. Like—it was like **in the room**, like a regular restroom [30]. [Recall that in the original testimony he testified that the restroom was "separate"[31]. Nothing was said about a shower.]
>
> Subsequently, Ware asks: "When you talked to her [when he told his mother what had happened] did you tell her about both times or just one time? A: One time. Q: When did you tell people about the second time? A: When I started talking with Officer Drummond." [32]

To say the least, the state is rather clumsy in trying to establish that there were two assaults, only one week apart. For some inexplicable reason, Jose, who becomes so eager to get everything off his chest to his mother, does not tell her there were two rapes, but does tell an officer whom he has just met, when the issue was not how many crimes were committed, but whether he could pick out a photo.

Ware passes the witness and Somoza commences a cross-examination that consists of only nine brief questions. He asks Jose to confirm that

---

[28]   Vol. V, 14:4.

[29]   Vol. V, 25:7.

[30]   Vol. V, 15:16.

[31]   Vol. IV, 27:12.

[32]   Vol. V, 20:12-18.

he was never struck by the defendant (implying to the jury that Carlos raped the victim but did not hit him). He goes on to reiterate that no physical violence was involved. Somoza does ask: "He didn't call you [for the year subsequent to the incidents], didn't ask your mother can he come work with me? A: No. Somoza: That's all I have Judge."

Proceedings were halted for the day and the jury was instructed to return on Friday. However, due to an illness of one juror, the punishment phase did not resume until Monday, February 11.

DA Ware prepares to call Antonio Luzan to the stand. She says he is eleven years old and asks that Ms. Constanza, the social worker, be allowed to stand next to him. The Judge compliments Ms. Constanza on how well she behaved in the first part of the trial and permits her to sit next to Antonio.

When the jurors return, the Judge greets them "…welcome back on this beautiful day." One might consider this somewhat odd, as their task was to decide the fate of a man's life. Mr. Somoza mentions to the Court that he has two witnesses and they will need an interpreter.

> Ware calls the witness to the stand and asks him his name. A: "Antonio Rivera. Q: Do you ever go by Antonio Luzan? A: Sometimes. Q: Where does the name Luzan come from in your family? A: I don't know. Q: Okay. And how old are you? A: Twelve. Q: When did you turn twelve? A: October 29. (About three months earlier)….Q: And what grade are you in? A: Sixth…..Q: And what is your favorite class? A: Math.
>
> Q: "I want to talk to you a little bit about some things that happened in 1998, like around September of that year. A: Okay. Q: Or in the summer. Were you in school that summer, 1998? A: I don't remember. Q: Do you ever remember meeting somebody by the name of Carlos Rojas? A: Yes, ma'am. Q: When did you meet that man? A: I don't know. I don't remember. Q: Do you remember what season it was, what time of year at all? A: It probably was April. Q: And why do you think it might have been April? A: Because I think it was summer. I think —I don't think I was going to school.[33]

---

[33] Vol. VI, 8 to 12.

Q: "And how did you first meet him [Carlos] A: By my friend. Q: What friend was that? A: Hector. Q: How old was your friend, Hector?" A: Probably like thirteen or fourteen. Q: How long have you known Hector for? A: I don't remember. Q: Had it been a long time or short time? A: Probably like a long time. Q: So did you ever go places with Carlos? A: Yes. Q: What sorts of places did you go to with Carlos? A: Like where you get parts off cars. Q: Do you remember what part of town it was that you went to get the car parts? A: Used to be like anywhere or something like that. Q: So when you went off with Carlos, did anybody ever come with you? A: Yes. Q: Hector." Q: Did Hector know Carlos first or did you know Carlos first? A: Hector knew Carlos first.

Q: "So how often did you go to the Go Kart place with Carlos? A: Probably like once—once a week. Q: Do you remember how long you knew Carlos for, how much time you spent in contact with him? A: No. Q: Was it more than a month or less than a month? A: More than a month. Q: When you would go to play Go Karts with Hector and with Carlos, did Carlos ever ask you to do anything else with him? A: Yes. Q: What else did he ask you to do with him? A: He will tell us like []…and I will give you free tokens. Q: When did he first ask you to do that? A: The first time he told Hector to tell me. Q: Who asked you the first time if they could do that to you? A: Hector.

Q: "What did you say when Hector asked you if Carlos could touch you? A: I said no. Q: Did Carlos ever offer you anything else to try to ask you if he could touch you? A: Cigarettes. That's when I said yeah. Q: So, when he offered you cigarettes, what did you agree to do? A: To let him []… Q: Where were you when you made this agreement? A: The place that—when Hector told me. Q: Was—what kind of a place was that? A: It was kind of close to here. It was that way. I don't remember the street (indicating). Q: Were you inside or outside? A: Outside.

Q: "When Carlos asked you to do this, where did y'all go at that point? A: To his house. Q: Do you remember what part of town Carlos' house was in? A: By [] county jail. Q: So, was it near downtown or where was it? A: Near downtown. Q: What did the house look like? A: It was behind an old lady's house.[34] Q: How big was the house? A: Smaller than this room. Q: Smaller than this room? How many rooms were there in the house? A: Just one. Q: What sort of furniture was in the house? A: Beds, couch, a drawer, and probably a bathroom and kitchen. Q: How old were you when this was going on, do you remember? A: Like eight or so. Q: So was it a few years ago that this happened? A: Probably. Q: When you went to the house, was there anything unusual about the door that you noticed? A: It didn't have a doorknob.[35] Q: Was there anything else about the door that you noticed? A: No.

Q: "What happened when you first went into the house? A: He told us to take our clothes off. Q: When you say us, who are you talking about? A: Me and Hector. Q: So, when he asked you to take your clothes off, what did you and Hector do? A: No, ma'am. The first time that he asked me to do that—[36]. Q: Un-huh (affirmative). A: —We went to the hotel. Q: Okay. Let's talk about the first time then. What hotel did you go to? A: I don't remember. Q: Do you remember what part of town it was in? A: No. Q: Was it here in [] County? Was it kind of near to your home or anything? A: Kind of near to my home. Q: Who went with you to the hotel? A: Me, Carlos, and Hector.

Q: "[At the hotel] And what was the defendant, Carlos, doing when you and Hector were taking a bath? A: He was in the bed. Q: After you took a bath with Hector, what did you do at that point? A: Told us to lay on the bed. Q: So, who all was [sic] laying on the bed at that point? A: Me, Hector, and Carlos." [Note: Assuming the Court reporter has recorded their exact words, both Ms. Ware and the victim always use incorrect grammar when referring to the position of those

---

[34]   Vol. VI, 19:13.

[35]   Vol. VI, 20:5.

[36]   Vol. VI, 20:16.

on the bed, saying "laying on the bed"[37] instead of "lying on the bed." This would not be significant if not for the fact that the "victim" has a pattern of repeating words used by the prosecutor, suggesting leading and coaching of the witness.]

Q: "And what did Carlos do when you laid down on the bed? A: He—he told me to—he was going to []… Q: How did that make you feel when he did that? A: A little bit uncomfortable. Q: Were you wearing any clothes when that happened? A: No. Q: Was Carlos wearing any clothes when it happened? A: I don't remember.

Q: "Okay, Antonio. One second. What were you given to go to the hotel room with Carlos and Hector? Were you given anything to do that? A: How? Q: I mean, did he reward you? Did the defendant give you anything or reward you at all for going to the hotel room? A: No, ma'am. Q: Did you tell your mom or brothers what had happened to you that day? A: No ma'am. Q: Because he had told me not to tell nobody. Q: Who told you not to tell anybody? A: Carlos. Q: Why did you feel like you can't tell anybody? A: Because I was kind of scared. Q: What were you scared of? A: Probably Carlos doing something to me. Q: When did you next see Carlos after that first day you went to the hotel? A: Probably the next day. Q: What happened the next day? A: I don't know. Q: Did Carlos touch you at all the next day? A: Sometimes.

Q: "Was there another time when Carlos touched you in a way that made you feel uncomfortable? A: Yes. Q: Do you remember how much later that was from the day you went to the hotel? A: No, ma'am. Q: Let's talk about that second time. A: Okay. Q: The second time it happened, did anybody ask you to do anything that day? A: How? Q: Did anybody ask you if they could touch you in a way that would make you feel uncomfortable? A: Yes. Q: Who asked you? A: It was Carlos, I think. Q: And what did Carlos ask you to do? A: He—just to let him []… Q: What did you say

---

[37]   Vol. VI, 22:9;23:4;30:20;31:11;33:9.

when he asked you to do that? A: I said, yeah. Q: Why did you say yes? A: Because that time he offered me cigarettes.[38]

Q: "Who was with you that second time that Carlos asked you if he could do that? A: Hector. Q: Did Carlos ask Hector to do anything? A: He used to do the thing, like to him. Q: The second time, where did you go? A: To his house. Q: Is that the house you described to us a little earlier? A: "Yes, ma'am. Q: What did you do after you and Hector too off your clothes? A: He told us to lay on the bed. Q: How many beds were in the house? A: Two. Q: So who laid where? A: Me and Carlos laid on one bed and Hector laid on the other bed. Q: What was Hector doing on the other bed? A: Smoking. Q: So, you're laying on your side, where is Carlos laying? A: In the back in the—like direction. ....Q: And what part of his body touched your body? []... Q: Did he []...? A: I don't know.

Q: "So when you say you changed beds, where did you go? A: I went to the other bed and Hector came where I was laying.....Q: And did you ever see Carlos touch Hector? A: Yes, ma'am. Q: How did Carlos touch Hector? A: The way he did to me.....Q: So what were you doing while Carlos was touching Hector? A: Smoking.....Q: What happened after Carlos stopped touching Hector? A: We changed again. Q: Then what happened? A: The thing. ....Q: What happened after Carlos stopped touching you the second time that day? A: Hector came to bed again.....Q: After Hector was with Carlos for the second time, what happened at that point? A: I think I went to the restroom.

....Q: "So after Carlos took two turns with you and two turns with Hector, what did he do? A: I think we put our clothes back on. Q: And where did you go? A: Fix a car. (Citations present highlights of the testimony and omit questions/answers that have lesser significance.)[39]

Q: "Did you ever tell your mom what Carlos had done to you? A: Yes. Q: When did you tell your mom? A: I don't

---

[38]   Vol. VI, 29:17.

[39]   Vol VI, 13-35.

remember.....Q: More than a week. Why did you first start talking to your mom about it? A: Because one day I was playing basketball and this man asked me who did I live with, and I got scared by that.....Q: The man who asked you where he—he—you lived, did you recognize him? A: He was my next door neighbor. Q: Did he know Carlos at all? A: No. Q: So why were you scared when he asked you that? A: I don't know.

Q: "When you got scared because he [the next door neighbor] asked you where you lived, what did you do? A: I just went in.....Q: Where did you talk with your mom? A: My room. Q: What did you tell your mom about? A: I told her the whole story. ....Q: So your mom called the police pretty quick? A: Yes. Q: After you talked with your mom and you talked with the police officers, did you ever see Carlos again? A: No ma'am. Q: Did he ever stop by and try to see you or talk to anybody about what happened? A: He stopped by my home. Q: When did he stop by? A: Yeah, I did see him once. Q: When did you see him that one time after you talked to your mom? A: It was like two days after I talked to the police and my mom. Q: Where did you see Carlos? A: He came and knocked on my door.[40]

....Q: "When you slammed the door on Carlos, what happened at that point? A: My mom said, no, let's get his license plate. Q: Why were you trying to get his license plate? A: So the police can know his last name and like catch up to him. Q: What name did you know him by? A: Just Carlos. Q: Did you know his last name at all? A: No.[41] ....Q: Was Carlos driving a car at that point? A: Yes. Q: Do you remember what the car looked like? A: No, I didn't really see it. Q: Were you able to get a license plate number? A: Yes. Q: How did you get that license plate number? A: When he was leaving, we saw out the window and we wrote it down.[42]

---

[40]   Vol. VI, 46:2.

[41]   Vol. VI, 47:6.

[42]   Vol. VI, 47:14-23.

….[At police headquarters] Q: "Did anybody ever show you any photographs? A: Yes. Q: Who showed you photographs? A: The police. Q: Do you remember how many photographs they showed you A: It was like four lines of four [that would be 16]. Q: So do you remember how many that was altogether? A: Eight. [Consider that math is Antonio's favorite subject,[43] he is in the sixth grade and his mother will later claim that he is now an honors student.]

….Q: "Before they showed you the photographs, did the police officer tell you anything, give you any instructions or anything? A: How? Q: Did they tell you how to do this at all? A: They told me to pick a photo that looks like Carlos or that is Carlos." [This rather sounds as if Antonio was guided to pick the "right" photo.][44]

Mr. Somoza's cross-examination: He begins with several questions to reinforce the idea that although Carlos may have raped the boy, he did not use a knife, or gun, or baseball bat to enforce his will. He goes on to establish again in the jury's mind that the offense happened two or more times:

Q: "After—you're saying the next weekend that this happened again, after that, wasn't that the last time? A: I don't remember. Q: Well, wouldn't you agree with me that you're saying here today that it happened on two successive weekends or two days and that was it? A: It was more than two. Q: Okay. How many times? A: I don't remember. Mr. Somoza: Pass the witness, Your Honor."[45] [Note that in spite of all the inconsistencies or weaknesses in Antonio's testimony, Somoza does not challenge anything.]

The state next calls Marta Rivera Luzan, Antonio's mother.

---

[43] Vol. VI, 10:9.

[44] Vol. VI, 49:5.

[45] Vol. VI, 51-52.

Q: "Do you remember what year it was that you lived in La Casita? A: '98. Q: How did you first meet the defendant? A: He would go to La Casita to look for another boy. Q: What was the name of that other boy? A: Hector. Q: How old was Hector? A: Ten or 11.[46] [Antonio had said he was "probably about thirteen or fourteen".][47]

....Q: "Who first introduced you to the defendant? A: Hector. Q: When you met the defendant, did he ever ask to spend time with Antonio? A: Yes. Q: What did he ask Antonio to do? A: That Antonio—for Antonio to go with this person. Because he works on mechanics and it was to teach him.....Q: How much time did he spend with Antonio, the defendant? A: Not a lot of time. Two or three hours. Q: About how often? A: Once or twice a week. Q: How many weeks did the defendant spend time with Antonio? A: Not a lot of time because sometime [sic] Antonio would look at him and his gesture was of rejection. [Again we see the strange circumstance where a mother allows her young son to meet at least several times with the defendant, if not more, and yet does not even know his full name, even after her son reacts "badly" to him.][48]

....Q: "Let me go back and try to figure out something about the timeline. Okay? How long did you live at La Casita? A: About two years. Q: Do you remember when it was that you moved from La Casita to the next apartment complex? A: January 21 of 1999.....Q: When did Antonio stop spending time with the defendant? A: In '98. Q: So altogether, how many months did Antonio spend time with the defendant? A: It was about two or three months, something like that. Q: How old was Antonio when he was seeing the defendant? A: He was about seven or eight years old.[49]

....Q: "Did Antonio's school work change at all? A: Yes. Q: How did his school work change? A: He was violent

---

[46]   Vol. VI, 54:6-15.

[47]   Vol. VI, 14:2.

[48]   Vol. VI, 54-56.

[49]   Vol. VI, 57:1-18.

with everybody, and his grades dropped. He would shout at his teachers, everything. Q: What did you do to try to help Antonio? A: I would talk a lot to him. I was always asking him what was happening, why was he this way. We received help from counseling. Right now, he is very high at school, in honors.[50]

....Q: "When did you find out what happened to Antonio? A: It was around year 2000, March or April. [This would have been about nine months *before* the trial victim, Jose, supposedly told his mother on New Year's, 2001, what he said happened to him and was able to produce a picture he had of Carlos.] Q: You told us about the time that you saw the defendant at La Casita after you moved. When did Antonio start telling you what had happened to him, after that time you saw the defendant? A: It was later. He had gone to play. He went to play basketball. There was another guy playing basketball, and he asked him where he was living. And my boy, since he was afraid, went inside to the room. And he was crying and told me what had happened."[51] [In Antonio's testimony it was not "another guy playing basketball" but the next door neighbor, who doesn't seem to know that Antonio lives next door! No one asks the simple question, "Why would you be 'scared' if someone asks you where you live, so frightened that you would begin crying and run to tell your mother how you had been raped almost two years earlier?"]

....Q: "When you saw the defendant the time after La Casita, how much later was it? [This will be the time when Carlos—not having been around for quite a while— suddenly appears at the door] A: I don't recall. Q: Was it before or after Antonio had told you what happened to him? A: **BEFORE** (emphasis added). Q: What happened that time after he came over to your home? A: ...There was a knock on the door, and my boy went to open it. And when he saw it was this man, he slammed the door....This man

---

50   Vol. VI, 58-59.
51   Vol. VI, 59.

was already going down the stairs and I said to him, I'm sorry, Carlos, I don't know what's wrong with my son. I'm going to talk to him. And that's when I told to him that we were going to take down the license plate... Q: Why were you taking down the license plate numbers? A: I wanted them to get this man so that he would pay for what he had done. Q: So that time that the defendant came to your house, was that before or after you knew about the abuse? A: **Afterwards.**"[52]

[Before she knows what the line of questioning will be, the witness says that Carlos came to the door before Antonio had told her what had happened to him. But once she testifies that she took down the license plate number, because of what Carlos had done, Ware leads her into "correcting" her testimony.]

> ....Q: "Looking back now, do you remember anything going on during the time that Antonio was seeing the defendant that would now help you to understand what might have happened?: A: No."[53]

As we saw above, the witness had testified only a few minutes earlier:

> Q: "Did Antonio change in any other ways after he started spending time with the defendant? A: He is even afraid to sleep alone. Q: When did those fears start? A: After he had been seeing this man.....Q: Did Antonio's school work change at all? A: Yes. Q: How did his school work change? A: He was violent with everybody, and his grades dropped. He would shout at his teachers, everything.[54]
>
> ....Q: "When did you call the police and tell them what had happened to Antonio? A: That day he talked to me. Q: Did you go any place with the police? A: Yes. Q: Where did you go? A: To the place where this man lived. Q: Was

---

[52] Vol. VI, 2-22.

[53] Vol. VI, 62-63.

[54] Vol. VI, 58:10-23.

the house there when you went? A: No.[55] [So, between the summer of 1998 when the crime/s allegedly occurred and April of 2000, the house where Carlos was supposed to have lived mysteriously disappeared.]

….Q: "At some point did the police ever show you photographs? A: Of this man, yes. Q: How many photographs did they show you? A: One. Ware again has to get the testimony back on the track she wants: Q: Did they show you one photograph alone or were you shown a bunch of photographs at the time? A: With a lot of pictures. Q: Were you able to recognize any of the people in those pictures? A: **NO.** (emphasis added) Not the response Ware is expecting, so she rephrases the question: Q: Did you ever see a photograph of the person you knew as Carlos? A: Yes. Q: What did you do when you saw the photograph? A: I only said, this is the man."[56]

Mr. Somoza then begins his cross-examination:

Q: "…Isn't it true that Antonio never told you that Mr. Rojas was violent with him? A: Never. Q: Isn't it true he never used a weapon with Antonio? A: No, he didn't tell me that." Mr. Somoza: That's all I have, Judge. Pass the witness."[57]

Once more, in spite of all the contradictions, inconsistencies and "misstatements" in the testimony of Antonio's mother, nothing is questioned or challenged.

The state calls police Officer Josh Straight, assigned to the Juvenile Sex Crimes unit.

….Q: "How did you first begin that investigation? A: The case was assigned to me, I believe, on April 21, 2000, by my Sgt.. Q: How did you go about your investigation?….A: He [Antonio] gave information as to where it occurred in [the

---

[55]   Vol. VI, 63:18.

[56]   Vol. VI, 64:3-20.

[57]   Vol. VI, 65:16-22.

city] and from that point I conducted a check on people that lived at those addresses, at the address of where Antonio said this occurred, and found that the defendant had once had a driver's license at that address.[58] [Recall that Antonio did not have an exact memory of the location of the house, much less its address. He testified that "It was kind of close to here. It was that way, I don't remember the street," "by [the] county jail," "near downtown."[59]]

"In the meantime, while I was doing that, an Officer Alexander had received a call from Antonio's mother stating that the defendant had driven up to the house, she had gotten a license plate number on that vehicle, it come [sic] back registered to the defendant."[60]

Officer Straight then testified that he obtained a photo of Carlos as follows: "…in this instance I had contacted our Criminal Intelligence Division. They have a data bank of driver's license photos. And I provided them with the defendant's driver's license number. They obtained his photo…"[61]

Straight next explains how a photospread is created and how he showed it to Antonio. Q: "And how did Antonio react when you showed him the photospread? A: When I showed him the photospread, he immediately pointed to the defendant's picture… Q: Did you show that photospread to anybody else? A: I don't recall. I don't believe I did. Q: Did anybody show the photospread to Ms. Rivera, the mother? A: I don't recall."

Officer Straight had just testified that Ms. Rivera was in the room with him and Antonio while he was showing Antonio the photospread, though not "directly right with me".[62] Why would he not have also shown her the photospread at this time? Ms. Rivera did testify that

---

58   Vol. VI, 69.
59   Vol. VI, 18:12;19:9,11.
60   Vol. VI, 69:21-23.
61   Vol. VI, 70:6-10.
62   Vol. VI, 71:10.

she had been shown the photospread, although she was not asked who showed it to her.[63]

Mr. Somoza cross-examines Officer Straight. Once more he merely tries to establish that Carlos was not violent with Antonio and passes the witness.[64] No questions about how he got the address that was unknown to Antonio, no questions about the inconsistency between his testimony about how the photospread was used and that of Antonio, no insistence that the driver's license used by the officer to identify Carlos should be placed in evidence as an exhibit. [The dating of this license—if it existed at all—could have shown whether Carlos was in the country in 1997, or could indicate that—if he did have a license—it was dated 1999 or later, after he entered the U.S. in 1999.]

Ms. Ware claimed she had another witness (unidentified), but that he was not present. The Judge permitted an early break for lunch. After lunch the supposed witness did not appear and the State rested.

Mr. Somoza called Maria Nueces to the stand, as a character witness for Carlos.

> Q: "Would you please tell the jury how you know Mr. Rojas?
> A: While I have been preaching in the street, he would be
> there. He would always help us a lot by giving us food for
> the homeless. And also when there was a funeral, he would
> contribute with money when we would have to send the
> deceased back to his country.
>
> ….Q: "As far as you know, has he [Carlos] ever been
> placed on adult probation in Texas or any other state? A: No,
> neither. Q: Ms. Nueces, I'm going to be asking for the jury
> to consider placing Mr. Rojas on probation.….Q: Do you
> understand that if the jury were to place him on probation
> that a condition the Judge would impose is that Mr. Rojas
> could no longer ever associate with children?[65]

---

63 Vol. VI, 64:3-23.

64 Vol. VI, 73-74.

65 Vol. VI, 82.

Ms. Ware: "Objection, leading. The Court: Sustained.[66] ....Q: And do you understand that we're asking the jury for mercy on Mr. Rojas? Ms. Ware: Objection, leading. The Court: Sustained.[67]

Somoza passes the witness and Ware's cross-examination begins.

Q: "Have you ever talked with the defendant about his criminal record? A: No, never had the chance to talk about that. Q: So are you aware that the defendant has been previously convicted of illegally entering this country? A: Well, no. [This claim had not been previously raised, either in the guilt phase or the punishment phase of the trial, nor was any evidence of such a conviction submitted. In fact, a review of historical charges against Carlos in the [] county records, does not show such a conviction.]

Q: "Did the defendant tell you what he did to Jose Lunes and Antonio Luzan? Mr. Somoza: Objection, Your Honor. Improper questioning, not relevant here. The Court: Overruled. A: Never. He never mentioned those people."[68] [If Carlos had been called to testify in his own defense, he would have told the jury that he had never seen either boy until the day of the trial.]

Ware questioned the witness in detail about all the sexual offenses for which the jury has found Carlos guilty. She clearly did not know about any of this (if these acts had never occurred and Carlos had never met these boys, how could she know anything?), but her questions served to reinforce the horror of the crimes in the mind of the jury. Somoza objected and made a motion for a Mistrial, which the Court denied.[69]

....Q: "And what if you were to learn that the defendant is accused of sexually molesting another child?" A: "Well, I am

---

[66] Vol. VI, 82:21-22.

[67] Vol. VI, 83:2-5.

[68] Vol. VI, 84:6-17.

[69] Vol. VI, 86:3.

surprised. I don't believe he would do that.....Q: Do you now understand that this defendant is accused of molesting two children? A: Yes. Q: And do you understand this happened more than once? A: Yes. Q: Does that change your opinion of the defendant's character? A: No, I would have to see it myself."[70]

Somoza passes the witness and asks "Could you ask for Anna Santana, and see if she is here?"[71] There is a brief pause (suggesting the witness was not present) and the defense rested, without calling any witnesses or offering any defense.

[Later we shall see that Ms. Santano had come to the trial at its beginning and wished to testify during the guilt phase, was sworn in, but never called. It is not surprising that she would not be present several days later, but this ruse allows Somoza to give the impression he did try to use her. At the start of the guilt phase of the trial, Somoza had told the Judge that he had **two** witnesses for the **punishment** phase of the trial and wanted them sworn in. The Judge replied that they needed to be sworn in in front of the jury. After the jury entered it appears one of the witnesses was sworn in (this would have been Maria Nueces who in fact testified as a character witness during the punishment phase). The Judge then asked about "the lady in the back row" and was told by the interpreter (because the woman did not speak English) that this lady had been sworn in on the previous Friday).][72] This must have been Mrs. Santano. According to the transcript she was sworn in **before the trial started and not in front of the jury**! Somoza then appears to call her at the end of the **Guilt** part of the trial (when she could have testified that Carlos did not arrive in Houston until 1999), when he knows she is no longer present.]

Ms. Ware calls probation Officer Rosa Mendez as a rebuttal witness. The gist of the testimony was to show that Carlos was unlikely to be deported and should not be given probation because he was likely to

---

70   Vol. VI, 87.

71   Vol. VI, 90:3.

72   Vol. VI, 5;2-7.

offend again. This effort is helped by Somoza's question: "The fact is, he could successfully complete his probation? A: My experience has not been like that as a probation officer."[73]

The attorneys and Judge discuss the instruction to the jury and the technicalities of life and eventual eligibility for parole (after thirty years if the sentence is Life). Closing arguments ensue:

Somoza begins:

> "…I wish I had some evidence to present to you."[74] [In other words, he has no "evidence" to persuade the jury they should not give the maximum penalty, such as the fact that there was no physical evidence of the crime, only the testimony of the "victims," there was continual inconsistency (if not errors or what appear to be lies) in what the witnesses claimed, and there was the testimony of the character witness about the good things Carlos had done.]
>
> "As you can tell by now, I'm here to plead for mercy."[75] He then devotes about ninety lines of the transcript closing statement to the timeworn Old Testament story of King Solomon determining which woman should get the baby, in the midst of which he is interrupted by the Judge:
>
> THE COURT: "Excuse me. Pardon me just a moment. Pardon the interruption. I want to make sure the interpreter is interpreting everything for Mr. Rojas. THE INTERPRETER: He has taken the headset off. He says he'd rather hear in English. THE DEFENDANT: I'm sorry, I understand better in English. Because this— this— the phone is too noisy. [In other words, there is so much static in the headphone that he cannot fully understand the proceedings.] THE COURT: Mr. Somoza, I'm so sorry to interrupt your argument, but I think we need to get this straightened out on the record. MR. SOMOZA: May I have extra time, Your Honor? THE COURT: Of course. Jurors,

---

73 Vol. VI, 94:7-10.
74 Vol. VI, 100:3.
75 Vol. VI, 100:4.

if you don't mind stepping back to the jury room. All rise, please."[76]

THE COURT: "Thank you. My impression, although I haven't heard Mr. Rojas speak much, my impression is he doesn't really understand or speak a lot of English, is that pretty much correct, Mr. Somoza?" [Somoza does not really answer the question, but says "Judge, I believe his primary language is Spanish." Somoza had been the attorney of record from at least May 2, 2001, and can only say that he "believes" Carlos' primary language is Spanish.][77]

THE COURT: "…I think it would be in your best interest [Mr. Rojas] to be certain that you understand everything that's being said during the trial. And it appears to me that up until this point, he has been utilizing the interpreter. Do you wish to use the interpreter? THE INTERPRETER: He says that there was static on the headset and he wasn't hearing well and didn't hear anything."[78]

There is a little more discussion, it is decided to continue using the earphone, and the jury returns to the court room.[79]

One can only wonder at these mysterious proceedings. The guilt phase of the trial is long past, the punishment phase is all but over, and, in the midst of the story of Solomon, the Judge becomes concerned that perhaps the defendant is not understanding everything. Rojas tells the Interpreter he has not heard [understood] anything, and the trial continues, using the earphone.

The Judge tells Mr. Somoza he has eight minutes left and the attorney resumes his exegesis of the Bible at verse seven: "Now, O Lord, my God, etc.…",[80] concluding almost three pages and fifty lines later with "And in verse twenty-eight, the Bible says that everyone stood in awe of his decision-making."[81]

---

[76]   Vol. VI,101.

[77]   Vol. VI, 102.

[78]   Vol. VI, 102.

[79]   Vol VI, 103:12.

[80]   Vol. VI, 103:18.

[81]   Vol. VI, 105:20.

He then asks the jury to exercise the wisdom of Solomon and pleads:

> "Ladies and gentlemen, I'm challenging you to please have
> some mercy here. Please have some faithfulness [sic] on
> Mr.—Mr. Rojas here....I understand the state's position
> and the family's position that he [Carlos] had no mercy on
> them [the two boys]. Now, please forgive what I'm going to
> say. In the scheme of things, this case, as offensive as it is
> to you, because you don't deal with this every day, it's not
> anywhere near as bad as these cases can get."

In his plea for mercy, the defense attorney highlights how the emotional lives of the boys have value, how they have suffered, how they have been violated and their families have suffered, but at least Carlos did not use physical violence. So he asks the jury not to give his client a sentence equivalent to the death penalty.

> "Ladies and gentlemen, twenty years is a fair sentence. Let
> him serve his twenty years, get deported and go back."[82]
> "Ladies and gentlemen, God doesn't make any junk. And
> right now, you're struggling to find anything of value and
> worth in Mr. Rojas. I'm praying that you try harder to find
> something of worth for him....All that stands between he
> and a life sentence is me [not that the facts of the case would
> have any bearing on the matter.] And if I have offended you
> in some way, I ask forgiveness....For a year now, over a year,
> I have been carrying this case with me in my heart, mind,
> and soul."[83]

Actually, it appears from court documents Mr. Somoza only took on the case in May of 2001, about nine months prior to the trial. During this time, Carlos told the court in pre-trial testimony that Somoza came to see him only one time.[84] Somoza claims that [over a period which he

---

[82]   Vol. VI, 108:6.

[83]   Vol. VI, 108:12-23.

[84]   Vol. II, 8:15.

says was more than a year] he saw the defendant four or five times.[85] The reader is left to Judge how heavy this case was weighing on the "heart, mind, and soul" of Mr. Somoza!

The Judge tells Somoza he has two minutes left and he immediately sums up:

> "I'm asking that you resist the state's demand to reach for the sword and split the baby. I'm asking that you implore [not exercise?] mercy. Mr. Rojas is asking for mercy. I'm praying godly wisdom upon you. Thank you."[86]

Thus, the only thing that stands between Carlos and a life sentence, is not evidence, not facts, not persuasive testimony, not the possibility that the defendant was not even in the country, but only King Solomon.

Ms. Ware commences her closing statement:

> "Life. That's the punishment that this defendant deserves. The maximum. Why the maximum? The legislature created the maximum for those cases that are the worse of the worst. Forcible rape on at least two occasions. Multiple victims.... Jose Lunes...Antonio Rivera Luzan...Hector. Now, you didn't get to hear from Hector.[87] Somoza: Objection, Your Honor. Improper argument, outside of the evidence here. THE COURT: Sustained. Ms. Ware: But you heard the testimony—Somoza: Make a Motion for Mistrial, ask the jury to disregard the last remark. THE COURT: That's overruled. Ware: But you heard the testimony about— from Antonio about what happened to both him and to Hector..."[88]

Yes, what about Hector? Where was this "victim?" Why was he never called to the stand, or at least deposed, to substantiate the testimony of Antonio? The question was never asked, much less answered.

---

[85] Vol. II, 8:18.

[86] Vol. VI, 109:3-7.

[87] Vol. VI, 109:11-20.

[88] Vol. VI, 109:21 to 110:6.

Ware continues:

> "What Life says is that his acts will not be tolerated in our society….It allows Jose to go home and Antonio to go home and not have to sit and wait and wonder when he will next appear on their doorstep. Somoza: Objection, Your Honor. THE COURT: Overruled.[89] Ware: It's not a probation case. He has the gall to stand here and ask you for mercy, to cloak himself in the Bible. And yet, he didn't show any mercy…"[90] [Of course it was not Carlos who used the Bible, it was Somoza spending half of his closing time on it.]
>
> Ware: "….And if you're unable in your hearts to return the verdict of Life, then I ask that you return a verdict of no less than 60 years. Give those boys at least that much peace of mind"[91] [if Carlos was paroled in thirty years, the boys would be over forty years old, Carlos would be about seventy-five and indeed they should feel secure.]

Ware concludes and the jury returns with its punishment verdict approximately forty-five minutes later. The jury was not polled, by consent of Ware and Somoza, and the latter said there would be a "Notice of Appeal." [92]

> THE COURT: "Well, members of the jury, that completes all your work. And it didn't take as long and [sic] we thought it might….But when twelve people listen carefully and deliberate together, I think they always reach the right verdict. My friend, Susie Ham, who was a mentor to many judges for many years always says don't go home and second guess yourself. Because if the twelve of you deliberated together, you reached the right verdict."[93]

---

[89]   Vol. VI, 110:15 to 111:2.

[90]   Vol. VI, 112:4-8.

[91]   Vol. VI, 113:10.

[92]   Vol. VI, 115:17-25.

[93]   Vol. VI, 116:6-18.

One may ask why Judge Carlson felt the need to dismiss the jury with this solicitous caution? Recall that in the guilt phase the State presented its closing arguments at 2:52 p.m. and the jury returned with its verdict of "Guilty" at 3:26 p.m., according to the Court's hand written notes taken on behalf of the Judge. In the punishment phase, the jury began deliberations at 2:30 p.m. and returned with its verdict at 3:15 p.m. Thus, total deliberations for guilt and punishment could not have taken more than seventy-nine minutes, not even an hour and a half. Given the nature of the trial proceedings as viewed through the transcript, jurors later might indeed have cause to reflect.

Judge Carlson had a few final instructions for the jury:

> "You can talk to anybody you want to about the case, or you don't have to talk at all. The only person you can't talk to is me, and that's because should the case ever be retried, and I'm certainly not implying it ever would be, but I would be the Judge to hear that again, and that's the reason I can't talk about it."[94]

Again, one wonders about what may have prompted this instruction.

Questions Not Asked, Thus Never Answered (Part II)

Why doesn't Somoza point out how imprecise Ware is in identifying the age of Antonio when the alleged offense happened?

Why doesn't Somoza ask Jose why he was willing to tell Officer Drummond that there were two assaults, when he did not tell this to his mother, at a time when he supposedly was trying to get forgiven for the guilt he was carrying?

Why doesn't Somoza point out how uncertain Antonio is about when he met Carlos. First it was spring (April) and he would have been in school, then it was Summer. Then, according to the prosecution, the rape did not happen until about September, 1998.

---

[94]   Vol VI, 117:1-5.

Why doesn't Somoza probe Antonio about his friendship with Hector. How did he get to know Hector? Why is he so uncertain as to how long he knew this boy?

Why doesn't Somoza at least argue that if there was a "rape" of Antonio, it was not "forcible," because Antonio testified he allowed it because he was given candy and cigarettes? Although improbable, this argument would show at least an effort to obtain a lesser sentence.

Why doesn't Somoza ask Antonio how he knew the alleged home of Carlos was behind an "old lady's house", since he was completely unfamiliar with the neighborhood?

Why doesn't Somoza ask Antonio how sure he was of the number of beds in the room? Why doesn't he probe him about the door without a door-knob? Obviously the prosecution wants Antonio to mention the steel door that was supposed to be there, but the boy seems to have "forgotten."

Why doesn't Somoza ask Antonio why he thought the hotel Carlos allegedly took the boys to was near his home, when he said he could not remember what part of town it was in?

Antonio says he consented to a second advance by Carlos because he was offered cigarettes. Again Somoza does not bring this up as a challenge to "forcible" rape.

Who was the mysterious "Hector" who introduced Antonio to Carlos and basically solicited him into a situation where the alleged rapes could occur? Why was he not found, or deposed, to confirm the story of Antonio? Why wasn't something done to protect him from predators such as Carlos was supposed to be?[95]

Why doesn't Somoza ever point out the improbability of the testimony that has Carlos sexually assaulting both boys several times within a few minutes, and Antonio not being able to remember whether he was [graphic sexual attack] or not?[96]

Why doesn't Somoza ask Antonio why he was scared of the man who asked him where he lived, since he said the man was his next door

---

[95]   Vol. VI, 30-31.
[96]   Vol. VI, 32:11.

neighbor?[97] If the man was his neighbor, why wouldn't he know where Antonio lived? Why would being asked such an innocent question cause him to tell his mother something he had been hiding for so long a time?

Why doesn't Somoza probe Antonio as to why he said he did not see Carlos after he had told his mother about the rape, but then changed his testimony when the prosecutor "reminded" him that Carlos might have stopped by his home?[98] No doubt Antonio would reply he just "forgot," but then the question could be raised as to how he could possibly "forget" such a dramatic visit from his rapist!

Why doesn't Somoza question the testimony about getting the license plate number. Supposedly Antonio had gone with Carlos many times, yet did not know what kind of car he had. He could not tell what kind of car it was at the time of Carlos's visit because he could not really see it, yet it could be seen well enough from the window to read the license plate! None of this is challenged in any way by the defense. The witnesses are not even asked where their apartment was located, to test the possibility of seeing the car, much less the license plate.

Why doesn't Somoza ask Antonio why he said the police officer told him to pick a photo that looked like Carlos?

Why doesn't Somoza probe Mrs. Luzan about the age of Hector. Why does she think he was only seven or eight, when Antonio said he was thirteen or fourteen?

Why doesn't Somoza point out the improbability of the time sequence: There is an outcry by Antonio in March or April, 2000. A police officer says he was able to get a photo of Carlos and his address from "an old driver's license" immediately after that.[99] Carlos is apparently well known in the downtown part of the city as "Carlos the mechanic," and yet he is not arrested until August, 2000, leaving this supposedly depraved predator on children on the streets for a number of months!

Why didn't Somoza probe Mrs. Luzan about the individual playing basketball with Antonio? Was he another boy? Antonio had said he was

---

[97]   Vol. VI, 44:6.

[98]   Vol. VI, 45:16.

[99]   Vol. VI, 70:6-10.

a man, a next door neighbor. Why would Antonio have been bothered by another boy asking him a question?

Why doesn't Somoza challenge Mrs. Luzan about the self-contradiction in her testimony about when Carlos came to their door? First it is **before** Antonio tells her about the rape/s, then, after prompting from Ms. Ware, she "remembers" that it was afterwards.

Why doesn't Somoza point out the inconsistency in Mrs. Luzan's testimony about the process of identifying Carlos's photo? First she says the police showed her only one photo, and has to be led into correcting this statement. Then she says she does not recognize anyone in the set of photos, and has to be led into saying that she did recognize Carlos.[100]

Why doesn't Somoza question Officer Straight about how he was able to locate an address where Carlos supposedly lived, when Antonio had only a vague idea of the area, and then, when an address is supposedly found, the house does not exist? If the police knew about Carlos as early as April, 2000, why did it take them until August to arrest him?

Why didn't Somoza press Officer Straight as to why he did not have Antonio's mother look at the photo spread, since she was in the room with Antonio?

Why didn't Somoza insist that the driver's license Officer Straight used be placed in evidence? What had become of it? What date had it been issued? Officer Straight said the police had obtained from Antonio's mother a plate number for the Carlos car and it was registered to him. During discovery why didn't Somoza demand a copy of the registration of this vehicle? If he was telling the truth, might it not show the date of registration and the physical address of Carlos at the time?

Why doesn't Somoza cross-examine Officer Straight about how he supposedly obtained the photo of Carlos? He says that he obtained it through the Criminal Intelligence Division, apparently very soon after being put on the case in April, 2000.[101] Just what crime was in question here? [] county criminal records do not show any case prior to May

---

[100]   Vol. VI, 64:7-17.
[101]   Vol. VI, 70:6.

12, 2000. It shows a charge of driving while license was suspended []
dismissed May 12, 2000. There was also case [], aggravated sexual
assault of a child under fourteen **dismissed** July 27, 2000. This would
appear to be the case of the alleged assault of Antonio Luzan, which
was so flimsy that it was dismissed at the time, then resurrected for
the punishment phase of the 2002 trial. Two other cases, [] and []
were merged into one, and filed January 16, 2001. The latter was the
case ultimately completed. This entire record is after April of 2000, so
why would the Criminal Intelligence Division have a photo of Carlos
Rojas? Rojas had also entered a sworn statement that he had never been
convicted of a felony in the state of Texas. Yet Somoza had no questions
for Officer Straight on this matter.

Why doesn't Somoza object when Ms. Ware tells the character
witness that Carlos had been previously **convicted** of illegally entering
the country, when no evidence to this alleged "fact" had been presented
during the trial?[102]

Furthermore, December 2, 2000, Mr. Valdez, Carlos' original
lawyer, filed a motion to exclude extraneous offenses:

"CARLOS ROJAS, defendant moves this Court to order the State
to not refer in any manner to any extraneous offense on the part of
the defendant until the Court has conducted a hearing and had an
opportunity to rule on its admissibility..." filed December 1, 2000,
page fifty of Clerk's Record).

The motion was sent to the DA, but the Court Clerk's file does not
include a copy signed by the Judge. On August 30, 2001, Mr. Somoza
filed a similar motion to exclude extraneous offenses, again sent to the
DA, but not signed by the Judge:

> "COMES NOW, CARLOS ROJAS... and moves this
> Honorable Court to order the District Attorney...to disclose
> and reveal to Defendant...any and all evidence...where such
> evidence ...be in the form of evidence of extraneous offenses,
> prior convictions...on the part of Defendant, which may be

---

[102] Vol. VI, 84:6.

> introduced into evidence by said District Attorney in the
> penalty phase of the trial...."[103]

Why didn't Somoza object to the introduction of this alleged
"extraneous offense" or "conviction?"

Motion for a New Trial

On April 29, 2002, proceedings were held before Judge Carlson seeking
a new trial, with Ms. Ware again from the District Attorney's office and
Timothy Crown, a new public defender taking up Carlos' side. In this
situation, Fernando Somoza, who represented Rojas in the trial, is now
the **defendant**.

Crown begins by asking Somoza

> "...are you currently a licensed attorney with the state of
> Texas? A: Yes, I am.....Q: Do you recall when the trial was?
> A: It was the second week of February, I believe. Q: Okay.
> And subsequent to that time, did you learn that your license
> had been under suspension at that time? A: Yes, I did."[104]

Crown shows Somoza a document labeled "Exhibit 2" (offered
by the **defense**), dated January 15, 2002 (almost three weeks before
commencement of the trial on February 5), which states that if an
attorney is in default of a student loan and does not cure the default
within sixty days of notice, that person's license will be suspended by
the Supreme Court. The suspension is removed if the attorney presents
satisfactory evidence that an acceptable repayment agreement has been
established.

The January 15 letter from the Supreme Court further states that
it had given notice on November 14, 2001, and had not received a
certificate certifying compliance. Therefore, Somoza's license was
suspended as of January 15, 2002. **Defense's** "Exhibit 1", dated March

---

[103]   Vol. I, Clerk's Record, 112.

[104]   Vol. VII, 11:6-21.

4, 2002, is a second letter from the Texas Supreme Court stating that it had received the required certificate and Somoza's license was no longer suspended. Thus, for the entire duration of the trial, he was practicing law with a suspended license.

Crown continues:

> "And at the time you were conducting the trial, were you aware that your license had been suspended. A: No, I was not. Q: Okay. And had you known, I take it you would have immediately stepped down? A: Yes, I would have. Q: Did you, subsequent to the trial, come into compliance and have your license reinstated? A: Yes, sir. Q: And what date was that, do you recall? A: This document states March 4th, but it was sometime before that **the loan was paid** (emphasis added)....."[105]

Ms. Ware next cross-examines Somoza:

> "...in fact, when were you told of the suspension? A: I— opened some mail sometime after the trial. It was on a Friday afternoon, and I was in shock. And that next Monday, I came to Court and the Court directed me to contact Mr. Crown (already selected to serve as the appeal attorney).....Q: And at some point after the trial you were notified of the suspension? A: That's when I became aware of it. I believe I had the mail for at least a week, I just hadn't opened it."[106] [Recall that the notice letter was dated January 15, 2001. The trial wound up on February 11, a Monday. He opened the letter on the following Friday, which would have been February 15, one month after it was written. If he had received the mail one week earlier, that would have been on February 8, over three weeks after it was sent.]
>
> Ware: "Now, Defendant's Exhibit No 2 does state that you are not actually suspended at this time, but you will be

---

[105] Vol. VII, 8-9.

[106] Vol. VII, 10:1-19.

> suspended if further action isn't taken; is that correct?"[107]
> [Apparently attorney Ware did not bother reading the
> second page of the Exhibit where it says "Accordingly, your
> name stands among the number who are now suspended
> effective Jan. 15, 2002."][108]

Somewhat befuddled by Ware's "assumption," Somoza stumbles through his reply: "I don't recall exactly what—I was—I was under the impression that I was under suspension during the time of the trial...."[109]

Somoza comments that he paid off the loan by phone almost immediately, and Ware asks him about the default:

> "And that would be a technical default that you were
> suspended for; is that correct, for nonpayment? A: It's referred
> to as an administrative suspension. Q: But you were not
> suspended for any misconduct or unethical behavior, were
> you? A: Correct. Q: And not suspended for incompetence?
> A: Correct."[110]

Ware passes the witness. She tells the Judge she has a case to present, which was given to her by attorney Crown. She says there are two cases wherein "both hold that a suspension for misconduct or ethical behavior, it basically [sic] as though the attorney was not suspended."[111] [We can only wonder about a suspension for "ethical behavior," but these are the attorney's exact words according to the transcript.]

Crown closes:

> "I would argument [sic] the motion be granted, Your
> Honor." Ware: "The State would oppose the motion, Judge.
> I think the defendant did get adequate counsel, there was
> no allegations [sic] of incompetence or unethical behavior,

---

[107] Vol. VII, 11:1-3.

[108] Vol. VII, Exhibit 2, page 4.

[109] Vol. VII, 11:5-7.

[110] Vol. VII, 11-12.

[111] Vol. VII, 13:1-3.

therefore we do not believe the defendant is entitled to a new trial. THE COURT: Thank you. The motion for new trial is denied."[112]

Thus ended this proceeding which, if anything, is even more curious than the trial itself. One would assume that the motion for a new trial was intended to exonerate Rojas. Yet both Mr. Crown (who will represent the defendant in his Appeal) and Ms. Ware do nothing but come to the support of Mr. Somoza, thereby undermining the argument for a new trial. Any number of questions could have been asked, but were not. For instance:

> "Mr. Somoza, did you receive and read the Notice letter of November 14 giving you sixty days to cure the default?" "If not, why not? If so, why did you not do something to arrange a repayment plan, so as to avoid the suspension?" "Given that sixty days had passed since the November 14 Notice, assuming you read the original letter, why were you not aware you were suspended as of January 15? Why would a letter be necessary to know this fact?"
>
> "Why was your student loan in default? What was the balance on the loan? What were its terms? Were you so short of funds you could not even negotiate a repayment plan? You said you had been representing Mr. Rojas for over a year. Could you not have anticipated payment for this service that would enable you to resume paying on the loan? How were you able to suddenly repay the entire loan immediately after the trial?" (Could Somoza's financial predicament possibly be related to how he conducted himself during the Carlos trial?)
>
> "Ms. Ware, why did you claim Exhibit 2 did not say Mr. Somoza was suspended, when it clearly stated just the opposite? Mr. Crown, why did you give Ms. Ware a case which she claimed [according to the transcript] proved that if a suspension was for "misconduct or ethical [sic] behavior" it was as if there were no suspension? Would not this case

---

[112]   Vol. VII, 13:12-22.

be prejudicial to your motion for a new trial? Mr. Crown, why in your closing argument did you not summarize the reason/s you were asking for a new trial?"

But now it is time to move on to the Appeal.

State's Appellate Brief

The Brief was submitted by Charles Rosen, District Attorney of [] County, Texas, and Shirley Preston, Assistant DA It begins with the statement that "the State requests oral argument only if oral argument is requested by Appellant." There is nothing in the file to indicate whether Rojas was apprised of this right or not. It is improbable, since he says he never met with his Appeal attorney.

The State's brief first lays out a "Statement of the Case" and a "Statement of Facts." Using an alias for Jose, "Pepe", it rehearses the "facts" of the case when Pepe was assaulted in the summer of 1997. It asserts:

> "Appellant then forced Pepe to sit on his lap."[113] [RR is the state's method of designating Vol. IV of the trial transcript.] This is an important point, because to justify a Life sentence, the rape has to be "forcible." The testimony we find at page twenty-eight is: Q: "And what did he do to you?" A: "He told me to sit on his lap." Q: "Did you want to sit on his lap?" A: "Yes." Ware seems somewhat surprised at this answer: Q: "You did?" Jose then seems to take her cue and adjusts his answer: A: "Yeah, because he grabbed me by the arm."[114]

After covering the rest of the State's version of the facts, the Brief presents a "Summary of the Argument," which is a reply to the Appellant's "**sole** (emphasis added) point of error," "the factual sufficiency of the evidence."

Immediately following this section, the Brief issues a "Reply to Points of Error One and Two." So now there is more than one point

---

[113]   Vol. IV, 28.

[114]   Vol. IV, 28:4-9.

of error to be refuted. The Brief reminds us that a verdict can only be overturned if it is "clearly wrong or unjust." The Court cannot set aside a verdict "merely because [it] believes a different result is more reasonable."[115]

An element of "aggravated sexual assault" is that the [] of the child must be contacted by the [] of the actor. As it happened, Jose was careful to use the exact legal terms "his [] when describing the alleged rape.[116] So the Brief assumes this part of the evidence is factually sufficient.

The next supposed "error" is an attack on the credibility of the victim. The response is that the testimony of one witness (the victim) to a crime is sufficient, the details provided by the victim were sufficient, and his testimony was supported by his mother. The Brief recalls the mother testified "that prior to the summer he was raped, he was a good child and a good student."[117] In fact, when she was asked "How was Jose doing in school in third grade?" she replied "Very badly. His grades were dropping."[118] But Jose (Pepe) was already in the third grade prior to the summer he was raped.

The Appellant's attack on credibility because of the delayed outcry is also dismissed. Pepe was afraid to testify, because he thought Carlos might "do something to him" if he told others.[119]

The lack of physical evidence and the disappearance of the home where Carlos allegedly took the boy is also discounted. After several years there would be no physical evidence and it would not be unusual for a house to be torn down and replaced by another.

The Brief concludes "Accordingly, Appellant's sole point of error should be overruled."[120] A copy of the Brief was mailed to Mr. Crown on November 19, 2002.

---

[115]   Vol. VIII, 8.

[116]   Vol. IV, 30, 23.

[117]   Vol. IV, 68, 70.

[118]   Vol. IV, 68:20-22.

[119]   State's Appellate Brief, 11.

[120]   State's Appellate Brief, 12.

Brief of Appellant

The Appellant's Brief had been mailed to the District Attorney's office on September 9, 2002. After its own "Statement of the Case," it discusses "Point of Error One." "The verdict of the jury is so contrary to the great weight of the evident as to be manifestly unjust." It should be noted that the State's Brief never replied to the charge of "unjust." This is significant because, at the very least, it could be argued that the **punishment** was disproportionate to the many weaknesses in the testimony of the supposed victim/s.

The Brief provides its own "Statement of Facts," in order to attack the "factual sufficiency" of the evidence. It uses the actual name of the victim, Jose, not bothering with the State's recourse to an alias. The Brief does not question the "facts" of the case as subsequently framed by the State.

It recalls that Jose's mother said he began having problems in school from 1997 onwards. It does not point out the inconsistency in her testimony where she says that he was doing badly in the Third Grade, which would have been prior to the supposed rape.

The Brief mentions that Officer Sandra Drummond helped determine the location of the offense by consulting the mother and child. It was in the 1700 block of Lyons, Houston.[121] The Appeal Brief does not mention that Jose testified he did not identify the street of the house but merely said it was "Downtown Houston. Like in north side",[122] and when he went with the officers to point out the house, it no longer existed.

The subsequent section of the Brief is described as "Summary of the Argument" and again lists "Point of Error One" but this time it is a different error: "The complainant's testimony was so vague that it seriously undermined its credibility."[123] Then "Point of Error One" is reiterated as a verdict that is "manifestly unjust."[124] The line of

---

[121]   Vol. IV, 104.
[122]   Vol. IV, 23-25.
[123]   State's Appellate Brief, 10.
[124]   State's Appellate Brief, 11.

argumentation cites Johnson v. State, 23 S.W. 3rd. 1 (Texas Crim. App. 2000) on factual sufficiency. The material included in this citation works against the rationale of the appeal, not for it.

Ward v. State, 48 S.W. 3d 383 (Texas App. ...2001) is then reviewed. The Brief makes the point **"The State never effectively challenged the alibi defense** (emphasis added) which consisted of the testimony of the coworkers which was corroborated by the time cards." It goes on to observe "The Court of Appeals held that the evidence taken as a whole was factually insufficient and the verdict was contrary to the law and the evidence (13)." **What is of interest here is the fact that the possibility of an alibi was never broached at any point during the trial.** As we shall see, this was a critical omission!

In the material provided by [] County, there is no information about the result of the Appeal. Since Carlos Rojas, as of October, 2013 was still serving his sentence in TDCJ (Texas Department of Corrections) Allred, it may be presumed that the Appeal was rejected, no doubt because the Court found the evidence to be "factually sufficient."

In assessing the sufficiency of the evidence and the justice of the proceedings, we might keep other "facts" in mind. Judges and attorneys in our system are driven by ambition for their careers. Judge Carlson has had a very successful career. Her web site indicates that as of 2010 she was completing her fourth term as the Judge of the [] Criminal District Court of [] County. In that year she was honored with two prestigious awards. Conversely, the *Texas Observer* (2/10/2006) once listed her among the worst judges in Texas, especially for partiality. In 2018 she completed her final term.

If the web is current, Jenny Ware is still an Assistant District Attorney in [] County.

Web information on Fernando E. Somoza in [] is a bit more difficult to decipher. There are several entries under this name, all for someone who received his doctorate from []... in 1988. He was born in 1955, making him about forty-seven at the time of the trial. According to the entries, he may be contacted at various addresses. He is listed in Martindale-Hubbell, but declined to have his ratings disclosed.

Although he was in private practice since 1989, he only became a member of the State Bar of Texas in 1997.

He represents that he is (apparently in 2003) a member of the Unauthorized Practice of Law Committee for [], and is a mentor for the []…Middle School "I Have a Dream" program and is a Class Facilitator for the "Leadership [] class 2002-2003.

[A number of years later an attempt was made to contact Mr. Somoza to obtain key documents he should have retained relative to Carlos's case. He could not be reached. A relative reported he had suffered a serious stroke, had been moved by the family to [], and the documents were no longer available].

Mr. Crown is listed on the web as an attorney in [], but no further information was available.

It also is to be noted that there are certain subsets of our population that are extremely disliked by many people. Included among these are both "illegal aliens" and (often with good reason) child molesters.

When we bring together a jury that apparently includes no "peers" of the defendant (in this case those with Hispanic lineage) and judges/attorneys with a need to advance the cause against sexual abusers of children, what are the chances for "due process" to prevail?

In the course of the trial, the witnesses repeatedly testified that the boys had gone with Carlos on many weekends to ride go-carts, to visit businesses to purchase used car parts, and even to a hotel. Yet **not one witness** other than the interested parties (the boys and their mothers) was ever brought to testify that he or she had actually seen Carlos with the boys at any time! Why was this fact not mentioned by Somoza? Would it not help to raise "reasonable doubt?

The Alibi

Carlos Rojas had spent more than eighteen months in the Houston county jail after his arrest and prior to his trial. This would have been ample time for a competent, well-motivated defense attorney to collect affidavits, depositions, etc. and identify witnesses who could testify on behalf of Carlos. Unfortunately, he had no money and no such attorney.

After his incarceration, Carlos began to put together documents to establish his innocence. He had collected his trial transcript and some affidavits, which he gave to a friend, Harry Winters, an offender at Allred who tried to help other inmates with attempts to get a new trial and such matters. Winters was disliked by the Administration because of his legal efforts and his cell was raided. The system calls this a "shakedown." During the search, all of his legal papers were seized, declared "contraband," and destroyed, along with everything Carlos had provided. (Winters was subsequently transferred to Clements, where he died suddenly).

Carlos began to rebuild the evidence of his innocence and eventually accumulated the documents which follow in chronological order (the author has in his possession certified copies of these documents but cannot present them here because they contain real names):

Diploma: This is a document of The Ministry of Higher Education in the Republic of Cuba. It states that the Rector of the Universidad de Oriente grants the title of Licentiate in the History of Arts to Carlos Rojas for having completed the necessary requirements as of June 17, 1997, with the document being executed on the second day of July, 1997. The document is signed by the Rector, the Secretary General, and the Dean.

Contract for Work, dated August 4, 1997. This too is a document issued by the Cuban Ministry of Higher Education. It states that Carlos Rojas is authorized to teach Humanities in any school of the Republic of Cuba for the seventh, eighth, and ninth grades. Carlos signs the document and gives his age as forty-four years old, and address of []… Cuba. The document includes two of his finger prints. It is attested by the Secretary General.

Cuban Ministry of Education documents dated August 11, August 15, August 20, September 15, September 30, October 1, October 6, and October 20, 1997, related to courses held from June 2, 1997 to May 20, 1998. They show that one of these courses was in the Humanities and was taught by Carlos Rojas.

Homeland Security document dated March 10, 2007, indicating that Carlos entered the United States at or near Brownsville, Texas, on or about **1999**. Although the person completing the document addressed it to "Carlos Manrique Rojas", it is clearly for Carlos Rojas, because it includes his date of sentencing (Feb. 11, 2002), Life sentence and offense. Attached to the document is a "Certificate of Service," apparently signed by Carlos on September 24, 2007. The document verifies Carlos's story and an affidavit (see below) stating that he entered the country through Brownsville in 1999. We shall see below that "Manrique" was in fact part of Carlos's full name.

One thing was puzzling about the Homeland Security document. If Carlos entered the country undetected, how did the Agency know that it was in 1999? In a letter of February 27, 2012, Carlos explained this matter. He wrote that when he tried to cross the border, he was caught several times. The first time it happened he gave them his name as Carlos **Manrique** Carlos. "Manrique" was the middle name of his father and he used this with Homeland Security at the time he was caught. Later he was successfully smuggled into the country, so this had to be no earlier than 1999.

Affidavit of Jorge A. Santano, dated and notarized on January 8, 2009. He states that he lives in a home in [], which he began purchasing in 1993. He first got to know Carlos in 1999, who was brought to his city by a Mr. Bernardo Chavez. He met him on the day of his arrival. Chavez paid someone to bring Carlos to town so he could work in his shop as a mechanic. The Affidavit is self-explanatory, but the main points are that it confirms Carlos' story that he came to the city through Brownsville in 1999, gives the reason for his entry to the United States, and mentions that the affiant's wife wanted to testify at the trial, was sworn in, but never called. It gives the address of the shop where Carlos lived and worked, which was very different from the alleged address where the offenses supposedly took place. This statement was officially notarized.

Sworn oath of Jorge Santano, March 5, 2009. Mr. Santano gave this testimony in a city in El Salvador, before two witnesses. One of the witnesses also notarized the document.

He says that for many years he was the neighbor and friend of Rosa Rodriguez and her son, Jose Lunes (the alleged victim in the guilt phase of the trial) in []. Mrs. Rodriguez came to his house on November 20, 2008, the day before he was to leave for El Salvador, to tell him something very personal. She said she had used his name in Court in order to condemn an innocent person by saying that she knew the defendant through him (Mr. Santano).

She did this because she was deceived by Jose, who was under the control of his Sunday School teacher. Jose had stolen a photo of Carlos Manrique Carlos from Santano's home. It had been taken on December 24th for Christmas. The teacher had persuaded Jose to tell his mother that the man in the photo had taken him to his home twice to have sex. The motive was to divert attention of the Church, because some of its members knew that Jose and the teacher were having homosexual relations and were about to accuse them. This teacher was the one who told Flora and Jose what they needed to say in court. And they did it.

Jose complied because the teacher was his lover. Floras did it because she believed what she had been told was the truth. But when Jose became eighteen, he went to live with his teacher. Before leaving, Jose told his mother they had used her and the photo in order to avoid the teacher being accused by the Church.

She said that Carlos Manrique Carlos was innocent, that he had never seen Jose until the day in court.

Santano finished the sworn statement by indicating that if more information was needed, he could be written at an address he provided in El Salvador. However, he has since passed away.

The Notary confirmed that the other witness, a woman thirty-seven years old, a person known to him, had witnessed the testimony given by Jorge Santano (sixty-five years old).

Affidavit of Andres Munoz, retired Director of the school at which Carlos taught, dated June 25, 2010, testifying that after an extensive investigation he was able to certify that in folio 32 of book 10-3 of the school he found the record stating that Carlos Manrique Carlos was sent to the school to perform his "Servicio Social" from August 11 to October 20 in 1997 and 1998 [the social service required in return for education received.] This document independently confirms the evidence provided above. It was notarized.

Affidavit of Miranda Garza, April 12, 2010: This document is also self-explanatory. In 2010 she is still a resident in the city in Cuba where Carlos taught her, when she was in the seventh and eighth grades (1996-1998). She states that she would be willing to testify to this in court. Her statement is also notarized

This is the evidence that Carlos Rojas, after years of patient effort, had been able to assemble to prove that he could not have assaulted Jose and Antonio in 1997 to 1998, because he was teaching in Cuba, as confirmed by a number of independent witnesses and documents. The evidence also provides an explanation for why Jose lied during the trial, and why his mother unknowingly gave false testimony. It does not explain why Antonio and his mother gave false testimony, but since they placed the event no later than 1998, they could not have been telling the truth. The prosecutor's office must have also had misgivings about Antonio's case, since they were not willing to introduce it as part of the guilt phase of the trial.

The Aftermath

So, what is it like to spend years in prison, knowing that one is innocent and may never be able to prove this innocence to the satisfaction of the Texas system of justice?

> April 27, 2011:
> "Of course you have my permission to do whatever you please it [sic] with my letters and poems. I wish I could send to you the true stories of what I have seen—the rape, abuse, suicide and killing, but these things are forbidden to talk about it [sic]." [Later in this edition of the story we shall see what consequences this knowledge had for Carlos].
> Notwithstanding this declaration, Carlos continued: "Now I am living in a living Holocaust itself. The very first day I came to this prison (I didn't know anything about

prison), I heard a moaning inside of Cell 48. I thought maybe someone needed help. I went to see, and as soon as I approached the window I asked if they needed help. But when I got in front of the door, I saw that a black man was raping a white boy. I looked to the picket and waved my hand to the guard. He waved in return, laughing, letting me know that he knew, but didn't care. When I looked around, everybody was looking at me, everybody knew. I was the only one who didn't know what happened. That monster had the impudence to come down with that kid by the hand, compelling him to walk around the day room, like a bridegroom's attendant at his wedding, challenging anybody who didn't like what he was doing to fight with him, who was so proud of being abominable and the most despicable creature on earth.

"The whites together in a corner like a bunch of animals huddled against the storm, unable to say anything. I told to the other Mexicans, 'That man must be killed for what he had done.' 'Not,' they answered. 'We can't take part, unless they ask it. That's the game of prison where the blacks humiliate the whites. They left that boy alone at the mercy of these monsters because they are scared to fight.

"That lasted almost a year every day and every night until finally the monster was moved. I felt myself disgraced for not doing nothing and acted cowardly like the rest of criminals who indulge in such actions of depravity. Years after I talked with that youngster, who is called SPOOK. I wanted to know what really happened and asked Spook his permission to write what I saw. He said it was ok, but don't use his name.

"Spook was the only child of a middle-class family in [], Texas. He attended at a Catholic school, When he was in eleventh grade his father, who owned a construction company suddenly in [], Texas, when he went to supervise his workers, as he climbed onto the roof to tell his workers how the job would be done, a tornado hit the place, throwing him to the ground and killing him instantly.

"Spook's dream to study a career suddenly came to an end also. His dad didn't have life insurance and the equipment and trucks were repossessed. His mother had to work as a school teacher again, but her salary wasn't much, with all the payments she had. Spook has to work on something. He never had been done [sic] anything because his father adored him and always gave him everything he needed. Spook never knew what it was to desire anything which he could not have it.

"He hadn't any skill nor experience on anything. The only job he could find was in a day-care facility. He worked there almost a year, but a lesbian who worked there hated him by apparently not reason [sic].

"That day, when an accident happened, he came late to work and he almost didn't come at all because a distracted driver crossed a red light and hit the car where he was (his friend was driving, not him). When he entered into the room where the children were—one of them was asleep; but after a while he had to feed them he went to see why he hadn't awakened nor even moved.

"As he inspected the child, he realized that was pale and still—dead. This was the instant that fated the rest of his life forever; this is the moment when our ignorance can doomed us to an eternal damnation (forgive me the redundancy). He called the child by his name and in desperation lifted and shaken him, trying to resuscitate him. But that was only what the camera showed and they said he was shaking the child not in desperation but anger and he killed him by shaking.

"With the corrupt system of justice of this country and without money anybody who is accused of a crime like this is dead. Spook hardly escaped the death penalty….

"How queer life is! How easy changes! And how a little thing can destroy us…because we don't live in a world ruled by love, but by the power which the possession of money conveys and that's the cause that has corrupted the societies of all ages and all times and has brought the civilizations to destruction.

"…Spook was convicted and sentenced to serve a capital Life in prison and was sent to this prison (Allred near [], Texas. When he came he was barely nineteen years old. He never had seen a monster too close. He grew up in a good neighborhood and never attended at a public school.

"When the blacks saw that kid coming to prison, they were casting lots to know which one of them will be the first to have sex with him. An easy prey had come to their kingdom of darkness and perversion, where the most wicked, ugly and evil humiliate those who are weak and better than themselves. That's what they call it 'Justice.'"

In a later letter, Carlos wrote:

"One of Spook's 'friends' told me that Spook was confined in Building 11 [solitary confinement pending transition] waiting to be transferred. In 2005, Spook's mother was coming to visit him. On the way she collided with a big truck belong to Pepsi cola. They investigated and found out that was the truck who invested [sic] the lady's car, taking it out of the road and the impact was terrible that Spook's mother only survived two months in coma. One of his friends told me the insurance gave Spook four millions of dollars, but someone else told me that he had to share that money with somebody else and what he got was just little more than a million." [These funds became a means for Spook to get into trouble through misuse of his Trust account. For example, inmates can use their account to purchase stamps or items from the commissary and then trade them for drugs obtained with the cooperation of corrupt guards and other offenders. The "commissary" is a kind of store. It is the only means inmates can use to purchase personal items. Access is strictly regulated.]

"The pervert is exalted for his perversity and the cruel for his cruelty. That's prison, the great failure of humanity and the shame of any society who makes profit of crime and the suffering of the weak and poor. The wealthy and powerful who possess [so] much money that they think they can reshape the world; they built these prisons with much time in advance because they wanted that millions of American youngsters to turn themselves criminals and good for nothing, so they can easily enslave them.

"They' pander to the most beastly and lower instincts of human beings to debase human's nature below the level of beasts. I think you still remember that youngster, Abhay Pazan, because you visited him once when he was confined in High Security. He gave me permission to write everything he confessed me: He was eighteen—just graduated from high school, his parents gave him a new car and a trip to India, to visit the holy city of Madras, where is a golden temple of the Sikh religion. That is the religion his parents practiced. Both of them came from India. He and his brother were born in [], Texas.

"The first day I went to the rec yard I saw a youngster squatted on his haunches in a corner. For several days I saw him in the spot—he never talked with nobody. I began to say 'Hi' and he answered. A couple of days later I went to talk with him and he agreed to talk with me about anything. I think the fact that I also had come from [] gave him a little confidence to talk with me openly.

"A few days before, I had met a Pentecostal pastor who invited me and other friend of mine named Sammy…to pray and read the Bible in the rec yard. The pastor was obsessed with talking in tongues, but he saw the youngster talking with me. He came and introduced himself, then started to preach to the young man.

"That evening, of a hot day of August, 2002, that young man introduced himself as Abhay Pazan. He barely had turned twenty, from [], Texas, and was serving capital Life for killing his parents. He was very interested about the Bible. He said he never had read it before. The pastor asked [him] to explain why he killed his parents; he said a demonic spirit chased him and often heard a voice telling him that he had to kill to have power and the most easy victims were his Mom and Dad.

"I asked if he had ever used any kind of drugs, and he said, 'Not.' The pastor promised him to cast out the demon and invited to pray close to the wall for Abhay to be him liberated from that demonic spirit—who have tormented him from long ago. We did pray it, but nothing happened. 'The demon is still there,' Abhay said.

"After that, Abhay separated from us, he knew the attempt of the pastor had been a failure, but I didn't believe the story of the demonic spirit because he had not signs of such things as demonic possession.

"It was more than a year later that Abhay began to talk with me again. One day he told me to go to rec because he wanted to tell me something. It was March 6th, 2004. He told me he was thinking to write a book to say the truth that it wasn't any demon who induced him to commit the crime he did it. He was enticed by the images he saw on TV, the superstars with the fancy cars and beautiful women, he said he wanted to be one of them.

"But he found any way to achieve his desire [sic]. Then he thought if his parents die, with the money of their life insurance he would be able to buy an expensive car and being like a celebrity.

"With every detail he explained me how he planned to murder his parents without his brother suspected anything. He waited until December 31, 1999, after his brother left to party in the neighborhood. When no one else was there, he took a baseball bat and went to his Mom's room. He killed her of one blow on her forehead. He saw her glasses were scattered into pieces all over the room. He told me he never could forget how his Mother by the time she died how she looked at him with a singular leer. Then when his father heard, he came to assist his wife—and he broke his legs first, then finished. After that he changed his clothes and went to the party. He took the baseball bat and the stained clothes and threw them in to a dump on the way to the party. He said he didn't know that he even could face prison for that.

"Why you didn't tell someone else, a friend or another person what you were thinking to do before you did it? I asked. 'I never trusted anybody else except my Mother,' he said. He looked at me with a profound anguish. 'I need to be punished for that,' he told me, very sad. Later he was taken into close custody because he had behavior problems. After that I heard that he had found refuge in the penumbra of the insanity."

June 12, 2011:

"…To me, there is no such a thing that one language is easy than other, poetry is the most difficult form of expression because it put aside all the trivialities of human's life and appeals to the spirit; is the anguish that every human being experiences as we see the evanescence of this life—how we will disappear—from this planet one day. We all love and we all hate—forever to never return and as time passes on nobody will remember that we past through this world too as others also will do after us and they also will pass in the way. [Much of these letters is left exactly as Carlos wrote them, revealing both his linguistic skill and struggles with his English.]

"The mission of a poet must be to enhance the most noble instinct in his fellow humans and suppress the beastly nature which all of us possess in our unconsciousness; to elevate human's spirit beyond all good and evil to the level that we can see what is the cause of all our suffering and misery.

"My mission just begun and will continue till the last day of my life. Often I put myself to proof what I believe when I find or someone comes to me and tell me that he's abandoned; that he starves at night waiting for the oatmeal or grits they will serve for breakfast; when he tells me that he's tired of having sex for a soup or a postage stamp—that he doesn't like to do that but sometimes he did it because he had no choice.

"Sometimes I have to cry till the morning to see too much misery, injustice and cruelty among human beings. Many times I sent almost all the stamps I had to that person who is in that situation of hopelessness and I feel a lot better myself to think that this person will have something to eat that night and will thank God for it.

"One day I told to one of a female prison guard who pretend to be a Christian: 'do you know there are kids who sell their bodies for a soup?' ....'Ah!,' she said. 'That happen everywhere.' Many people know that children are sold in India, Thailand and other countries for a hundred or a thousand dollars; the US is the nation who tells the world about moral values, Human Rights and Christianity. How come kids are selling for twenty-five cents in US's prison...?

"I don't know how this government has convinced the US's people that all the prisoners are monsters who don't deserve any less but to die in prison? And tells to the world that there is nothing wrong in America; that they're who can tell to other governments what is good and bad for them?...

"Through history we know that the errors of all the empires that have existed in this world—all have been the same. Power and prosperity had corrupted every human being who had possessed it, and the consequences have been the collapse and utter extinction even of their people; no one knows what happened to the Romans as a people; still exist the coliseum and the catacombs as a stigma of cruelty and shame for mankind, but the Roman people were extinct. Italy was formed just one hundred fifty years ago.

"The Soviets didn't know they were an empire and what they most wanted was to get rid of that evil and oppressive regime. Now the US has adopted the Soviet tactics to oppress the American people."

July 26, 2011:

"...During the Fourth of July I was reading a book of the History of the Jews people, how they have survived 4,000 years among several civilizations which now days are lost and gone and they still exist as a nation.

"The US is a great nation with many great people. The problem is the government and a group of people reactionaries who rule this country under the shadows. They don't care about human rights nor race or anything; they want absolute control of anybody—illegal aliens and citizens alike.

"Of course, to cheat an illegal alien and send it to prison for life is much more easy than a citizen, because at least the citizen is able to understand what are talking about in the Court—the illegals do not; the attorney the Court appoint it to help them are even more crook than the Court itself.

"….There are thousands in prison convicted and sentenced to long sentences than no other nation in the planet has such a justice system to incarcerate human being indefinitely for something that in the rest of the world are not crimes. The whole world knows the hypocrisy of this government—they call it PURITANS because their mentality it goes back to the seventeenth century.

"Paradoxically these judges all of them claim to be Christian and use the Bible to make the accused to look bad in front of the jury panel, knowing well that they're committing a crime in front of God's eyes because they're bearing a false testimony against an innocent person violating the tenth commandment. They do that almost every day and nothing bad happen to them, they're happy with their lifestyle of wealth and comfort and to keep that way they have to dwindle [sic] more families sending more innocent people to prison for life.

"Paradoxical is also the propaganda the government use against crime. How will survive the bunch of parasites who work in the courts, who don't know anything else but to lie and cheat? They can't afford it to stop crime, rather the government encourage and promoting in a subtle way that people never can detect it—they're criminals; they have license to steal and kill, they have converted millions of youngsters of the poor families into criminals, thousands are trapped in prison without knowing anything to do for living but crime. Prison is nothing less than perversion and destruction of human nature itself.

"….I know my poems—most of them are saturated with anguish; it's not only the anguish of those who longing and fading in prison abandoned and hopeless…but also the anguish of millions of people throughout the world who have not future and will face death by starvation because the world in which we live are ruled by the most ruthless criminals who have designed all these miseries to oppress and kill us, and we are powerless to fight back for our lives. They have the power to kill us by imprisonment, wars or starvation—nothing can stop them.

"We have the illusion that we're human beings and we're worthy of many things, but we are dying like worthless things which don't have any value…Our lifetime is too short that most of our plans are only dreams that never become true.

"I have talked with some youngster here who still believe they gonna be riches,—I don't see any form how they can build their dreams. But their dreams are just dreams and anybody has the right to dream in America.

"But what I see in the corner of history is a baleful storm that will wipe out millions of human beings from the face of the planet and I don't know if I will survive. That's the anguish I feel, the anguish of millions who're dying with me miserably without knowing what is life and without knowing what death is … to die and disappear forever and nobody will remember that we also past through this world one day.

"Human Beings are seeking happiness and never find it because we often search in the wrong places; though to be happy we just need a few little things, but our ignorance blind us and we undertake a battle, we want to conquer the world to be happy and that almost ends in our suffering and own damnation. That's what happened to me, if I only would know it before I would never come to this country, but that's the price we pay for our ignorance or stupidity. [Carlos is reflecting here on the fact that he was enticed to enter the country illegally in 1999 for what he thought would be a good job as a mechanic repairing cars in a major Texas city.]

November 30, 2011:

"My poetry [during his years of TDCJ confinement Carlos has created a portfolio of over forty poems] is the voice of those who don't have any, those who are fated by birth to be nothing better than criminals and come to die in prison. The Machine pandering to the most bestial instincts in human nature unfettered the sense of crime in the young generations of poor families to corrupt, oppress and impose the Machine's will upon them.

"When no hope arises in the solitary road of life…the future seem uncertain and obscure, only darkness surround the pathless way [Carlos always has trouble with how to write the tense of his verbs.] My poetry is a cry from the heart…a clamor from the human spirit appealing to the infinite, hoping a Divine force will hear one day and raises the human hearts from the present spiritual blindness and save mankind from self-annihilation.

"…I …wrote to Innocence Project in New York asking them to please to reconsider my case, because my evidence is even strong [sic] than DNA. They sent me a letter in 2010 saying they only accept cases where strong evidence is involved like DNA; you gave me a hindsight saying that my evidence is even strong[er] than DNA because I can prove that my physical body wasn't here by the time the supposedly crime was done. They haven't answer yet, but I believe that whatever their decision may be—they will answer." [As of October, 2013, there had been no reply.]

December 7, 2011:
"Merry Christmas to you both. [Another inmate] told me he will write to you this week. He was telling me about a document which the Court maybe can provide to you. According to …is very possible that the indictment the Court presented to me was not even signed by the nine members of the Grand jury but by the District Attorney himself. [The Court file includes an indictment with regard to the alleged **second** offense (Jose Lunes) dated March 2, 2001, and apparently signed by the jury Foreman, Karen Winston.[125] There was no indictment for the alleged offense

---

[125]   Vol. I, Clerk's Record, 6.

against Antonio Luzan because when the incident was brought before the Court, it was dismissed.]

"They gave me an indictment about Antonio Luzan [it is not clear what was shown to Carlos, but there was no actual indictment for this case] and three months later the attorney told me that if I didn't plea guilty they would bring more people to accuse me. The attorney was harassing me by almost two years trying to make me fall in the trap. Finally when they realized that they never will convince me to sign nor write about anything. One day on February 9th, 2002 [Carlos is writing from memory, without the help of documents; the actual date was February 5th] they had prepared a trial for someone else who they wanted to send to Death Row, but that person refused to go to trial that day. That was the jury they used for me and the person who they used was not Antonio Luzan but Jose Lunes.

"The attorney before going to trial offered me if I could sign for twenty years and I refused, then derisively told me: 'They know that you did nothing, but they can do whatever they want to you have to sign for twenty years.' They are slay [sly?] and crooked. They don't write nothing about that. They make a mockery of the law and justice and even about God when they read the Bible putting God as a witness when they know that everything they are saying is false. God bless you. Sincerely, Carlos Rojas."

December 13, 2011:
"….They discharged the case of Antonio Luzan because they hadn't trained him and when they asked him if he had been hurt having sex, he laughed and said 'not'. That part of the trial is not on the transcript because that makes them look bad."

December 18, 2011:
"….I have many things which I like to put into writing; many things that many people can't believe that happen in this country; others just don't want to know and close their eyes by not to see the cruel reality while the Nation heading

to a cruel tyranny; they will not be better than servants or slaves. The majority of the population have been brainwashed, that's why no one knows what to do and the tyrants have free hands to do whatever they please it.

"The method they use in prison to make them to obey and respect that is terror and intimidation,—they don't know nothing else, they use the tactics outside. If Harry Winters died by kidney failure as …says, poison also cause kidney failure and that is what might had happened to Harry, but I can't talk more about it because it's top secret, but one day when I am out of prison—wherever I go [there has been some talk that in 2013 many illegal immigrants in Texas prisons will be deported] I will write to you to tell all the untold stories….I haven't heard anything from Innocence Network yet."

December 26, 2011:

"One more Christmas past, one more Christmas behind bars, seeing how others have fallen…fallen on the way, sadly, they not even could see the end of the tunnel, not the least gleam. But I believe that Mother Nature is subject to God's laws which they call 'Laws of physics' and not the laws of men.

"That is why I believe this world can change anytime, in any given moment could happen the unexpected and there is nothing what the most powerful men can do to avoid the sternly [sic] command of Mother Nature. That's we're waiting for…a miracle. To me every day is a miracle in my life, because every day is a gift from a Divine Being who has the power to do whatever He wants and He has chosen give me life today…life which is not under my control nor under any human mortal like me, only on God's hands. Every day that I can see this wonderful planet full of living creatures, every day that I can comfort other humans who have been less fortunate than I am, that's a blessing to me. Because only God can give me the strength I need to overcome this indescribable perversion and misery. [When I first knew Carlos at his prison unit, he professed to have become an atheist, although he never acted much like one. After several years when he began receiving documents that would help prove his innocence, he perceived God working on his side, and regained his faith, which had never really left him.]

"I still don't receive any answer from any of these places, despite of my requesting to let me know if they had received the questionnaire. I think that from [a Texas Innocence Project there] is the one which never respond, I don't know why."

December 29, 2011:

"I just received your letter an hour ago at 8:00 p.m. and I had to get out of the cell because the guard came to search the cell— even though we are in lockdown since Tuesday, 27th...

"I know I have grammatical problems. The problem is, here there is no one who can help me. The immense majority of these persons barely can read the newspapers and fiction novels and the few educated— they just don't like poetry. I think, for most of the people in this country, poetry is something outdated—something belong to the eighteenth century. I know and I don't write for that bunch of lazies and vicious who were spoiled by the abundance of this nation in the years of splendor, like the Romans when their lives were **bread** and **circuses** till the day that was ransacked by a bunch of primitives.

"I write for the new generations who will grow in poverty and will see things differently. That lady [a literary agent to whom he had written] maybe not even will write me back [she has not] and will throw everything—even the self-addressed stamped envelope—to the garbage can. Maybe she think that **Rap** is poetry....We are living in an age of darkness, spiritual darkness, a very dangerous time."

"I want to send the rest of the poems to you in case they deport us. Then, wherever I go, I will go to work hard and will not have much time to write poetry. Poetry take a lot of time, but I have enough information about many terrible things this government has done to many people—terrible things that could surprise even the most conservative of the Republicans, with real names of persons and places which actually exist, to write a non-fiction book no less than five hundred pages…"

January 7, 2012:
"….I didn't know that what these people of the Court were doing while I was held in the county jail [were] trying to find someone who they could train to accuse me of what they wanted—but they dismissed it because they couldn't learn the questions until they found Jose Lunes, even he almost forgot the questions [recall how during the trial Jose contradicted himself or stumbled frequently when trying to answer the questions put to him.]

"The attorney told me during the trial that he couldn't question him because the Judge would object it.

. [Pages 3 and 4 of the Court Clerk's Record indicate that on January 16, 2001, the date the District Attorney filed the official "Complaint", Carlos declined his right to have his Consulate notified of his arrest. They bear what appears to be a clumsy imitation of his signature.]

"The sign [signature] on that paper about the Mexican Consulate is not mine. They never asked me if I wanted to see any Consulate. I only signed when they appointed me the attorneys twice. I don't remember the first one's name [this was Ramon Valdez who was the court-appointed attorney from after Carlos's arrest until he was replaced by Somoza in May of 2001.] He was bad and the second [Somoza] was even worse.

"In 2006…I was very excited because I believed that if I could contact the Pastor [of the church attended by Jose and his mother] I could have a recantation from Jose, but when Sister Maria [the character witness at his trial] tried to investigate, she didn't tell me if she found the church or not.…She didn't tell me how she found out that these persons who I was looking for were no longer there, not even the Pastor. The one who is now preaching doesn't know neither

Jose Lunes nor Flora Rodriguez and the Sunday Schools' teacher. I couldn't find any clue of where they could be.

"I still had hope that maybe Jorge Santano who returned to El Salvador—he might know where they are, but he died in 2010.

"Every day I ponder; where can Jose be? [One might also wonder about where the Sunday school teacher may be. Is he still out there preying on, possibly enslaving, another young boy?] He's the one who knows what these people of the Court promised to him in exchange —in recompense for accusing me; that's what I would like to know. He's twenty-five years old now. I don't think his conscience gives him peace knowing well now that what he did is awful wrong—unless he's a psychopath. I think they all will return to El Salvador as the economic crisis getting worse here and sink into another great depression."

February 15, 2012:
"I hope you have had a wonderful Valentine Day. I apologize for the lateness, I must answered you two weeks ago. The reason is that I have been struggling with something unusual to me: since the beginning of the year I have struggling against a bad energy that has been trying to bother me. It was like if someone has unleashed all the demons from hell and all of them are hovering upon Allred prison.

"When I tried to write—nothing came to my mind and every night I had the terrible feeling that something terrible would happen in the world. Everything it seem different now. The first positive thing was your letter, it was of great comfort...

"....I would like to know if exist in the world any organization who cares about Human Rights, but not Human Rights itself because they are a joke—they don't see nothing wrong in the USA. A nation with four million inhabitants in prison [actually there are about 2.5 million], how come could be called Christian and Democratic? China only has eight hundred thousand prisoners and has 1.3 Billion inhabitants."

February 27, 2012:

This letter begins with several reflections on the public's attitude toward poems. "Poetry is the less thing people want to read and the publishers and the publishers don't see future in it—no money.

"People are interested in writing which discuss about the end of time—as if they know when the world will end. Poetry describes the glories, miseries and vices of an epoch. Most of the poets lived miserably and their writing were unknown during their lifetime. Thousands of books have been written about the end of 2012, and what gonna happen the year ends and nothing happen of what they have said it, those writers will be seen as charlatans.

"….Many things have changed from bad to worse during the time I have been here and I think that still will be more changes—not for good but for worse. We are already dying—many people abandoned, what's the worse that could happen to us?"

This brings to a close the letters I had from Carlos as of this date. This part of his story ends with three of his poems. The first of these, *When Tomorrow I Stare,* expresses much of the anguish Carlos has manifested in some of his letters. Use of the word "Stare" is perhaps not the best English, but there is scarcely a word in our language that more eloquently captures his dreadful anticipation of the future, springing possibly from the pain he has experienced. Again, with a few exceptions, I have not attempted to correct the minor deficiencies in his grammar.

When I Tomorrow Stare

When I feel before me the tumult of years,
Madness and disaster they prepare;
The morning light finds me watered in tears;
When my eyes tomorrow stare.
The future unrolling its ample page,
A dark cloud arose with eternal wings;
Chasing the light with inhuman rage
Engulfing in darkness all human beings.

Mother Nature there is no place to hide! When
Unleashing the intolerable day;
The world ruled by greedy merciless men,
Begin to arrest, torture and slay.
Your voice warned me of human fate,
But I believed too late!

Not all of the poetry of Carlos Rojas is weighed down by such pessimism. He can also write beautifully of love, as we see in:

Sunset

Love of my life I will never forget,
The Sun's rays trembling on the floating tides;
In silence fell the beautiful Sunset,
The Heaven's light reflecting on your eyes.
I will never forget that dying day,
Its tenuous rays with renewed might;
Stir my heart when I fade away
Like dissolved dream with love's delight.

I will forever love the freshing Sea,
And everything that breathes and moves;
The wind that blows happy and free:

Lead my heart to thoughts of love,
And my Soul lingers to the Shore
I feel my life like water rolling evermore!

Finally, one of the first poems Carlos shared with me aptly depicts his solitude in this prison far from his homeland.

I Always Feel So Alone

When the light of life has vanished, and all the good has gone,
The joy also is finished, and I always feel so alone.
O Lord, come to my life, I don't want to be the same.
I lift up my eyes to the dark and cloudy heaven.
Is there nothing I can change?

O Lord, come back again, this world suffers too much pain.
There is no love, no friends, we all have forsaken you,
And no one seems to understand.

Come to my heart, O Lord, it seems the light of life is 'ore,
And time exists no more.

O Lord, come to my life, I don't want to be the same.
I lift up my eyes to the dark and cloudy heaven,
Let me see what I can change.

Carlos Ismael Rojas

CHAPTER TWO

MEDICAL SERVICES AND AN AGING PRISONER

Ned Parker had been in the system for many years He was white, over seventy, quite frail and suffered from COPD. His hair was white and thinning, his bearing kindly. With his somewhat oval face framed by aging wire-rimmed glasses, he could pass for a mild-mannered accountant or attentive male nurse. At the time of this writing he had been isolated in one of several small cells in the Allred Unit infirmary for approximately four years. He is of medium height and on the thin side. His stomach protruded considerably, due to a hernia job botched by TDCJ. He was well educated and successful in the world of business

He deeply regretted the kind of life that brought him to prison, but also challenged the way the legal system adjudicated his case. Over the years of confinement he underwent a religious conversion and did what he could to atone for the way he had harmed others—by doing his best to help those around him.

No doubt there are those who would be quick to assert that he had merely caught "jail-house religion" and used it to obtain certain advantages. Having known Ned for about ten years, however, I firmly doubt that this was the case.

Ned was somewhat unusual, in that he had a relative on the outside who occasionally put money in his trust account, but he did not hoard the money for his own purposes. Often he used some of it to purchase something for one of his indigent brothers in white. The system forbids prisoners to help each other in this way (they call it 'traffic and trade"), so when he did this he always ran he risk of "catching a case."

Cases can be major or minor, depending on the whims of the officer or prison employee who writes the case. Punishment can vary from denial of recreation or commissary privileges for forty-five days or more to time in the "hole." The "hole" is no longer what the word suggests. Typically, it is a small cell in solitary confinement, which is not absolutely "solitary".

Ned studied Christian music and became somewhat adept at coaching other prisoners in singing at services. Over the years he was selected to guide both the Protestant and Catholic choirs.

One of the Chaplains at the unit was of an evangelical persuasion and some of his services featured faith healings, "slaying in the Spirit," and religious experiences along those lines. On one occasion Ned was joking about some of this with a few friends. He found the possibility of some of his tough acquaintances actually being "slain" by the Spirit rather problematic. Unfortunately, one of those he regarded as trustworthy ratted him out to the Chaplain.

Not long after that, Ned was in the Chapel area without a pass. Ned's unit enjoyed a Kairos ministry (an interfaith activity) that met regularly on Saturday mornings. Following the gathering, some of the Kairos leaders would take musical instruments from the gym back to the Chapel for storage. Ned would regularly accompany them, to help out, never having an actual "pass." After storing the equipment, he would return with the others to their assigned quarters. He enjoyed a high level of trust within the unit and no one seemed troubled about this practice, until one fateful day.

In this particular instance, the Chaplain, knowing that Ned did not have a pass to be in the area, accused him of being "out of place." According to prison regulations this can be a very serious charge. Since the Chapel was only a few locked doors from the front gate to the prison, being "out of place" could be construed as an escape attempt. The Chaplain immediately had an officer write a major case against Ned. Apparently the Chaplain intended to make it clear to all prisoners that no one should dare make light of his religious services.

Ned was interviewed by an officer friend of the Chaplain (Capt. Wintry) and told that if he objected to his case, he would be "shipped" to another unit or placed in Building 8 (medium security) where "he wouldn't last a week." The prospect of transfer to a distant unit had quite an intimidating effect, because it meant Ned would lose all of the remaining friends he had in the world, other than his one elderly sister.

The result of the case was that Ned was removed as director of the two choirs. He was also prohibited from even singing in either choir for at least a year. Since his participation in the choir's activities had become the focus of his life, much of his Self was in effect being executed by this sentence.

Subsequently, several volunteer Chaplains and others interceded with the Chaplain to ask that the case be reduced to a minor case, but without effect. The punishment stood, but Ned's troubles were only going to get worse.

The Cancer Episode

July 17, 2009:
"This has been an incredible thirty days since June 15th. I had talked with you several times between December and May about the 'spot' on my right lung that showed up on a series of four chest x-rays. Then they did a CT scan on March 5th to further explore what it was. Well, on June 15th, the PA…called me to medical. Three months and ten days later [since March 5th] the radiologist 'read' the thing and PA…said 'you have cancer—a malignancy and we're sending you to Clements for a CT scan enhanced biopsy of the tumor.' I asked him how he knew it was cancer/malignant. He responded by saying 'they can tell by the density of the spot.'

"Well, if you want someone to create acute anxiety in you and upset your whole world, let them tell you that you definitely have cancer. Nine days later I actually got to see the CT scan report by requesting a review of my medical records (which inmates are allowed to do by law every thirty days). The report said **'suspicion'** malignancy—spot is 1.8 x 1.3 cm. Anyhow, anxiety is a great weight loss program—ten lbs. in two weeks.

"On Sunday, June 28th, a boss comes frantically looking for me at 6 p.m. saying 'we've got thirty minutes to pack you up. You're on a special medical chain to Clements leaving in thirty minutes. You have a doctor's appointment tomorrow in …' Hurry, hurry, more anxiety—more bad decisions on my part. I gave all my coffee to my friends. I expected my plight to be—biopsy -determine type of cancer—chemo— death, acting on the best information I had at the time.

Well, I was in Clements by 11:30 p.m. Sunday. For two days I was housed in Building 11. 24/7 noise, inmates screaming, kicking doors, bosses refusing to come when you need them, no showers, no shaving, cold food. Finally, on Tuesday the 30th, they took me to the infirmary to sign NPO orders and told me I would have the biopsy on Wednesday the 1st. They kept me in the infirmary that night.

Wednesday was a day of pure hell. Two guards took me to the Hospital complex. The female guard was determined to make this as unpleasant an experience as possible.

The actual CT scan/biopsy was done by a PA, not an M.D. Belly down, hands/arms above my head, handcuffed, legs chained, the tech marks my back for puncture, CT picture of the 'nodule' (they call it now). PA deadens skin and muscle, punctures back/skin/lung with a long biopsy needle with a tiny snip inside it. The process is probe/picture, probe/picture, probe/picture until the film shows the needle is in the nodule. He then snips three times to obtain tissue samples for the pathologist to 'determine the type of cancer.'

The problem is, with the probing and digging in my lung, there is a hemorrhage and I start coughing up copious amounts of blood. Remember, I'm cuffed with my hands/

arms above my head. No way to catch the blood. It's either spit or swallow. Did a bit of both. My lung did a partial collapse, so I had a huge problem breathing. Up to this point little had been said about my long-standing COPD.

I was supposed to go to 'recovery' for two hours, then back to Allred. The clinical measure of my breathing/oxygen saturation…was so bad they immediately put me on oxygen. By this time the guard had re-chained my wrist to a waist belt so I could not do anything—spit up, drink water, etc. The guard refused to loosen the handcuffs. I had to swallow the blood that continued to be coughed up/couldn't eat or drink, couldn't use the bathroom.

The two hours dragged on to six hours, breathing got worse. Guard (female) was upset because she had something she wanted to go to at 3:30. Hospital was refusing to release me because my lung condition was continuing to deteriorate.

Finally, after six hours, hospital agreed to release me **provided** guard would transport me on continuous oxygen. Hospital even provided a portable oxygen canister. Finally I was 'wheel-chaired' out to the van. The sadistic guard put me in the caged back of the van, put the portable oxygen canister in the front seat with her and off we went back to Clements. I've since wondered if I was supposed to conveniently/accidentally die on the way back to the unit.

Needless to say, I was in pulmonary crisis by the time I arrived back at the infirmary. For thirteen days I continued to cough up blood. My pulmonary oxygen measures remained at critical levels, even on continuous oxygen.

On July 10th, the pathologist report came back. The way they worded it was 'based on the tissue samples provided there is **no** evidence of a malignant process.' (No cancer). The unit's MD's first reaction was that it was a faulty tissue sample. On Monday he called the supervisory MD at BSA. The film was in front of him. The needle was **in the nodule,** the samples were good and there was no CA. So they decided to send me back to Allred immediately.

Now dr. Noolan [Perkins often uses lower case for "Dr." as an expression of his assessment of Noolan's competence], who is Medical Director at Allred, tells me I've reached the **downward** spiral in COPD, that I **may**/must remain on continuous oxygen. I'm housed in room two of the infirmary [where Ned by this time had been confined for about twenty-two months.] I get out once a day to shower and sometimes once a day to walk. My lung function is stabilizing but I must learn to function with a nasal cannula in my nose. I'm not sure I accept that this is all there is. I was once assured I had CA, but God disagreed! I believe as long as there's life in Christ, there's hope."

Ned's COPD worsened. Since his arrival in the infirmary, his treatment had become increasingly punitive.

Prison administration has a procedure given the label "Grievance System." If a prisoner feels he has been unjustly treated, he can file a Step I Grievance. After he receives a reply, if he is not satisfied he can file a Step II Grievance, which is reviewed at a higher level than at the original unit. Most prisoners will tell you that this system is not effective. The responses to Grievances typically merit the descriptor "boiler plate." The Grievance responses invariably read "insufficient evidence was found to support your claim." More or less identical wording is typical at both Step levels.

Ned did not take his treatment (mistreatment) lying down. He began to file Grievances regularly. This activity led to retaliation by the system, as evidenced in a number of subsequent letters Ned gave permission to share.

Grievances and Retaliation

Letter of January 31, 2010:
Ned asked "Have you been able to determine if infirmaries statewide are administratively/security under Ad-Seg?" ["Ad-Seg" is shorthand for "Administrative Segregation." Prisoners in this area of the unit are typically considered very high risk and are confined to their cells 24/7, except for brief periods of exercise or a scheduled shower. Such activity might be in

an enclosure open to the sky, with a netless basketball goal. Normally the individual exercises alone. Men treated this way have often belonged to gangs. They are being kept away from other gang members, or being protected from them.]

"This last item has daily consequences—comfort and access. For example, the Warden here imposed lockdown on Ad-Seg (thus us) [prisoners in the infirmary] Thursday thru Saturday because there was ice on the roads and some staff didn't come in. Thus, no phones, no walking, no day room for us….Is there any way to find out if the ACLU Prison Project has…access to Minimum Standards of Care for Prison Inmate/Patients infirmary Care?"

(When I asked the state's prison health department if it would share the TDCJ standards for minimum security prisoners in Infirmaries, the question was not answered but dispatched to the TDCJ Ombudsman's Office, which then contacted the Warden. The result was that I was barred from activities at the unit as a volunteer chaplain, with no opportunity to explain my question to the Warden.)

> March 6, 2010:
> "More and more days I am dealing with the discouragement of my failing health. When I first arrived in the infirmary and was allowed the exercise of walking a sufficient distance to make a Cardio-pulmonary-vascular difference, I could walk at a good clip for thirty minutes and tolerate it fairly well. Now, after eight plus months of almost total confinement in my cell, I can barely walk three minutes.
>
> "I am convinced I would not have decompensated [deterioration of a system or structure previously functioning satisfactorily] this rapidly if this unit had followed the spirit and Court orders of the …lawsuit the Department of Corrections agreed to abide by. **The problem is there is no one 'out there' willing to do what it takes to make the appropriate people accountable** (emphasis added).
>
> "Second shift—"Two Card"—has three incidents of either unnecessary use of force on a disabled inmate (he

has Huntington's Corea) or in two other instances blatant disregard of medical treatment—coming awfully close to "Life Endangerment"—all in the last forty-five days. [A "Card" is a shift of officers on duty during certain hours each week.]

"Yet Grievances are a sham—they say 'no evidence to support complaints…' and are signed off by the Warden, who probably didn't even read them. Yet, no one's willing to contact OIG [the TDCJ Office of Inspector General] to see if they're even aware of this institutional disregard of Court orders, inmate abuse and failure to 'police the police.'"

Subsequent to these events, between 2010 and 2016 Ned experienced a continuous series of poor medical treatment, bogus cases, grievances, retaliation (e.g., denial of access to religious services). Excerpts from a few more of his letters follow:

April 25, 2010:
"Four months ago, Medical hired a male nurse, LVN, older guy, shaved head, recent graduate from LVN school. Ms. Jenkins, RN, his supervisor, took him around to show him Building 10 from front to back. He was so new he didn't have his name tag. Ms. Jenkins introduced him to nursing, officers AND inmates as "Tunney." At the time, I thought to myself—Hmm—a fifty something, head shaved, short, new issue (not graduate) from LVN school wants to call himself a …. 'Tunney'. <u>Whatever!</u> So, for January, February and March, when he delivers my meds at 2 a.m., waking me from sleep, I simply say 'thank you, Tunney.'

"I don't put my glasses on when he wakes me up, so if he's got a name tag with any other name, I couldn't see it. Now, in sixty-eight years I've never known a mother to name her son Tunney something. It never occurred to me his first name could be Tunney. See, shoulda' called him 'Mr. Tunney'.

"Well, one fateful morning, meds are late, 3 a.m., eggs, fried, have been in 'hot box' for one and a half to two hours and are reduced to the size of a quarter. [Prisoners on some meds have to take them with or after food.] So, I think, let me show Tunney what happens to our food when meds are late. So, an officer walks by and I ask her if I can speak to Tunney. She starts screaming, almost hysterically, 'you don't call an employee by their first name.' So I scream back 'I don't know any other name for him. What's his name?'

"She answers, 'Mr. Inlet' I ask her to speak to Mr. Inlet. The other guard brings Mr. Inlet over and opens the door. When he opens the door, I tell him the guards are telling me I'm addressing him by his first name and I ask him what is the proper name for him. He says 'Mr. Inlet.' I ask him if that is what he wants to be called. He says 'yes,' and I said I would be pleased to address him as such.

"End of story? No! Officer Pumpkin writes me a MAJOR case for 'attempting to form an inappropriate relationship' by calling Mr. Inlet by his first name, Tunney. The rest was a slam dunk. Case served at 8:20 on March 31. Hearing held in my absence (I did not agree to that). Guilty 45-45-S3 to L1. The reduction from S3 to L1 was the key. In doing so, they 'suspended' my OTS (offender telephone system) so I can't call my sister …or my social worker friend … who had initiated efforts for a transfer to the ___unit. That was done in the third week of March. I signed authorization for release of medical records, etc. Maybe I should be positive and say no news is good news.

"I appealed the guilty via Grievance, as prescribed, but of course they upheld Disciplinary. I'm yet to do the Step II appeal, but don't expect much.

"I believe I told you about the guard who refused to get the nurse for me on January 16th. I wrote a Grievance on that after two nurses and two guards advised me I should. I'm sure it's coincidence it was the same shift, same Card, who wrote the first case.

August 8, 2010:
"Haven't seen or heard from Deacon Banner for past two months. I tried to get approval to even watch our 'Christian' TV—Daystar, since Warden Vrumpkin shut the door on

<u>any</u> infirmary patient attending G.P. (general population) religious activities. This disregarded what had been allowed since '96 when the decision was left to the physician whether patients could leave the infirmary for two hours….No one even answered the I-60s. [When offenders have a complaint, the first step required by the system is that they send the I-60 form to the authority within the unit with supervision over the issue.] Finally, Lt. Fumes said 'No way!'

"I'll try not to rush to judgment but to ignore the [prison] problem will not make it go away. My heart breaks when I see these young Hispanic gang members come into the infirmary psychiatric overflow, their spirits broken, their hope dashed, long sentences in Ad Seg, abandoned by family and, I guess, Church….Jesus told Peter three times, 'Feed my sheep.' Will today's Catholic Church farm out the feeding?

"[My friend] Shirley first contacted [Health Services (HS)] in March. They sent her a written reply in late April. She sent me a copy in June. And since the HS response was full of <u>untruth</u> and clearly demonstrated a total lack of any investigation, I responded with a six page explanation of how things really are here. HS then said they assigned a 'Medical Investigator'. Whom HS and this Medical Investigator is talking to is very unclear. I checked with Doctor, Nurses and infirmary Charge Nurse. None has heard from anyone from HS.

"That leaves Mr. (ex-Warden) Doolittle, who is now Medical Administrator. He is clearly pro-security, won't answer I-60s. Told one nurse to stop asking questions, etc. Anyhow, SOMEONE- ALLEGEDLY is telling []: (1) In April said inmates were allowed to freely walk one hour in dayroom. <u>Neither is true.</u> There's an IOC [interoffice communication] from Capt. Frimke attached to the wall in front of officers' desk [stating] that any walking will be done in dayroom <u>during</u> regular dayroom time (they incorrectly [illegally] call our dayroom time 'Recreation time.) Currently to do that I have to take my nine steps in each direction, avoiding two wheelchairs and two oxygen machines. Because of the twists and turns I'm now having hip pain and can't walk but three to five minutes without resting. In short, my endurance continues to suffer <u>unnecessarily</u> and as any Physiatrist (specialist in Rehabilitative Medicine) would predict, other circulatory, digestive and physical problems continue to intensify, never mind the decline in mental acuity from isolation....

September 24, 2010:
Ned included in this letter a *New York Times* article published in the *Dallas Morning News* September 19, 2010: "Cost may be factor in sentencing." The article points out that the cost of a thirty year prison sentence is $504,690. This assumes an annual cost of about $17,000. Conversely, the cost of keeping Ned in the infirmary runs about $100,000 a year.

"Things were made worse on Thursday, 23rd, when the guard I had to grieve [named in a Grievance] in January finally struck for her revenge. I went to the dayroom at 6:45 p.m.. Wouldn't have done that had she been here when they called dayroom. She came after I was in the dayroom and did her shakedown. Took my new $75 Bible, all my devotionals, plus seized two <u>unopened</u> mailroom packages of books sent by my friend in Florida. Also missing are some newly issued inhalers. She later came in my cell by herself, stood at the door, made sure I could hear her and said something to the effect that if I wrote her up like I did before, 'it would be on' and the only way I could live would be to be transferred off the unit. To emphasize her threat she had one of the male bosses come paste his face in the door window, turn on my light, stare threateningly, pound and kick on the door <u>throughout the night</u> (after he took off his name tag so I wouldn't know who he was. I wonder if he'll be the one she gets to physically abuse me or even kill me?

"...There's nothing more to say about [] and my circumstances that hasn't already been said. I am certainly <u>no</u> security threat, although I'm an easy target, very vulnerable, to a guard like Ms. Espinosa. There are now seven of us G-2s (a minimal security classification) in this infirmary. None of us is physically able to go anywhere if they should leave the doors open. There's no reason we need the restrictiveness of Administrative Segregation. But who will listen when we plead our circumstances? No one willing to or able to do anything about it."

November 25, 2010:
"....NO ONE initially, not Allred and not [TDCJ headquarters] (Ombudsman or Internal Affairs) will objectively look at the subtle and not so subtle abuse of elderly, medically/physically disabled inmates. The Prisoners' Rights Program doesn't even acknowledge receipt of documentation or evidence from inmates. This failure to acknowledge compromises the safety of inmates reporting internal abuse. It makes it possible for the mail system to open and compromise the mail.

"What puzzles me is the inability (or is it unwillingness?) of people to see how interrelated rape, abuse, retaliation, failure to investigate, Rank's failure to supervise, and any and all officer misbehavior are part and parcel of the thing. The structure is there to remedy, but NO ONE CARES. Any officer who properly does their job does so out of their own individual integrity. When there's enforcement, it's for the ridiculous (as you well know!)."

January 22, 2011:
"....The Step II response was received by me on Dec. 27th. Of course, they denied all my claims <u>but</u> said I <u>could</u> receive my books/Bible back. Problem is tho, it appears Allred will ignore Region 5 determinations. [TDCJ is divided into a number of 'Regions.' The Allred unit is under the supervision of Region 5, to which Step II Grievances are sent.] Go figure. Anyhow, I'll be sending a copy of a letter I sent to Region 5 [and to] Internal Affairs, refuting their findings and showing how the Grievance investigation <u>ignored</u> what a nurse, officer and Medical Administrator saw/knew and how the officers violated eleven personnel rules."

February 14, 2011:
"Am almost finished with a letter to Larry Winston [a reporter who has written a number of articles dealing with prison issues.]

In his letter to Winston, Ned commented on how TDCJ has abandoned what the Federal Court decision accomplished. He addressed four areas of concern:

Medical: Ned mentions his background in health issues with the U.S. Army Medical Services Corps, the Medical College of Georgia, then Kaiser-Permanente. He writes "I mention this foundation so you won't think I'm just upset because the same nurses keep giving me the wrong pills. They probably do the same to the Alzheimer's [patient] in Cell 8, but when I verbalize concern I'm told I don't have the right to speak of another inmate's care (whistle-blower)…. TDCJ is unable to meet in any cost effective, reasonable quality of care way the huge increase of elderly, disabled, sick, dying inmates. The Alzheimer in Cell 8 wasted away to 110 pounds before anyone noticed he wasn't eating and was confused and urinating on himself in dorm housing.

Safety and Security: "….When you look closely, you see how, for example, an arrogant, upwardly mobile Lt. or Capt. can refuse to allow the disabled inmate permission to ambulate….The stroke [victim] with left side paresis makes no improvement if he doesn't walk (ambulate).

Safeguards: "Multi-page Policy and Procedures assure a fair and equitable mechanism to protect inmates from officers' abuse of power. These are summed up in 'Grievance and Disciplinary.' You have been sent samples of where these have collapsed….The legislature was told [in 2007] that although eighty-five percent of inmates testified the [Grievance] system did not work, their conclusion (AG Office) was it was 'achieving its objectives'!….They also failed to mention that some fifteen percent+ of inmates surveyed could not read or write!

<u>Chaplaincy:</u> "….Senator Tanner did a press release proudly proclaiming every unit has a Chaplain. Nobody mentions that the real source of care is the volunteer chaplain. Has anyone looked at [the system's] <u>severe</u> limitation they've put on what volunteers can say or do? There's nothing left to sustain their interest or motivation.…The Chaplain here has run off most volunteers. They <u>fire</u> the volunteer who tries to 'intercede for an inmate.'

"….I would hope you would not evaluate my credibility based on what I did twenty years ago to end up in prison. I don't deny it nor do I try to excuse it. I abhor what was done but cannot continue to exist if I don't turn the page or close the door on that as past.…

"….Anyhow I don't really have to fear being killed because of my crime. <u>Twice,</u> officers have tried/threatened to cause my death—another story.…I am not writing to you from a psychosis, unrestrained rage, desperate neurosis or secretive agenda. But I see what only an inmate can see!!! [The system] has gone to…extraordinary lengths to 'cover over' where it fails to perform by its own standards. I would like to contribute to that being brought to the light and submitted to public scrutiny, even if it must be at my expense."

Medical Challenges in TDCJ Confinment

February 18, 2011:

Ned commented on a *Dallas Morning News* article of February 11, 2011 concerning the cost of incarceration of older, sick prisoners. The article pointed out that of 1,000 offenders potentially appropriate for medical release in a recent year, only fifty-nine won discharge by the parole board. The Budget Board staff estimated that caring for a critically ill inmate can cost the state more than $10,000 a year. The article noted that in 2009, seventy-four inmates died of natural causes.

Parker challenged the report on several fronts. The true annual cost of caring for an offender in this category is more like $100,000 a year. And at the Allred unit alone he knew of eleven who had died in the past year. "Violent" offenders are excluded from consideration for release. But the scope of "violent" is poorly defined. Even with murder, there is an immense difference between a cold blooded killer and a one-time act of passion.

Offenders with sex crimes are not eligible, so the prison continues to lock up an eighty-one year-old offender with Alzheimer's who is habitually disoriented. Also refused was a terminal man who killed in revenge twenty-seven years ago. He has been denied parole five times and is so disabled with cancer/stroke he can barely walk, can't eat, and is otherwise severely disabled. Then there is another sex crime offender who is sixty-nine, incontinent, requires help to get out of bed, totally dependent for care and certainly "non-violent."

"A little more detail: A year and a half ago, Cal Summers was told he had cancer and was terminal. He was placed in Cell 12 and hospice isolation. For a short while he would be taken to day room in a wheel chair for short periods. He was unable to ambulate to shower. He continued very slow deterioration. After a <u>long</u> wait he was denied release to confinement in a community near his family….He gave up and stopped eating—wanting to hurry dying.

"Finally, at the beginning of 2010 he was transferred to Montford for some reason (I guess because he wouldn't die). He was returned to Allred nine to ten months later, still alive, but barely. For the past three to four months he's bedridden, incontinent of stool, seldom can eat, on Ensure to add weight. **Death is a fickle lady—sometimes can't be hurried or given a time-line.** This man doesn't fit in "infirmary care," let alone general population….But Cal Summers can't be "paroled" because he has a charge of aggravated sexual abuse of a child!

"The security needed for the elderly, disabled, sick and dying inmate is <u>totally</u> different from that for a thirty-year-old gang member/murderer! And the [Ad Seg] guards shouldn't be assigned. That's how my <u>abuse</u> was triggered in January, 2010. And we don't <u>need</u> our doors locked shut 24/7. We're not going anywhere—we can't!

February 28, 2011:

"There's also the question of reprisals. While offenders are <u>required to be permitted access to legislators, courts, public officials, etc.,</u> it is well known that retaliation is common for doing so, even though to do so is a Level One (most serious) PD-22 violation (#22). In the instant case, the denial by Officers Lindley, Espinosa, etc. is also a Level Two offence (denial of privileges or entitlements) (PD-22, #23). The range of disciplinary action <u>may</u> include probation, suspension without pay, reduction in pay, involuntary demotion and dismissal. For Level One, <u>dismissal</u> is recommended.... What makes the actions of Espinosa and Lindley even more <u>actionable</u> is that Sgts., Lts., Capts., and Majors AND the Warden (via Grievance) have known or should have known of Espinosa, Lindley and Allen's PD-22 violations beginning January, 2010 and continuing through the February 23rd "disappearance" of my ID, and thereby <u>knowingly</u> denying the privilege of commissary. There's "Grievance issues", but also the <u>questions</u> of (1) Did this occur subsequent to my letters to McEntire [Congressman] and Grand [church official]? (2) Is there any connection to the <u>conjecture</u> (calculations) on lost revenue via commissary that were mailed to a state legislator....There's even the question of whether those mail communications have been illegally opened. Or (3), is any of this the unit's (Allred's) response to the letter to [the reporter] Mr. Winston?

"What I suspect would be the greater offense in the eyes of Warden Buster is the continuing pattern of leaving their post and falsifying documents that began in January, 2010.

"....I think, surmise, guess, conjecture, etc., etc. that officers who work in Ad-Seg are often so stressed by so many of the psychopathic/psychotic offenders confronting them every day that maintaining integrity and adhering to rules becomes very difficult. The question is does it make it OK to abandon the rules when overseeing a G-2 medically disabled, elderly, sick/dying sixty-nine-year-old in the infirmary who has done nothing to provoke them, unless doing what he's legally permitted to do provokes them?

"Now, here's another ramification. If failure to enforce rules, falsifying documents, and covering up officers' PD-22 violations at the unit level is well known AND sanctioned, then is it not also so that gross misinformation (lies) is forwarded to the Regional level, (thus the letter to Region 5) and from there the misinformation is forwarded (in enhanced form) to [TDCJ headquarters]? (You can see an example of this when the Ombudsman investigated and dismissed the allegations AND [] refused to release their findings and "work product" to State Representative Jim McEntire." [Ned goes on to mention that there were two staff witnesses to some of his more serious allegations.]

March 21, 2011:
Ned critiques the standards used by the Parole Board to determine who is eligible for release because of poor mental or physical condition:

"Sex offenders are not eligible unless they are in a coma or persistent vegetative state. Violent offenders who have committed such crimes as murder or aggravated robbery are only eligible if terminally ill or requiring long term care. Death row inmates and those incarcerated for life without parole are not eligible. In 2010, 457 of 1,443 cases referred were considered and 102 were approved. Fifty-four were terminally ill, forty-six needed long term care (coma, etc.). One was mentally ill and only one was released because of advanced age."

159 inmates who had been referred for medical parole died behind bars in 2010. Anyone who has spent any time visiting geriatric or

hospital wards in the TDCJ system readily sees the absurdity of keeping many of these men and women in prison, when they could be readily maintained and monitored in nursing homes, at much less expense to the state.

In his letter to the MN editor, Ned comments:

> "The public needs to know 'the whole story.' Remember the Sounder/Mulvaney article on the [] Commission's [youth camp] evaluation? The very infrastructure collapse that led to that scandal is 'business as usual' in TDCJ. The Federal Court mandates … now ten + years later, are basically common jokes officers share. Incredible compartmentalization rife with $130,000 a year administrative jobs designed to 'cover-up' manifold multiple violations of [Federal requirements] is what limitlessly inflates costs, not inmate milk cartons that are to be replaced with powdered milk.
>
> "There are very few politicians willing to tackle the bottomless money pit that TDCJ has become. There are no 'Father O'Brien's' to take on the cause (TDCJ fires Chaplains who speak out for abused inmates). And it may be that no reporter (or newspaper) wants to respond to the inmate 'scum' (America's 'Most Wanted' term) speaking out and revealing what you will never hear or come to know if you listen only to mysteriously based statistics and politically motivated spin from highly paid TDCJ spokespersons or the Chairman of the Board of Pardons and Paroles, where I assure you political pressure is a factor."
>
> "….I'm also sending you a copy of Step I and II [Grievances] regarding the ID card….See what I mean, data gathered at ground level that is falsely handled and replied to, then reported, then passed up the structure severely compromises what the big shots report to the legislature. I wonder if these politicians know that—or care?"

Ned next lists copies of several letters he wished me to forward to Larry Winston, to D. Sinister, M.D., Executive Director of TDCJ HC (six pages), to State Representative George Oxley (except for ACC, these are all fictitious names, substituted for the actual names of legislators, officials, etc.), to the ACA (American Correctional Association), and to Major Ratter of Allred.

> "But", he comments "the problem continues that USPO and other mail from/to the infirmary is taken to Ad-Seg control [where Officers Lindley, Espinosa and Allen work], then to/from the mail room. Mail comes/goes, but also disappears like my ID did. The mail room is aware of this. Suggested I write the Warden. I did, but nothing changed. As expected, the Warden doesn't believe offenders. I've had friends (inmates) who worked Ad-Seg as SSI (janitor jobs) who have seen officers tear up inmates' mail and I-60s."

In his letter to Dr. DiNoansora, Ned asks for clarification of minimum standards of health care for TDCJ offenders housed in infirmaries. He notes:

"This document is sent to you <u>only</u> after having exhausted <u>all</u> resources available to an offender, both those mandated and those within the organizational structure; Grievances have failed, the Patient Care Coordinator is non-responsive as is DON [Department of Nursing].

> "For the past fifteen months there have been continuous problems in nursing care/patient management involving, primarily, medication errors, charting inconsistency, lag between med disbursement and [prescribed] feeding [times], ambulation of patients, and nursing's responsibility when patients are abused and/or clearly prescribed treatment is thwarted or prevented by Security."

Parker provided five pages documenting in detail all these charges. He never received a response from Dr. DiNoansora. Instead he received a form letter from a TDCJ office telling him his letter had been addressed to the wrong office, and that he should seek redress within the unit, or Grievance system!

June 10, 2011:

"….Please forgive me when I seem to lose focus. The overall goal of enlightening the outside with the hope of improvement on the inside loses its focus from daily minutiae….

"I'm constructing in my mind the content of letter to CDC [Center for Disease Control]. The TCRP [Texas Civil Rights Project] report spends several pages on the perils of Managed Care in prison. One section deals with contagious diseases—TB, HIV, Hept. C, Staph and poor containment practices. I've seen *all* that here in the infirmary, except HIV. Right now, today, there are of nine medical beds (cells) three Staph, two Hepatitis C, and maybe one TB. Plus, there's one paralyzed man in Cell 11 who's incontinent of stool [problem with feces left in the shower described above.]

"….No one supervises the SSI to make sure the shower is adequately cleaned, all feces is removed and bacteria control applied. Laundry does not always do its job. But, it's not Nursing's responsibility to oversee the SSI, nor is it Security's. Whose is it? One of many offshoots of TDCJ indifference is the mantra 'It's not my job!'

"….Meanwhile, Security is not allowed to use medical latex gloves. When serving food trays, Security is *supposed* to wash hands after contact with Staph patients….Officers are seldom told which patients have Staph….

"….The latest state of TDCJ affairs is that [health liaison office] will not accept correspondence from inmates, Ombudsman will not accept correspondence from inmates, Grievance *assumes* inmates are lying, and legislators do what?

"The TCRP, page eleven, describes Govt. Code 501.064 that requires policies and procedures of medical be made available to inmates. Law Libraries are *required* to make state law/codes available to inmates. Allred law library *swears* it doesn't exist. Should I believe the TCRP or Allred law library?

"….From Governor to inmate, the idea of 'it's not my job' is what allows an already dead inmate to be pronounced a suicide. If you'll put the sum of your information in a bowl and analytically ponder it, you'll discover how & who!

[Ned appears to be referring to an inmate I knew fairly well who was declared a suicide, which seemed highly unlikely. This did not seem in his character. He was a "fighter." He was subject to asthma and possibly he was pepper-sprayed, leading accidentally to choking and death—which was then covered up.]

"….One of the comments I made in a one page update to the ACA letter that went out…was that before too much time passes: 'whether ACA, Texas legislators, Healthcare Licensing Authorities, or the Attorney General investigation of Govt. code violations are the most appropriate avenue of resolution must soon be resolved.' I also mentiond that the kitchen now serves cockroaches with cold food trays and reiterated razor, ambulation etc. issues continue."

August 8, 2011:

"Had problems recently about inhalers to handle my ongoing, decompensating COPD. dr. Noolan (DO) informed me in June that [medical employee unknown to Ned] deleted one inhaler (Atrovert) **and** 'added restrictions' to my Proventol, saying one inhaler, considered a 'Rescue Inhaler' **must** last ninety days. When my current inhaler ran out on August 5th, nurses refused to replace it, referring to Policy.'…Finally, this AM, dr. Noolan changed it to every forty-five days, but restated I should remember 'this is not a hospital, you are in prison, etc., while others clearly intimate I am out of line with my Grievances, reference to Policy and Procedures, etc.

"….I've repeatedly requested access to CCC Policies and Procedures. Finally, they let me see on August 3. The statute 501-064 passed in 2001, requiring inmate access, was **finally** complied with August 1, 2011 (four years later). That's when the law library said they received it.

"I wrote a second letter to CCC….When CCC returned the letter with their rejection form letter, the Allred Mail Room sent it to Medical who 'inadvertently' opened it by 'mistake,' instead of to me….If I die suddenly and inexplicably, there may be cause for an independent autopsy….Could occur if they take away my oxygen.

"Did I ever tell you about a **young** inmate, **maintenance worker**, with no known health problems? One hot day he started having trouble breathing. Since he was known and liked, several fellow maintenance workers (remember they occupy the highest inmate-status/rank in TDCJ) persisted and got a boss to come look at him because he needed to go to the infirmary. Boss came, said he was 'faking.' Some time passed (fifteen minutes I think). His friends went to the boss again, who said the same thing but then, because the inmate gasping for breath was a **maintenance worker**, said he'd call the infirmary. Came back and said the infirmary wouldn't bring a wheel chair. Friends said 'Look, he's in trouble. We're gonna take him to the infirmary. If you want to stop us, call the goon squad. Because they were **maintenance workers**, the boss let two (I think) walk him the quarter mile plus to the infirmary [From Building 18, where he was, to the infirmary was about two-thirds of the way across the unit.]

"I don't have information on what happened during the trek. Once at the infirmary, he was put in the cage [a holding pen where offenders are placed to await attention.] One maintenance worker was allowed to stay with him. He was left in the cage for a while (I don't know how long). **Before any** health care professional would see him, he lost consciousness, fell to the floor (in the cage), and stopped breathing. His fellow maintenance worker attempted CPR. After another while, a nurse finally came, put the unconscious inmate on a gurney, and took him inside the infirmary. We don't have any information on events/actions after that, but we know he ended up **brain dead**.

"After protracted ICU care (paid for by TDCJ), TDCJ released the inmate to his family who lived back East. This is perhaps four years later and, as far as we know, the family is still footing the bill for their brain dead son.

"Here's an outcome of a 'deliberate indifference' climate that combines physician/nurse indifference with Security indifference: ....Remember our Cell 8 Alzheimer eighty-two year-old who was getting 'whatever medication' but didn't know the difference? Several weeks ago Medical (dr. Noolan) received 'unsubstantiated confirmation' of his acceptance at one of the newly formed 'TDCJ Nursing Homes' (or whatever they're called). I guess dr. Noolan thought Cell 8's transfer was imminent, so without forethought he discharged him from the infirmary and Security put him in Building 11—Pre-hearing Detention [this building also houses 'solitary confinement' offenders.] (Imagine how confused Mr. Young was by then).

"When he didn't transfer [out], some unthinking Security decided to put him in dorms. Yes, dorms. [Dorms are housing sections comprised of open cubicles rather than cells. Normally, inmates with the best security classifications are placed there.] There he…probably had trouble finding the toilet or cubicle. After several days of not being able to figure out how to walk the quarter mile to the chow hall and even being turned back once by a Capt. who didn't have the skill to recognize his confusion, some boss sent him to the infirmary and dr. Noolan stirred up unusual mercy and readmitted him.

"The only thing Mr. Young can or tries to manage that's not set before him is he likes to watch wrestling on T.V. Of course he asks probably thirty times a week if 'wrestling's on tonight or is it time for wrestling?' God, spare me!"

August 10, 20211:
"Glory! Cell 8 and Cell 13 (seventy-two year-old with broken back) were transferred to the 'new' (nursing home) facility. I **think** they said it's in [], Texas. dr. Noolan told me I couldn't go due to being on oxygen machine [a nursing home that can't handle oxygen?.]"

August 25, 2011:

"….Want to pass on another sad, sad series of events: Approximately two and one-half years ago, Cal Summers was told he had cancer. He decompensated and became an invalid, unable to get about except by wheel chair. He was sent to M…'s 'extended care'/hospice and stayed there about a year. He was mostly unable to perform activities of daily living without assistance. What happened at M… was not clear, but at some point he was told he **did not** have cancer. By now he weighs probably less than 100 pounds, is bed bound and frequently incontinent. M… sends him back to his unit of origin [Allred], suggesting dietary supplement. In the year that has since passed, he's gained little weight, continues persistent cough, increased weakness and incontinence of stool. Nurses occasionally speak of him as purposely defecating on himself. I've seen him lay in it many days.

"The SSI's who clean (one in particular) are convinced he does this on purpose. He only leaves his cell when they (RNs, Officers) decide to bathe him. Officers feed him reluctantly. He stinks!

"I talk with him daily. A brilliant man, PhD in law, career with NASA, was referred for Medical Parole, but denied because of his crime (daughter). I have noticed a sharp decline in cognitive function. Suggested to RN a Psych evaluation. They looked at me like I'm crazy. I thought it would encourage more compassion. I wonder how bad his skin has become, since he lied on his back in feces hour after hour, day by day. His left foot has developed 'claw toes' because of his prolonged, extended physical neglect. I don't know if he can feel cramp-like things.

"I guess you can imagine how I project myself into this. If I have a stroke (my family all die from strokes), I guess my demise will not be as protracted since I doubt they'll feed me or give me water. 'God, what would you ask of me? What can I do?'"

"….Saw dr. Noolan for ten minutes today. Interesting. He's more administrator than clinician. I think he **thinks** as one would whose dealt with TDCJ for ten years and survived. It's possible that the effect of that is insurmountable.

"Oh, one last thing. In 2007, rules were passed that every elderly, chronically ill inmate would have an Individual Treatment Plan. I got mine 8/5/2011 (four years later). dr. Noolan diagnosed me with cancer of the lung (don't have), acrocyanosis feet & toes (don't have), said I was on 'regular diet' (I'm on diet for health), and said I agreed to limited physical activity due to medical problems (I argued for fifteen minutes for **increased** activity. Wrote him an I-60 to review, which he ignored)."

September 25, 2011:

"Well, another's been set free! The guy next door (Cell 3) departed this world around midnight. Ironic he should depart at the beginning of a Lord's Day he denied existed. Was adamant God doesn't exist. Well, he knows now, at 2 p.m. on this Lord's Day, fourteen hours later.

"Here's a little piece of denomination **stuff**! He said he was a born-again Baptist for many years. Father was a preacher even! So, if the Baptists are correct, he still made Heaven! But there's Scripture like Hebrews Six that seems to describe him. [Hebrews 6: 4-6, 'For it is impossible to restore again to repentance those who have been enlightened…and then have fallen away, since on their own they are crucifying again the Son of God and are holding him up to contempt.']

"He rejected Catholicism, so no Purgatory? Wonder if there's any place special in Hell for a doctor of law? Lots of inmates think so of lawyers. But then, he's **outta here**! When I go, let God decide my eternal destiny and celebrate, dance, sing."

At this point we will leave Ned's story, until it is taken up again in the **Epilogue**. As we have seen, he has reached a very low point, psychologically and physically. Yet he maintains a sense of humor and a hope that someone will pick up on his concerns, for himself and others, and take action.

CHAPTER THREE

THE REJECTED CHILD

My wife and I first met Curtis Hutchins when a friend brought him to our "choir practice," as we prepared for our afternoon service in the gym. These practices were always on the dramatic side as Ned, whose story we told above, tried to keep the peace as the "brothers in white" vied for who would play the guitars that day. At the time we met, Curtis was a white male, about fifty-eight years old, who looked much older than his age.

If anyone ever looked beaten down, it was Curtis. He was a very small man, probably less than five feet tall and very slender, creating the impression of someone who was never very well fed. His hair was thick, always slicked straight back with water, and somehow even more black than that of Carlos. His face was as wrinkled as someone much older, and his front teeth were broken.

My wife and I tried to visit with him for a few minutes each time we came to the unit, but did not really know much about him. Eventually he let us know that he was in prison for sexually assaulting a child, a crime which he said he did not commit. Apparently his case had been appealed a number of times and one day he showed us a letter from the Supreme Court indicating he had been denied "Certiorari," meaning that his case would not be reviewed.

One day he brought us a hand-written manuscript of about 200 pages, with the title *The Rejected Child*. He begins his story when he was about the age of ten. A bit later he returns to earlier years when he was around four. These were pleasant years, when he lived in Florida with his parents and three brothers. (When he was in the second grade his fourth brother was born).

He wrote that not long after this his mother underwent a change that would be devastating for him. From this time until he left home in his teens he would be denied food, beaten, and tortured in ways that can only be described as diabolical

Upon reading Curtis's manuscript, I was both puzzled and stunted. How could this mousy little fellow write so vividly of his unbelievable abuse by his mother? How could any child be so terribly treated? How could a man of almost sixty, a man so obviously crushed by life, recall his childhood in such detail, even given that some of the experiences were certainly unforgettable?

One day my wife and I were taking a walk through a mall when she stopped at her favorite vitamin shop. While chatting with her, the young female shop attendant began telling her she was enrolled in a course in criminal justice. Her teacher had required the students to read a book entitled *A Child Called It*.[126]

She proceeded to tell us something about the book. She noted in particular a horrifying story about the mother of this child, who forced him to drink ammonia (an incident Curtis narrated in his manuscript). Not only did it include the tale of the ammonia, Curtis's manuscript replicated the entire book, practically word for word. *A Child Called It* was written by Dave Pelzer and originally published by the Omaha Press in 1993. It carried the endorsement of one of his teachers when he was a young child, Steven Ziegler.

Upon discovering the apparent plagiarism several years after we lost contact with Curtis, we could only ask ourselves "Why?" Why would anyone go to so much trouble?

Possibly Curtis's experiences in prison were a factor. He told us once of having been raped twice by a large man placed in his cell. After

---

[126] Dave Pelzer, *A Child Called "It"*, Omaha Press: Nebraska, 1993; Health Communications, Inc.: Deerfield Beach, Florida, 1995.

Curtis filed a complaint against this offender, the man was removed from his cell, but continued to be housed in the same pod. Each time he saw him, it struck new fear into Curtis's diminished capacity to cope.

[The problem of rape is endemic in U.S. prisons and has recently provoked new legislation. Joaquin Sapien's 8/30/2013 article *"In Effort to End Prison Rape, Questions About a Monitor's Independence"*[127] in **Pro Publica** reports that the American Correctional Association has been selected to conduct the first series of formal audits to implement "The Prison Rape Elimination Act." The ACA has been criticized for its failure to effectively monitor prisons it has accredited, but Representative Charlie Scott of Virginia, who helped author the legislation, has said he is comfortable with ACA handling the work.]

Possibly this book so accurately mimicked Curtis's childhood he was moved to reproduce the story as his own. Perhaps he desperately wanted us to appreciate what he had experienced in his formative years.

We used to visit the Estelle Unit (to which Curtis was moved from Allred) on a regular basis. Curtis had a friend there, the one who had brought him to choir at Allred, who encouraged him to attend the service. He did so twice. Whereas formerly he would like to visit a bit, now he did not seem to have time and quickly left the service, saying little. We did not see him again.

We asked his friend if he knew what was transpiring. He shook his head and said all he knew was that Curtis had stopped taking his "meds." Later I wrote to Curtis, but the letter was returned as undeliverable. I called the unit to see if Curtis had been moved to another unit. No, Curtis was dead.

We will never know what caused his death. TDCJ does not release this information to inquiries from volunteers. We do know that while he was at Allred and thought his cancer was in remission, the system neglected his six month checkups, sometimes conducting them more than six months late. His transfer to the medical operation at Estelle

---

[127]   Sapien, Joaquin. "In Effort to End Prison Rape, Questions About a Monitor's Independence," *ProPublica*, August 30, 2013. http://www.propublica.org/article/in-effort-to-end-prison-rape-questions...

suggests the return of his cancer. Or, the fact that he stopped taking his meds, may mean that he had simply given up on his very, very hard life.

No notice of death. No obituary. No one to claim the body. No funeral. After learning of his death, I wrote to one of his brothers to see if the family would like to have my copy of Curtis' manuscript. There was no reply. Truly, Curtis was the "rejected child."

CHAPTER FOUR

MADNESS OR MISTREATMENT?

The TDCJ Chaplaincy operation has a process through which volunteers can become qualified to serve as volunteer chaplains (CVCA's). With this certification, the CVCA is given a special badge and is permitted to visit offenders throughout the unit, including in the Ad Seg pods, High Security wings and infirmary. It was as a CVCA at the Allred infirmary that I first met Charlie Gilmore, Jr. (Bobby Randolf, Jr. in the original edition)

While visiting an ill inmate, I heard someone behind me call out "Chaplain" through the heavy, sealed cell door (the doors in the infirmary have a small window constructed of something like very thick Plexiglas). Turning around, I saw frantically staring at me through the window a rather emaciated African American man with a badly bruised face and two black eyes. It was Charlie Gilmore, Jr. He appeared to be about forty to fifty years old. He was quite thin, with a narrow, pock-marked face. Light skinned, he appeared more Latino than Black. He was clothed in a tee-shirt tattered with holes. [TDCJ provides decent white shirts to inmates as part of their "necessities," but for some reason Charlie typically wore this tee shirt.] This was in October of 2004.

On October 9, 2004 I received the following letter:
"….Well for me, I told you alright. But I feel real bad. That's why I'm writing you. I **lied**! No, I am not alright. And things are getting worse. I just saw that officer right in the back of you. And I knew telling you would make it more worse for me. And I can see you are getting Old, but you still are trying to do good work for God and his people. [When inmates communicate to us in this manner, we always start by wondering if their remarks come from the heart, or are they setting us up for a con? Only Time tells.]

"See, I just would feel real bad if something happen to you by you trying to help me with these **Devils**! [Eventually something rather bad did happen. After about ten years serving as a volunteer, I was dismissed from the Chaplaincy by the Warden for trying to help Charlie reach one of his sisters, as well as for asking a question on behalf of Ned Parker.] It is much of Satan working here. Now I know I asked for your help.

"But see I have been in here for fifteen years and I have Life & 99 years so I'm never going home. And I know how much wrong these people will do.

"But please know I do appreciate all you have did. And I do know you would try to do more to help. But now I'm **scare** [sic] for you. Because it's a Big Gang of Outlaws that work here. And they will do crazy things! So I don't want nothing to happen to you. I can take it. I'm much younger!

"God be with you! Always!"

Around this time Charlie sent me a copy of a Step I Grievance he had submittedApril 6, 2004:

"On the last time I was saw by Medical I saw the PA, Mrs. Berryhill, and I was telling her I be feeling bad that my blood pressure be up like the medication is no good no more. My head be killing me! See I ask the LVN to take my blood pressure on that machine so I can read it too! But he said No! Now when I'm not having problems with my blood pressure, they are always use it! The LVN's name is Mr. Mistka…

"....Now by her being mad [Mrs. Berryhill] she knowingly and intentionally wrote in my medical records for me to get this water pill that I am **allergy** to! And it's in my medical records that I am allergy to it. I am sending you one of the water pill and to show you she is trying to cause me harm.

"....I need to see the Dr.! Now I am **seriously scare** of the PA! Please let me see someone that will do they job and not try to hurt me! [If it were not for the health care experience of Ned at Allred, which has been documented above, this might be considered the paranoid raving of a mentally ill offender—but was it?]

"....And I know that is discrimination by the LVN. Mr. M. is using that machine to see if the other inmates' blood pressure is high! But not on me! Like I'm Dog!....Please, let me see the Dr. so I can get the right medication! And to stop me being showed harassment or retaliation. I need to see someone else." [Here he inserted the name of the medication as Triamterene HCTZ 37.5/25]

On May 4, 2004, he received this response:

"You were asked by Ms. Berryhill if you had any allergies, to which you replied no. Medication was prescribed and it was later determined you had an allergy to it. This medication was discontinued and collected from you. You were then prescribed a different medication. Additionally, you are being monitored to ensure there are no ill effects." [The medications are not specifically identified and the signature of the Medical responder is illegible.]

On December 6, 2004 Charlie indicated a desire to file a law suit because of the abuse he claimed:

"To whom it may concern: This is very **serious** and important! For the last five months I have been going through much cruel and unusual punishment, physical abuse assaults and now it have come to **sexual abuse!**

"Yes I have been writing **Serious Life In Danger** I-60s, Grievances and complaints before the assault would happen. But the officials would ignore the reported threats! ["Life in Danger" is the technical name for a specific type of complaint offenders are permitted to file. Offenders are told to notify a certain office if they believe their lives are in danger. This notice is then supposed to be investigated.]

"Well I lost a tooth in one, two black eyes and hit in the head on one [the result of which I witnessed in the infirmary], and right now I got a broke hand from trying to help myself from a knew Predator that was showing **sexual abuse** and harassment to me!

"Because the officials will not help me. Now five times is no coincidence. All of this is knowingly and intentionally, by putting mentally ill inmates in the cell with me. See I can prove this by you just talking to the inmates. My cellie is the one I got into it with. And have me take a polygraph examination and the officers I gave the I-60s too! That will show you I'm not lying on them. One was just trying to assault me with a pen! See I had wrote on a I-60 a week ago that my cellie is crazy and he have threat me! And that I feel my **life is in serious danger**! And gave it to Officer F… and asking would they Please Help Me! By moving me or the inmate. And I told them about what had happen with me and the other cellie I had that was mentally ill! And that I was trying to stop from something else happening to me. And that I have a broke hand and cannot help myself too good. But no, no one did nothing!

"Now for this to keep going on and on, you must know it is Serious Criminal Activity going on by the officials! And now Medical is showing Conspiracy with them by not doing nothing for my broke hand! The Dr. had said it was broke on 10-12-04 and they did not do nothing for it. Please if you cannot help me, will you send this to someone you feel can. God knows I'm not lying. Please help me soon!

"I sworn under the penalties of perjury and I declare that the above is true and correct under the penalty of Perjury. Signed pursuant to 28 U.S.C. 1746, etc…."

January 5, 2005:

"…But we must do something about these Devils because if it's not me again, it will be someone else! Now everyone cannot take what I have took. Some will kill they self. And these people will have gang inmates kill for them too! I do know what I'm talking about. I have been in here sixteen years! Yes inmates do dirty work for them!"

January 24, 2005:

"…I must say God is good. See, when he keep someone like me in control, showing love and having a good attitude with my enemy, that's God working with me. And I give all thanks of Him! I know I couldn't do nothing like this on my own….Now I know that God be wanting me to take care some of those wrong evil doing people. See it's some criminal activity going on here that need the Law to take care of! They are out of control! What's so bad about it is the Warden is not trying to stop it! Well today is my Birthday and I cannot relax! Please keep praying for me…"

March 14, 2005:

"….But it's one thing I do want you all to know. Yes these people will do wrong things with our mail. Like not send it out. Or not give it to us! I can prove it to you. And if you want me to send proof to you I will."

This letter had attached to it copies of Step I and Step II Grievances. The first was filed December 21, 2004 and the second January 24, 2005. They concerned Charlie's fear for his life. He admits to snitching on a Lt. and the head of Crips (reporting to the Warden something he considered serious wrongdoing). The fact that he had done this was known to other inmates, resulting in his fear that he might be killed by the Crips. The official response to Step I was "You were reviewed by UCC on 1/6/05 for life endangerment. Your request was declined." (Signed by Warden Winslow). The response to Step II was: "Appropriate investigation was conducted at the unit level. There is no evidence to

support your life endangerment claims. No further action is warranted."
(Signature illegible)

> March 28, 2005:
> "....Now I'm sick and I know I need the right medication
> for my Hepatitis-C that the Dr. say is real bad, and the right
> antibiotic for my skin that I'm not allergy to. But now let's
> use common sense it's several other things that have been
> did wrong. Now to me it's not intelligent to take the <u>chance</u>
> to take some medication from them. And I do understand
> it's not like I can go to another hospital and see some other
> PA and nurses. But I feel I will die soon if I take some
> medication from them."

[This becomes an ongoing concern. Because of what had happened in the past, Charlie has no confidence in the unit to provide medication he can trust. If he takes the medication provided, it might harm him. If he does not, he will definitely suffer from his diseases.]

Attached to this letter was a copy of a Step II Grievance submitted December 20, 2004. Charlie explains that he allowed TDCJ to operate on his shoulder and was told it could not be fixed. It would slip out of joint from time to time. Nevertheless, he was assigned a top bunk and could not manage to get into it when his shoulder was "out." At such times, he had to sleep on the floor, with nothing but a sheet.

Next, his hand was x-rayed and the Dr. determined it was broken. He was told he could not have a cast. He was given nothing but the cover of a splint, because it could not have metal in it.

Finally, he again noted that he had a constant problem with pimples exuding pus and blood. His complaint was that he was not receiving the treatment other inmates were getting for these types of medical conditions. He declares in the Grievance

> "I'm not a Dog! And it's nothing I can do because I'm Black!
> No one deserves to be ignore with serious medical needs! I
> need your help!"

A response to this Grievance was dated 12/31/2004. It stated that Charlie had "received treatment in accordance with the complaints presented to the medical department." It went on to inform him that he had not provided specific dates for other complaints and referred him to the Office of Health Care systems in…. It judged "no action through the Grievance mechanism is warranted." (Signature illegible)

November 7, 2005: Charlie wrote that he thought he was suffering from a Staph infection, which was getting worse because he believed they were again offering an antibiotic to which he was allergic. He was also told by the doctor that his "enzyme is real high from the Hepatitis C. I will be dead from Hepatitis C soon!…I need your help real soon, please!"

> April 27, 2007:
> Charlie submitted a Step I Grievance to Senior Warden Buster and OIG Officer Junior McGurk stating "This is a real serious emergency! Where I been beat to the wall and floor with my face real bad, out of retaliation for the exercising my right to file Grievances and complaints to public officials! On 4/18/07 Sgt. Rimco and these officers beat me real bad and I had on handcuffs.…It's nine days after it happen and no one will help me. It's something broken in my face! The hold [sic] left side of my face is numb and my eye is still black and blood red and give me problems seeing out of it. And I'm hurting in seven other places. But you can see it with the eye, my leg, hand and balls. And to show you they was lying! Said I attempt to kick Officer Beem. It would be common sense to put **leg cuffs** on me after they beat me like that, but no they didn't…But they know I didn't try or do nothing. They beat me out of retaliation! And the **camera** that's on the wall in medical in the hall will show everything, and I will pass a polygraph test to everything I wrote on here and my Use of Force papers.…And Sgt. Rimco…saw my leg had got real big. And I showed them I was spitting up blood for three days. I'm in pain. Help!"

"Use of Force" refers to a practice where by an offender is forcibly removed from his cell when he won't exit voluntarily. Typically, about five officers dressed in riot gear from head to foot, giving them the appearance of a swat team, descend upon the cell. They often pepper spray the offender until he collapses on the floor. The team then enters the cell and places the inmate in cuffs. Next he is stripped and placed in a shower to wash off the remnants of the spray. Finally, he may be placed naked in a cell so small he can only stand erect, visible in his nakedness to all who pass along the corridor. While this is taking place, one of the members of the team holds a camera, giving the appearance of filming everything that happens. Although Charlie will appeal a number of times for the film on the camera to be reviewed, there is no evidence this was ever done.

On May 24, 2007, the Warden's office replied:

> "Your claims have been investigated. The use of force that involved you was because you became aggressive to staff.... Your face did not get broken. Medical noted a superficial abrasion to the left side of your face. I find no merit in your claims."

On May 28, 2007, Charlie filed a Step II Grievance. It was marked received by UGI on May 29, and HQ on June 5. He notes that after the beating the RN did not give him any medical care. He felt like he had been hit with a brick, yet no x-ray was taken to ensure that nothing in his face was broken. He adds, as he did in Step I, that the woman officer holding the camera told the other officers that the camera was not working, and they began beating him again.

The response at the regional level on June 22, 2007 was:

> "An appropriate investigation was conducted at the Step I Level. No evidence was found to support your claims that your life is in danger. If you feel your life is in danger, you should contact Supervisory Staff and provide the substantiating evidence. No further action is warranted at this time."

In other words, the findings at the unit level were not re-investigated. No questions of the Warden or his staff were asked. No independent person ever examined Charlie as to whether or not he showed the effects of a beating.

By the year 2008 Charlie had been moved to the Clements unit (where Ned Parker had his torturous cancer exam), but the same problems continued:

> July 10 and August 5, 2008: Problem with high blood pressure and medication.

> March 5, 2009: Pimples and pus on his face.

> May 27, 2009: His mental health was found to be stable, not delusional.

> June 8, 2009: Property and pictures taken. Charlie claimed this was retaliation for his grievances.

> July 2009: Meds to which Chalie was known to be allergic were prescribed.

> August 19, 2009: Excessive dosage of blood pressure medicine prescribed.

> November 29, 2009: Charlie set aside focusing on his problems temporarily and sent a considerate Thanksgiving greeting:

> "Old School God sent Angel!....And that's what make you a real Special Angel. You are over sixty and still putting in work and not just praying about situations! If more people that say they love God would take time and put a little work to showing it, others would too. Because they would understand that love is a Action Word!....A late Happy Thanksgiving and much happiness for Christmas Days with you and your loved ones! You are like a real uncle I never had!"

March 29, 2010 Charlie filed Step I Grievance #...6369 claiming that Officer Guzman had denied him food "3 days back to back." When he was fed, his food tray was placed on the floor. This was alleged to have been caused when Charlie filed a separate Grievance against the officer for working with gang members to get them to fight and hurt or kill him in the process. The filing received the standard response:

> "Your complaint has been investigated and reviewed.... Sufficient evidence has not been found to indicate retaliation for the use of the Grievance procedure or any other staff misconduct."

Step II Grievance followed on April 14: Charlie asserted his claims could be supported by other officers and the cameras. The response dated May 4 said that "an appropriate investigation was conducted at the unit level" and "no Policy Violation" was noted. Officer Guzman denied the allegations.

May 3, 2010:

> Charlie filed Step I Grievance #...8108, with the complaint that Officer Hellbent had threatened him, took his ID card and destroyed it. "He said now that to make me do something he is going to take me out of my cell and not put the handcuffs on right so I can fight back!" The Warden replied that Officer Hellbent denied all this and investigation did not reveal "sufficient evidence to indicate retaliation..."

June 24, 2010: Charlie received a letter from Special Agent, Thomas Cornwall (by Conrad Quirk) of the U.S. Department of Justice in reference to his letter dated October 13, 2009:

> "....A review of your complaint found no basis for a criminal civil rights investigation." However, the complaint was forwarded to TDCJ, Office of Inspector General.

July 21, 2010:

> **Well, it's much going on I need to tell you! So someone will know when something happen to me. Yes, it's that serious!"** [Emphasis added].

August 8, 2010:

> "….the Ombudsman [after papers were faxed from the office of a Senator] was supposed to be doing a Investigation. I wrote a three paper complaint. But it look like they always go with what TDCJ say. It's clear evidence that all of this is intentionally on-going retaliation! Torture!"

September 1, 2010: An affidavit was written by inmate S… stating:

> "I have witnessed several times the deprivation of [Charlie's] food by officers. I have also witnessed the harassment. The officers come on the pod and tell [Charlie] that they are going to beat his ass because he write Grievances. Officer Hellbent has denied [Charlie's] food on a regular basis. They walk right by his cell without even attempting to feed him. I will testify on his behalf concerning this matter. I certify under penalty of perjury that the foregoing is true and correct."

September 6, 2010: Charlie was accused of a disciplinary offense. The complaint stated he "did possess contraband, namely three towels, three sheets, four pair of socks and a line. Offender [Charlie] was ordered by Officer Hellbent to get off his knees and go back in his cell, and said offender failed to obey the order." Charlie's side of the story is that the officer had come in his cell and "destroyed everything." He was on his knees begging that a Sgt. be called to the cell. As a result of the "offense", his security status was downgraded. [He was already being housed in "High Security," the maximum level of security. Reduction of status meant that the few "privileges" he had were being reduced and more items normally allowed could be classified as "contraband."]

On September 3, 2010 Charlie had submitted an I-60 noting that his blood pressure medication had expired and asking for renewal of his Verapamil. On September 8th an LVN replied that an e-mail had been sent to the MD "to review chart for renewal." This was followed by a second I-60 written for the Senior Warden, Culpepper, Safe Prison, and O.I.G.:

> "Now look here he is again trying to cause my death! It's common sense that it take **all** of my medication to keep my blood pressure down so I don't have a stroke or a heart attack! It's been **ten days** without it! I'm sick. I really feel bad! And I'm scare to death. Please help!" [With his letter, Charlie sent a "Medication Print Pass" documenting the fact that a morning dose of Verapamil had not been prescribed as of September 13, 2010, and a second pass dated July 29, 2010 showing the morning 180 mg. dose of Verapamil expiring August 31, 2010].

October 11, 2010: Charlie received a reply to his Step I Grievance #...7693

> "....The provider renewed your medication, but ordered it to be received in the evening and increased the dosage to 240 mg. **This was done in error** [emphasis added] and was corrected on 9/15/10 to where you would be receiving 180 mg in the morning. According to medication compliance records, you began receiving this on 9/16/10."

October 13, 2010: Charlie wrote to the state Classification Committee at his unit: "Please safe [sic] my life and transfer me and have them to replace my property. Your help is needed. Please!"

October 13, 2010: Charlie filed Step II Grievance #...7693 reiterating that mistakes had been made nine times in two and one-half years. He believed this was purposeful retaliation and not honest error. He wrote "Please! Have O.I.G. and Safe Prison to help me soon. It's a need, before they cause my death!"

The reply (November 17, 2010): "There is no evidence of the medical department attempting to cause you harm by this action....No further action is warranted through the Grievance process."

November 12, 2010:

> "....This is just some of the mentally ill inmates they put me in the cell with for them to harm me! Like the one had did the first day I saw you!
>
> Hallow, P., 8/19/04; Butterworth, J., 10/12/04; Kringle, J.; Calista, K., 12/6/05; Johnson, R; Moreno, 1/29/06; Vincent, D. [Prison I.D. numbers were supplied by Charlie, but are omitted here.]

November 21, 2010: Charlie sent a brief note letting me know he had been moved to a new location, Estelle. "No matter what's going on here it's no way it could be worse than ...on Clements. [Unfortunately, it seems this expectation was not to be realized.]

> December 10, 2010: "This is a serious medical need. Some time I feel real bad! My feet is swelling real bad! I have Hepatitis C and High Blood Pressure real bad. I need to see the Dr.!" A sick call was provided on December 12.

January 9, 2011:

> "Yes, ...the Dr. have stopped the meds again Verapamil 180mg that I take in the a.m. Now what really look bad is that when I saw him on 1/5/11 my blood pressure was high! And he said to keep my feet from swelling and take my BP down he is going to order me another BP medication to go with my other meds. No new meds was order and this one was stopped!...Now what's a good excuse for this? I have not did or said nothing wrong to no one!...I guess I just have to take more of my KOP meds to stop from having a stroke or a heart attack and die! What you [sic] would do?"

March 7, 2011: "….I do understand what you said, thank you! And I'm doing it! About the Hepatitis C."

Sick call request February 20, 2011: "I'm having some real serious problems with my neck. It's a on-going thing with me not getting blood or oxygen to my head! Please help soon!"

March 24, 2011: "I just saw the Dr. on 3/24/2011. It took thirty days and still didn't do nothing for me!"

March 27, 2011:

> "….No, I'm still not getting no help from my sisters and it's getting hot in this cell [his new unit is located in Southeast Texas, which becomes very hot and humid in late spring]…. when it's hot it make my blood pressure high too! In this cell with no **fan, radio** and just a little **hygiene** to make it on, is not a good feeling. [Charlie added a reference to Hebrews 13:3, one of his favorite quotes: "Remember those who are in prison, as though you were in prison with them; those who are being tortured, as though you yourselves were being tortured."]

April 21, 2011: Charlie sent an I-60 to the Chaplain's office requesting several cards to send his sisters and a friend for Mother's Day: "Dear Chaplain: With all due respect! On the envelope it do say 'in addition' to these four cards, you may request special holiday cards, Mother's Day. Do I have the wrong understanding of 'in addition'? Please help with this matter. Thank you."

He received this response from the volunteer chaplain:

> "Mr. Gilmore, I am sure that you have a correct understanding on 'in addition to,' but your etiquette could certainly use some polish! First of all (1) This applies on an 'as available' basis (we currently do not have any special occasion cards). (2) Copping an attitude instead of asking a 'civil' question will **always** get a similar response!"

Charlie frequently does not receive a reply to his requests, but on the rare occasion when he gets one, this is what it is like. I have known a number of very compassionate volunteer chaplains, but it would seem this was not one of them. Nonetheless, a few weeks later my wife did receive a Mother's Day card from Charlie.

May 22, 2011:

> "....I do hope that you understand why I asked that inmate to write to you. He said he think he know you and I feel from his Book (Charlie is referring to the work of TDCJ inmate John K. Murray, *The Texas Department of Corruption: Keepers and the Unkept*) you will more so understand that it is all real intentionally [sic] what's been going on with me. This is how they work."

> "Now to show you just how much it is still going on. They say that they send me to this unit to take the danger off of my life! But look now the inmate that was **next** door to me on [Clements]... is here now and have told all the inmates & officers what was going on over there! And now it's the same things!" [Charlie cites the name (Roberto Pena) and the number of this inmate.]

August 14, 2011:

> "....Well this is just a note to say No, I have not received no mail from you in over 120 days and I write to you two times a month! [I had written to Charlie on May 7, July 14 and July 18.]

> "....wrote to the Senior Warden, Mr. Stanley, begging for his help with this on-going abuse out of retaliation with clear evidence to prove it! It's cameras everywhere and they don't lie! Taking my food, giving it to other inmates. Inmate assaulting me and the officer with him and they do nothing about. Lied and it's on the camera!"

August 24, 2011 (going out on September 5):

> "See I had wrote and told you that I told the Dr. that I would take the medication for Hepatitis C. Yes, because of

what you said! Well, they say that they was going to take some more tests. Some of my liver. That's why I was at the hospital in [] on July 21, 2011. But back on the unit on July 22, 2011. Now it's been over thirty days and no one said nothing about it."

"….Serious abuse!….cameras everywhere that they can rewind and see that I'm not lying! They rewind it to see if we give another inmate some soap! And will punish us! All the time!"

"….Now on 8/22/11 the officers destroyed my Bible! I had it twenty-one years. My sister that's dead sent it to me. *A Life Application Bible.* And tried to justify it by lying and saying it was razors in it! Enough is enough. I cannot take no more!"

September 11: 2011: Officers had taken some of the Level 1 property of several black inmates, including radios. On September 7, Charlie sent an I-60 to the Warden stating that one of the officers had told an inmate that this had happened because of Charlie snitching to the Warden. He perceived this as another effort to get him killed by the inmates. He also complained that he was being served food on a paper tray (required for some offenders, but not him), and medication was being put in his food to make him sleep and have diarrhea.

October 23, 2011: "….Yes, I have been writing several High Public Officials letting them know what's really going on and it's cameras everywhere." This note was accompanied by a copy of a September 27, 2011 letter to Governor []:

> "….My life is in real danger. The Officials did conspire and have a officer tell several inmates that I wrote the Warden and told him that they are showing **racist hate & discrimination** on black inmates! We are all Level 2 inmates. But they just take the radios from the Black inmates….So it's no good excuse for them to give my name to supervisors or officers. This is a clear understanding that they are having inmates to hurt or kill me!…I was at SCC (state Classification

Committee) and the [] worker said for me not to write or say nothing about things like that 9/15/11!"

There follows a gap from late September, to early January, 2012. January 6, 2012:

"It's just that it's not like you to not write or send a card for Christmas [which I had done]. So, yes I'm thinking some of everything…But because I didn't receive no mail from no one. You know I understand it's these people! Because my sisters will say Hi and Merry Christmas and that they got my card."

January 22, 2012:

"Well, I need to ask you something. Do you feel that they was trying to let me die? Look how much time they took to send me back to see if it's **cancer** that they saw. Is that right? I was thinking it was something that should be took care of soon? The first test was 7/21/11 and now 12/28/11.…To die soon would be better than this torture!"

February 20, 2012: "….Something is not right you know. I write several people and places. No answers! The last letter I got from you was 1/14/12." [I had written Charlie on January 14, but also on January 21. One month later, Charlie still had not received this letter.]

March 12, 2012:

"….I did receive the letter dated 3/3/12 with everything on 3/8/12. But look I got the letter of 2/16/12 on 3/7/12 with the copies of the Grievances. See, most of the time it be the officers not giving us our mail".

March 13, 2012:

…This is no unit to do time on. I must get off of here.… No, I don't feel too good! Something is not right. When I was taking the Hydrochlorothiazide I was alright. I don't understand and this Dr. is no help!"

Charlie included with this note the prescription sticker from his Hydrochlorothiazide medication, showing an expiration date of 1/26/2013, and a notation that they had taken this medication from him, with no explanation. He was prescribed Hydralazine instead, but he had not experienced any trouble with the other medicine. The new medication was giving him problems. He sent an I-60 asking "Who, When, and Why?". There was no reply.

April 3, 2012:

> "I'm always praying that you all are doing alright. For me, I'm going to say o.k. But, no I'm not. I took a blood test and it was for Alpha-Fetoprotein or AFP. Well, it's suppose to be about 7, but is was 120! [Elevated AFP is not necessarily a reliable tool for diagnosis of certain types of cancer if the patient has Hepatitis C, but may be suggestive. Certainly something to be worried about.]
>
> "….You all please take good care of yourself and know it don't matter if I go tonight. I'm ready and do know I'm going to be with God. This **torture** and **abuse every day** is out of control!….As soon as I get back from the hospital, I'll write!"

This letter was received on April 21, 2012. As of May 6, I had not yet heard from Charlie. For the many years [since 2004] I have known Charlie, he has never ceased to fight for what he considers his rights as a human being. As his death in prison inevitably approaches, he continues to struggle to have a radio that works returned to him, not because he cares that much about the radio, but because it is his right!

CHAPTER FIVE

THE STEP-GRAND DAUGHTERS: VICTIMS OR LIARS?

The Investigative Narratives

Earnest Hutchins (we shall also refer to him as Pops, although the family gave him the nickname of Cootie) was an African American man who was sixty-seven when we met him in 2004. (Ben Higgins in the original version of this book). He had been in prison since 1997, charged with sexual assault of a child. We met him as volunteers participating in the Horizon program at the Allred Unit.

Pops was a kind-faced, congenial looking man. One could easily envision him as a gentle, caring grand-father, who might be firm with mischievous children, but never an abuser. He smiled easily, but tears almost always ventured to his eyes as we discussed his case.

On May 19, 1991, Officer FB was called to a residence in Austin, Texas. The call to the police was made by Lacy, a young girl about twelve years old at the time. (All names, except that of Earnest, are pseudo). Lacy was with her sister, Carly, who would have been about four years old. The police "Investigative Narrative",[128] dated May 20, 1991, reads in part as follows:

> "….The grandmother, [whom we shall call Violet Morse], took me [the officer] out to the back patio and had Carly and Lacy tell me what happened. Carly, [the four-year old] was hesitant, but Lacy, the twelve-year old, asked her to tell me what she had told Lacy. Carly said she came out to the porch and told Lacy 'that Pops was getting booty with Mamie [about five years old at this time].'

> "Lacy cried and related the following story. She said she was outside and her three sisters, Lettie (age three), Carly (age four), and Mamie, were in the house. She said she [Lacy] tried the door and it was locked. She said her grandmother, [Violet Morse], and her friend, B…, had gone to the store. They were gone about thirty minutes.

> "She said Carly came out the front door and said, '[Sweetpea, Lacy's nickname], can I come outside with you?' Lacy said 'Why' and Carly said 'We don't want to be in the house with Pops.' She said 'Pops was getting booty with Mamie.' Lacy said she went into the house, went into her grandmother's bedroom, opened the door and 'I seen him and her laying on the bed. He had [sexually graphic descriptions will be replaced by brackets here] and she had [] and he [] She said she said, 'What are you doing?' and 'he didn't say nothing and starting [sic] putting on his shorts.'

> "….I went in and placed Pops or Earnest under arrest, handcuffed him, and took him to the patrol car….I called victim services and LM and LL came out. They interviewed all the girls and spoke with Mrs. Morse. They called the sex crimes investigator on duty and were asked to pick up the evidence. I took sheets, pants, and waste paper towels…. Evidence of the bed sheet, Mamie's pants and under-clothing, and paper towels that were used to wipe up fluids [], were

---

[128] The "Investigative Narratives" are from an Austin, Texas Police Report dated February 17, 1998, pages 4-7.

collected and turned in at the evidence room. Earnest was booked for sexual assault with a child."

An "Investigative Narrative" dated May 29, 1991, submitted by the crisis team, LM and LL, added a few details, but did not substantially change the preceding. However, an additional narrative dated May 30, 1991, reported:

> "On May 22, 1991, TT of victims service conducted video-tape interviews with Mamie and Lacy. It was alleged that Mamie was molested. Following a pre-video interview with Lacy, a video-taped Mamie, who was very quiet and I managed to qualify her after several trys. We identified the body parts where she calls breasts [] and [] booty. She would not use the dolls. **I was unable to get her to disclose any abuse** [emphasis added]. The tape with Lacy was essentially the same as on the night of the incident. After the video's [sic] Sgt. G and I met with Violet Morse, the grandmother, who said that Lacy was a liar and a trouble maker. She did not believe the children….She whined about how her life has always been hard. We said that we understood but that we were concerned for the helpless children. Mrs. Morse left in a huff, not believing the girls. I told Lacy she had done the right thing and gave her my card."

On June 5, 1991, a final "Investigative Narrative" is issued:

> "This case will be closed because we have no outcry. The child involved refuses to speak with us. After speaking with the grandmother it is obvious she did not believe the children. **This case will be unfounded** (emphasis added)."

We are left to wonder what happened to the alleged physical evidence. At this stage there is no further mention of it. Apparently, without an "outcry" by Mamie, it became irrelevant, and at this time the testimony of Lacy was not considered credible.

But why would Lacy concoct a story like this, if it were not true? There were various tensions between Lacy and Pops that might lead a teenager to try to cause trouble for an adult, but—while the exact timeframe is unclear—it turns out she had begun a relationship with a boyfriend, Paul Mosely. Pops will testify that this boy was sneaking into the house at night. Pops was giving Lacy a lot of trouble about this relationship, and it appears that by fabricating the incident she may have been trying to put a stop to his effort to enforce some discipline.

Six years later, on August 13, 1997, a new "Investigative Narrative" was filed by Officer Tom Grudge. The text follows:

> "On 6/17/97 I was assigned case #97....to investigate. [The report does not say who first brought the charges.] The case was a aggravated sexual assault of a 11 year old girl and possibel [sic; the report contains numerous errors of spelling, grammar, and even the name of the alleged victim; these errors have been preserved in this text] her two sister that are ten and nine years old. While investigating the 97 case I located this old case 1991 case and felt there was enough information in the report and the new case to re-open the case. The suspect in the 1991 case is the same as the 1997 case. Most of the investigation is in the 1991 report. The victim and witness video's from 1991 were taped over since the case was closed.
>
> "On 6/23/97 Mamie [actual name misspelled] and her father came to the children's advocacy for a videotaped interview. The victim gave an outcry that the suspect sexual assaulted her. The victim said that the suspect []. The victim also gave a witness statement that the suspect sexual assaulted her ten-year-old sister, Carly. The victim was unable to give exact time and how old she was, but did give some of the same story that was reported in 1991....
>
> "On 6/27/97 Lacy M came to office to give me a written statement. Lacy [now about eighteen] was the witness in the 1991 case but was able to remember the details of the incident and gave me a written statement. This statement will be made part of the case jacket.

"On 7/2/97 I staffed this case with DB with the DA's office and it was decided to file the 1991 case on the suspect along with some 1997 cases.

"….In the 1991 case the officers recover some physical evidence at the scene. The suspect used some paper towels to clean up []. [In the "Narrative" of 5/29/91 it supposedly was Mamie who used paper towels to clean up the….] This evidence has been properly stored at the …PD property room. DPS lab said that if the evidence was properly stored they should be able to recover enough of a sample to compare with the suspect. (File documents show that when the "evidence" was examined no fluid was found on the jeans or panties. A small amount of [], which was not even tested, was found on a sheet).

"On 8/6/97 I prepared a search warrant for the blood, hair, and saliva of Earnest Hutchins. Judge C…reviewed the affidavit and felt there was enough PC to issue warrant #S…

"Earnest Hutchins is in the [] Correctional Faciclity. I went to the jail were Nusre W…assisted and collected the sample of blood, hair, and saliva from Earnest. After the sample were collected I turned them into the …PD property room and asked if they would get it refrigerated until I could take then to the DPS lab for comparison with the evidence collected.

"On 8/13/97 I went and took out the sample I had collected the week prior and the evidence that was collected in 1991 to take to the DPS lab. "On 8/14/97 I went to the DPS lab and turned in the evidence and sample to be examined and compared to the samples. A copy of the offense was given to DPS along with the evidnece and samples.

"The case has been cleared by arrest and when the result come from DPS I will forward them to the DA's office."

Other file documentation noted the following: A Dr. Bess Nolan… reported that Carly has said she had been [] by Earnest. But in A.L.'s report of 6/3/1997 it was noted Carly had denied that anyone had "tried to do it with her." We shall also see that Pop's common law wife, Violet

Morse, was persuaded not to testify on his behalf. It had been claimed that she had scalded one of the girls during a bath, leaving a large scar on her back. In his investigation, Officer Grudge, who filed the 1997 report, noted it was not possible to verify that the scar was from a burn.

The state's "Notice of Outcry" prepared by Assistant DA, JK, commented that Mamie said Earnest "did it to her." She also said he had [], at least twice. (As we proceed with the trial record, the abbreviation "DA" will be used to designate the Assistant District Attorneys conducting the case).

February 13, 1998, four days before the beginning of the trial, the DA gave notice of intent to introduce charges that offenses against the girls occurred between 1989 (when the girls were four and three years old) and 1997 (when the police first were called).[129] The DA had also prepared a list of "evidence" for thirty-five alleged offenses committed by Earnest, including numerous acts of sexual assault of a child, theft, burglary, arson, assault and robbery, and assault with the intent to commit murder. It was stated that this evidence would be used to prove the State's "case-in-chief," to impeach the defendant, and for the punishment phase.

There is no documentation in the "criminal record" of Hutchins supporting any of these claims, except "unauthorized use of a motor vehicle" (joy riding) in September of 1960. It appears the list was prepared only to intimidate Earnest and limit his defense options. [The list has these offenses committed in [] County, Texas. In the sentencing phase of the trial, one of the prosecuting attorneys cites an "Exhibit 8" that places the aggravating offenses in a different county. This is only one of the many instances of sloppy work that occur throughout the case.]

Jury Selection (Voir Dire)[130]

From a panel of fifty potential jurors, the jury selected was comprised of seven men and five women. According to Earnest Hutchins it did not include any African Americans. Not a single alternate juror was selected.

---

129   Vol. II, page 23, lines 18-22 of the Hutchins trial transcript.
130   "Jury Selection" citations come from Vol. I of the Hutchins trial.

At the outset of the trial, before the jury panel was admitted to the courtroom, several preliminary matters were handled and Hutchins pleaded "Not Guilty" to five counts with which he was charged. The D.A., JK, then asked the Judge to invoke "the Rule" (instruction to a witness about who they can talk to, etc.) with regard to Violet Morse (Earnest's common law wife and grandmother of the children). It was clarified that while Ms. Violet Morse was present, her attorney was not. However, his instruction to Violet Morse was that she should take the 5th Amendment. The Judge told Violet Morse to return the next afternoon. She was prohibited from talking to Earnest's attorney about the case.

The defense attorney, Mr. Daly, then asked for $500 to pay an investigator to look for certain witnesses, and requested a jury panel shuffle. Other than the fact that the state provided a court appointed attorney, the $500 was the entire amount spent to defend Mr. Hutchins.

The Judge introduced himself as a visiting Judge and hurried the process of getting the jury appointed. He made it clear he wanted the trial completed by the end of the week

The DA questioned the panel for a little over an hour. Several of the individuals who were chosen for the jury were not questioned by her at all during the period. Those that asked the most questions, generally, were not selected. No one who expressed a concern about wrongly convicting an adult, based on a child's testimony, made it onto the jury.

Mr. Daly, the defense attorney, begins his interaction with the panel by telling a long story about bias and prejudice and how he once misjudged his baby sitter. He then states "I should have asked to voir dire each person individually because it is so embarrassing to talk about whether you have been the victim of a sexual assault. But we just don't have the time to do that." For some reason there seems to be an urgency to hurry this trial along..

The defense then led a long inquiry into whether an indictment or the fact that five charges were brought implies the defendant is guilty. Only a few potential jurors responded to the question, but the impression was left that if there were five charges, surely there must be some evidence, which could be interpreted as an unconscious bias toward guilt.

The Judge intervened to offer the rather strange observation that he did not care what the lawyers thought. As far as he was concerned they did not know anything about the facts of the case and the jury should just listen to the witnesses.

Following this, the defense attorney calls attention to the fact that his client has very bad teeth and sometimes spits when he tries to talk. He hopes the jury will not hold this deficiency against the man! (One of the many ways in which the attorney demeaned his own client during the trial.)

The Judge completed the proceedings with a series of instructions to the jurors, told them to adjourn until 2:30 p.m. and advised them that they probably would work only a couple of hours in the afternoon, ending the day at 5 p.m.

The Trial

The trial began on February 17, 1998, a Tuesday, and concluded with the punishment phase on Friday, February 20th. At the beginning of the trial, Judge Mench—a visiting Judge—apologized to the jury for starting late. He assured them they would be finished by Friday.

The first seventy-seven pages of Volume II of the trial transcript consist of direct examination and cross examination of Grudge, the police Officer who filed the 1997 report, of Earnest Hutchins (not cross-examined), of Mr. Claude Lyons (a former felon, alleged father of two or three of the children, and a major witness), and Lacy, the instigator of the case. This process was conducted **without the jury being present.**

The defense attorney had moved to exclude the 1991 incident from the trial. The first witness called was not the police officer who filed the 1991 report, but Officer Grudge. He agreed that the charges in the 1991 incident were declared "unfounded" because there was no outcry on the videotape by the supposed victim. He testified that the videotape had been taped over [although it could have included exculpatory evidence], but other physical evidence was retained [clothing, bed sheets and paper towels.] The defense attorney does not ask any questions about any testing that may have been performed on the physical evidence.

The police officer was asked if the 1991 report included the statement by the grandmother that the girl who called the police (Lacy) and the alleged victim (Mamie) were lying about the incident. The officer responded by asking his own question, there was an objection by the DA, and this crucial question posed by the defense was never clearly answered.

In the cross-examination of Grudge, the DA established that in 1991 Lacy testified on the tape that she had caught the defendant [] with Mamie. This alleged incriminating evidence [if true] had also been taped over. She asks a question about retention of physical evidence on what she calls "suspended" cases, and wraps up without asking about testing of this evidence in 1991.

Mr. Daly calls Earnest Hutchins to the stand. He testifies that in 1991 he did not live at the house where the girls were living, but did stay there overnight from time to time. He was familiar with drug dealing that went on in the house across the street and said that Lacy (his accuser) stayed there more often than in her home. The people in that home were hostile to him. According to Earnest, it was the people in the house across the street who called in the police in 1991, and the police report that Lacy had made the call was incorrect.

The defense attorney next asks:

> "After this offense report, did you subsequently find out that
> Lacy had stated to Violet Morse that she had made up this
> story about you, that the neighbors across the street had told
> her what to say and had made up this story in order to get
> you out of the house?"[131]

The DA objected to this question on the basis of "hearsay" and her objection was sustained. Mr. Daly asks the Judge if he can make

---

[131] Hutchins Trial, Vol. II, 19:1-6.

an offer of proof as to what the defendant would have said—if he had been allowed to answer the question, for the purpose of eventual appeal. The Judge consents.

Argumentation proceeds with regard to whether or not the 1991 incident should be suppressed and what Mamie, who was five at the time, could accurately recall. The Judge asks whether the DA thinks the child will testify that the molestation was on-going.

> "DA: Yes, sir. I gave notice from 1989 through June 1, 1997. THE COURT: She didn't say 1989, did she? DA: No. There is a specific incident that this will relate back to. I have other witnesses who walked in on the defendant and the little girl."[132] [In 1989 she would have been only three years old!]

The 1991 incident, even though unfounded, will be allowed. Yet the Judge follows with a somewhat bizarre "allowance":

> "THE COURT: However, if we get to a situation where you wish to impeach her [Lacy] or something, I would be more than lenient in the manner in which you do it, even if you do it with another witness without **asking her directly if she didn't make a non-statement** [emphasis added] back in May of 1991. Do you understand what I am saying? Mr. Daly: I understand what you are saying. THE COURT: I would be lenient with how you get to do that."[133] [Perhaps Mr. Daly understands, but we might be forgiven if we do not readily understand how you ask a twelve-year-old child "if she didn't make a non-statement."]

The DA calls witness Claude Lyons to the stand (not in the presence of the jury). She begins by establishing that in 1970 he was given a sentence of three years for aggravated robbery. He was again sentenced for armed robbery in 1975 and was released in 1982. The DA emphasizes that Mr. Lyons had been "absolutely straight" since that

---

132 Hutchins Trial, Vol. II, 23: 18-22.
133 Hutchins Trial, Vol. II, 26:6-16.

release, and asked that these convictions not be introduced during the trial to impeach the witness.

Earnest Hutchins's attorney argued:

> "In response to that, I don't believe that we would use those convictions under Rule 609 to impeach the character of this witness. But we may want to introduce it because—as an essential element of his character under Rule 404 and 405 as an element of our defense. Our defense is essentially that Claude Lyons conspired with Lacy and another man by the name of Paul Mosely to falsely accuse Earnest of sexual abuse so that he could get custody of the kids and therefore obtain the $800 in social security support that the children are paid each month. Essentially his motivation was to obtain the money that the children get and they arranged to remove Mr. Hutchins from the picture so they could do that."[134]

To this the Judge ruled that he could not allow this line of testimony in until he had heard more other evidence:

> "THE COURT: There is no way I can do it. So therefore, I am not letting it in at this time until I hear some more about what you think your evidence is going to be."[135]

The Judge noted it was now past 3 p.m. and he had not yet heard any evidence.

The DA began to question Mr. Lyons with regard to the outcry.

Prompted by the DA's question, Lyons testified that about a month before the police were called to the home of Mamie's Grandmother, he received a phone call from Mamie. He said Mamie told him

> "She said no, he will come into our room and fondle [the term of an eleven-year-old?] our []."[136]

---

[134]   Hutchins Trial, Vol. II, 35:10-25.

[135]   Hutchins Trial, Vol. II, 38:2-5.

[136]   Hutchins Trial, Vol. II, 41:3-5.

Again prompted by the DA, Lyons said that two weeks later Mamie phoned him again and told him

> "[Pops] came into her room and woke her up and [sexually graphic assault implying penetration.]"[137]

Subsequent questioning by the DA established that Claude Lyons knew Lacy (the oldest girl) since she was five years old (she was eighteen or nineteen at the time of the trial) and that he is her step-father. It was determined that Lyons was not sure whether Mamie had told Lacy about the offenses before she told him or not.

Lacy was then called to the stand and sworn in. She was asked by the DA what details Mamie had given her about the molesting by Pops. She answered "very little details." This testimony followed:

> "Q. What were those details she told you? A. She wrote me a note and she wrote that [Pops] said that he was going to get her if she didn't behave or something like that, but I didn't keep the note so I don't have it now. Q. But she didn't give you any details about all the sexual molesting that Earnest did, did she? A. No."[138]

Mr. Daly's cross-examination ensued:

> "QUESTIONS BY Mr. Daly: Q. Did she, during the year 1997, did she [Mamie] make any statements to you that [Pops] was molesting her in any way? A. No. Q. Would you have expected her to tell you if something like that had happened? A. Yes. Q. Were you very close to your sister, Mamie? A. Yes. Q. If she was going to tell somebody about that incident, do you think she would have told you first? A. No. DA: Objection, that calls for pure speculation. And how is it relevant? THE COURT: It is sustained. Mr. Daly: I pass the witness."[139]

---

[137] Hutchins Trial, Vol. II, 41:11-14.

[138] Hutchins Trial, Vol. II, 50:7-15.

[139] Hutchins Trial, Vol. II, 50:19-25 to 51:1-14.

After some back and forth about what would be allowed and what would not be permitted, the Judge essentially ruled in favor of everything the DA wanted (the outcry coming from Claude Lyons) and against the defense (evidence about the character background of Mr. Lyons).

The Court had Mamie brought in and proceeded to question her. She said she was now twelve and in the sixth grade. The Judge inquired whether Mamie knew the difference between telling the truth and a lie, and what to do if she didn't understand a question or know the answer. Mamie was dismissed and her younger sister, Carly, was brought in.

She says she is eleven, and in the fifth grade. She receives the same instructions as Mamie with regard to truth, lying, etc.

The Court was now ready to bring in the jury, but the defense objected to the presence of Claude Lyons's wife in the courtroom, arguing it might put pressure on the children to deliver some pre-arranged testimony. It was established that the children were now living with Lyons and his wife, rather than with Violet Morse and Earnest Hutchins. The Judge denied Mr. Daly's request to exclude the wife from the courtroom.[140]

First Day of Trial in the Presence of the Jury

The Judge commented it was getting late in the day, but hoped to get through two witnesses. The jury entered the room, was sworn in and told they would hear the indictment and opening statements by the attorneys. The indictment was read by the Assistant DA (but the words are not recorded in the transcript), and Hutchins pleaded "Not Guilty."[141]

The DA, Ms. Anita Konchek, opened with a summary of the state's case:

> "What you are about to hear is probably the worst version of
> Cinderella you will ever hear. I don't mean that lightly. What
> we expect the evidence to show is [Mamie] was sexually
> abused by this man here. You will hear the heart-breaking

---

[140] Hutchins Trial, Vol. II, 74:22.
[141] Hutchins Trial, Vol. II, 77:18-23.

testimony of a twelve-year-old little girl about what Earnest did to her. But if that's not enough for you to convict, you will hear from her father [this paternity was not established with certitude], Claude Lyons, about the outcry that she made to him in June of 1997. She tried to tell him many times. She tried to tell people it sounds like a lot what was going on, but action was finally taken in June of 1997 when her real father, [apparently the DA means Mr. Lyons] got involved and said this is wrong, we are going to do something about it."[142]

The DA tells the jury they will hear from Dr. Bess Nolan, who will tell them that she examined Mamie and found what "was an abnormal exam and what she found is consistent with vaginal penetration."[143]

The defense attorney, Mr. Daly, begins his opening statement somewhat strangely:

> "I have no doubt that the evidence in this case will be that these children were abused and abused severely. The issue which the defense wishes to present is who is the real villain in this case."[144]

[In saying this, it would seem the attorney concedes the state's contention that there is indisputable evidence the children were severely abused, not distinguishing between sexual abuse and other forms. In fact, the trial will establish that the only "evidence" is one child's claim that she was abused, an older girl's claim that she witnessed sexual abuse, an absent possible father's report of what he was told, and an "expert's" opinion that Mamie's vaginal area showed damage "consistent" with penetration. Why would the defense attorney set in the jury's mind from the outset that there was **certain** evidence of serious abuse?]

Mr. Daly develops his contention that Earnest is the victim of a conspiracy by family members, Claude Lyons and Lacy, who manipulate

---

142 Hutchins Trial, Vol. II, 78:7-24.
143 Hutchins Trial, Vol. II, 79:7-9.
144 Hutchins Trial, Vol. II, 79:23-25,80:1-2.

the younger girls, especially Mamie, in order to get Hutchins out of the home and take control of $800 in social security payments. He follows this with a brief history of the family, pointing out that the girls' mother was into drugs and prostitution, and died at a young age, leaving the daughters to be raised by Violet Morse, the grandmother (rather than the "real" father, Claude Lyons).

He provides some background on Lacy:

> "The situation was that around 1991, Lacy, when she was twelve years old, began to associate with people who were drug dealers and began to go out with various men. Around this time and sometime after Earnest moved into the house, but not very long, she took up with a man [boy] named Paul Mosely."[145]

Daly explained that Lacy and Mosely developed a close, sexual relationship, and Lacy was able to control the grandmother, who was in her sixties at the time.

The attorney offered some comments about Earnest, which may or may not have helped:

> "Mr. Hutchins—I don't want to make Mr. Hutchins out to be a moral character. I don't think this is really a moral issue."[146]

[Earnest Hutchins has been accused of sexual molestation of young children, and it is not a "moral" issue? How would such a statement establish any credibility with a jury?]

Mr. Daly:

> "He [Earnest Hutchins] didn't like what was going on in the house, not from a moral standpoint because he thought they were Violet Morse's responsibility and it was her responsibility to take care of the moral upbringing of the children and he

---

[145]   Hutchins Trial, Vol. II, 82:8-14.
[146]   Hutchins Trial, Vol. II, 83:17-19.

didn't really want to get involved in that. But he didn't like drugs being brought into the house and he didn't like the stealing that was going on that was directly affecting him. So he began to take efforts to try to remove Paul Mosely from the house and also to try to control Lacy."[147]

After telling the jury in great detail about the incident where the police were called out in 1991 and stressing that no charges were filed because of a lack of outcry, as well as noting that later, in 1997, when there was an outcry, analysis of the 1991 evidence did not find any semen on the child's clothes, the attorney gets back to Lacy and her motivation:

"Lacy was living with her boyfriend, Paul Mosely [1997]. They were having a hard time getting money. About the time that Lacy turned eighteen, she began telling her grandmother that her grandmother is really not able to take care of the younger children because of her age and that the grandmother should give Lacy custody of the children. Of course, this would give Lacy control of the $800 a month that the kids had and thus solve her financial problems."[148]

Mr. Daly adds that Earnest and Violet Morse have now together bought the home that they and the girls are living in.

"He [Earnest Hutchins] kicked them [Lacy, Paul Mosely, Claude Lyons and his family] out of the house and said I don't want you to come back. It was shortly after that that these allegations were made. Within a month or so, maybe even less time, after Earnest was arrested, Lacy moved back into the house with her boyfriend, Mosely, and they are living there still."[149]

The now twelve year-old Mamie is called to the stand and is questioned by the DA. She says that she is now living with her daddy.

147 Hutchins Trial, Vol. II, 83:22-25, 84:1-8.
148 Hutchins Trial, Vol. II, 87:22-25, 88:1-7.
149 Hutchins Trial, Vol. II, 89:22-25, 90:1-3.

In response to Ms. Konchek's query, she answers that she is supposed to tell the truth and God punishes people who lie. For a while she had lived with her Grandma and her "boyfriend." Her nickname for him was "C…" [Pops]. She points to identify him as Pops.

Question of DA: "Is there any time during that time that Earnest or Pops did something to you that you didn't like? A: Yes."[150] She testifies that she and her two little sisters slept on a mattress on the floor in the dining room, because Lacy was using the bedroom. [It is the DA who first mentions the location where the children slept as the **dining room**. We will see that Mamie testifies they slept on a mattress in the dining room.] One night when she was sleeping, Pops came in drunk while the Grandma was asleep and "messed" with her sister, who was also asleep, then he "messed" with her. She says he put his "private" with her "private" and it hurt.

Her testimony then becomes a bit self-contradictory:

> "Q: Did you feel if it was []? A. I don't remember. Q. Do you remember if it hurt or it didn't hurt? A. It didn't hurt. Q. It did hurt or didn't hurt? A. It did."[151] Mamie has just said Pops put his [] and it hurt, then she does not remember if "it" was [], and it did not hurt, then it did hurt.

The DA shows Mamie some dolls that she had previously been shown in the attorney's office and tries to get her to demonstrate what had happened. Again, the testimony is fumbled:

> "Q. Whenever—see how—see down there where [] did you see his []? A. No. Q. Was it dark? A. Yes. Q. Did you feel his [] or not? A. No. Q. Did you feel it down in your [private area] though, or not? A: Yeah."[152]

The DA returns to the 1991 incident:

---

150   Hutchins Trial, Vol. II, 95:23-25, 96:1-2.
151   Hutchins Trial, Vol. II, 101:8-15.
152   Hutchins Trial, Vol. II, 103:16-25.

"Q. I want to talk about another time, okay? Do you remember a time when Lacy and Carly came into the room and caught Pops and you? Do you remember that? It was a long time ago. A. Sort of. Q. Do you remember how old you were when that happened? A. No. Q. Do you remember what Pops did that day? Do you remember where you were? A. No. Q. Do you remember if you were in his bed? A. No."[153]

The DA makes another effort to "refresh" Mamie's memory about the 1991 incident. [Because of its significance, this testimony will be presented here at some length. There is much more questioning about the 1991 event, when there was no outcry, than the alleged offenses of 1997 for which Earnest is being tried]:

"Q. "I want you to think back to a time—that time when Lacy came into the bedroom. Okay? A. All right. Q. Do you remember if your grandma was home? A. No. Q. Do you remember where you were with Pops, if you were with Pops? A. Grandma's room. Q. You said in your grandma's room? A. Uh-huh.

"Q. Did Pops—was Pops nice that day or did he do something nasty that day? [One might consider this leading the witness, but there is no objection from the defense.] A. Nasty. Q. Would you tell the jury what he did nasty that day? A. The thing. Q. The thing that you told us before? A. Yeah.

"Q. That time, was it during the day or during the night? A. The day. Q. Did you see his [] that time? A. Yeah. Q. Could you tell the jury what he did with his []? Do you want to show us with the dolls? A. (Nodded head up and down). Q. Could you show the jury what he did that day when he was in your grandma's room? A. (Demonstrating). Q. Was he []? A. I don't remember. Q. Do you remember if you saw his []? A. Yes. MS. K: Let the record reflect that she has the dolls with the—Q. Do these dolls have the []

---

[153] Hutchins Trial, Vol. II, 104:1-15.

touching each other? A. (Shakes head back and forth). THE COURT: Can't hear. Q. (By Ms. Konchek) Can you talk up? A. No. Q. When you have these dolls together, Mamie, are the [] touching each other when you are showing us what Pops did to you? A. Yeah. Q. So right there, right there, what is that? Is that Gramp's []? Is that what it is? A. Yes. Q. Please show the jury what he did with the dolls, the anatomically correct dolls, what he did on that day when Lacy walked in.

"A. He was laying there and I was right here. Q. You were right here. Were you standing up first? [Attorney prompting, even as to position.] A. Yeah. Q. Where were you standing up? A. On the floor. Q. Where was Pops? A. Standing up. [A few seconds earlier he was "laying there."] Q. Did he have his []? [More leading]. A. Down. Q. Did you see his []? A. Yes. Q. Could you describe to the jury, tell them what it looked like. A. It had []. Q. It had some kind of []? (Nodded head up and down). Q. Did he touch his []? A. With his hands. Q. What was he doing with his hands[]? A. []. Q. Do you remember if he was moving or was he []? A. []. Q. Do you remember if it was pointing []? MS. K: Let the record reflect my finger is []. Q. Or was it down? A. Down. Q. He was down. Do you remember if it was []? I know it has been a long time ago. A. I don't remember. Q. When he was [], did he look at you? Did he know you were there? A. Yeah. Q. How do you know he knew you were there? A. Because he was looking at me. Q. When he was doing that, did you have []? A. No. Q. Did you—did he []? A. He did.

"Q. What did he do to you once your []? A. When he got close to me, my sisters come in. Q. Were you on the bed when your sister and them came? A. Yeah. Q. Was Pops on the bed when your sister came in? A. Yeah. Q. So you said before he got close to you, your sisters came in. Do you remember which sisters came in? A Carly and Lettie [about four and three years old at the time]. Q. Carly and Lettie came in first? A. Uh-huh. Q. What did they say when they saw that? Do you remember? A. No.

"Q. So what happened? Did they stay in there or did they leave? A. They left. Q. What did Pops do after they left? A. He got up and put on his pants and started calling. Q. Did Lacy come in there ever? Do you remember her coming in? A. No. Q. Do you remember somebody coming in, though? A. Yes. Q. Do you remember how old you were when that happened? A. No. Q. Was it a long, long time ago or was it a short time ago? A. Long. Q. Do you remember if you were in school? A. No.

"Q. Mamie, has anybody ever told you to come in here and make this story up? A. No. Q. Has Lacy ever told you that you need to tell—make this up about Pops? A. No. Q. Has your daddy, Claude Lyons, has he ever said, 'Look, let's say this about Pops so you can come live with me,'? A. No. Q. Has your daddy ever said, 'Hey, say this about Pops touching your [] so you can come live with me and I can get your check.' You know, you get that check in the mail? Did you know you get a check in the mail? A. Uh-huh. Q. Have you ever heard your daddy say that? A. No.

"Q. Do you remember ever telling your grandma, Violet Morse, about what Pops was doing to you? A. Yeah. Q. Did she do anything about it? A. No. Well, she would cuss at us. Q. What would she say to you? A. Bitch, you need to go sit down somewhere. Q. Do you remember did you tell your grandma a lot of times or a few times about what Pops was doing to you? A. A few. Q. Did she ever call the police or try to get Pops to stop? A. No. Q. Did Pops do these things to you when your grandma was around? A. Sometimes. Q. Did he ever do it to you while she could see it and was in the room? A. No. Q. What do you mean your grandma was around sometimes? Where would she be? A. In her room or in the kitchen. Q. So are you talking about she would be in her room when you would be in your room? A. (Nodded head up and down). Q. Is that when Pops would come into your room? A. Yes. Q. Do you remember if Pops did this a lot of times or two times that you have told us? Was it more than you have told us? [Prompting again?] A. Yeah. Q. How did that make you feel, Mamie? A. I was sad.

"Q. Mamie, back whenever your sisters walked in on you and Pops, do you remember if the police came? A. Yeah. Q.

And do you remember going in and them taking a video of you, trying to make a video a long, long time ago? A. No. Q. You don't remember that? Were you afraid to talk about what Pops was doing? A. Yeah. Q. Why were you afraid? A. Because sometimes my grandma would threaten me. Q. Your grandma would threaten you? A. Yeah. Q. About what? A. That she will kill me. Q. She would threaten you. Was that about Pops or was that about something else? A. About Pops. Q. Why would she want to kill you if you told her, if you said it happened? A. I don't know. [Recall that in the case of Carlos Rojas, victims also testified that they were afraid to speak out because they might be killed. Soliciting this form of testimony seems to be a frequent prosecution tactic.]

"Q. Did Pops ever tell you anything about telling other people? A. Yeah. Q. What did Pops tell you about telling other people? A. That he didn't need trouble, something else. Q. What is that something else? You need to remember if you can. It is very important. If you can remember it, tell me. If you can't, then tell me you can't remember. A. I can't.

"Q. Were you afraid of Pops or were you not afraid of Pops? A. No, sometimes. Sometimes. Q. Sometimes. Sometimes you were and sometimes you weren't? A. Uh-huh. Q. Tell us about the times that you were. A. Like when he be sneaking around at night. Q. Is that when you were afraid of him? A. Yeah. Q. Some nights when he came into your room, did you smell anything? A. No. [Since she does not recall the smell of alcohol from the supposedly drunk Pops, the DA had to prompt her once more.] Q. Do you remember if Pops drank alcohol sometimes? A. (Nodded head up and down). Q. Are you saying yes or no? A. Yes. Q. Did he drink a lot or did he drink a little? A. A lot. Q. You said that this happened a lot with Pops coming to your bedroom. During any of those times, did Pops—did he touch up here on your—what do you call these up here, these []? What do you call these up here? We know you don't like to say words like that, but you need to say them in Court. Okay? Do you know what these are called? A. [The breast area]. [Earlier she had no trouble talking about fondling of ....] Q. Did he ever touch you there? A. No. Q. Any of those times, did he ever touch you there? A. No. Q. Mamie, is it kind of confusing to talk about all of this? A. Yeah. Q. Why is it confusing? Do you want to forget about it? A. Yeah. Q. Mamie, is everything you have come in here today to tell us, is it true? A. Yes."[154]

Not happy with all of Mamie's testimony, the DA sought to rationalize the "confusion." Even a cursory reading of the transcript and original police report readily reveals the inconsistencies. Previously we saw how Mamie "sort of" remembered when **Lacy** and **Carly** came into the room and caught Pops and her, but did not remember if she was in his bed or what he did to her. Immediately after this, with the DA's help, she "thinks back" to when **Lacy** [the DA's words] came into the bedroom. She did not remember if her Grandma was home, but the incident took place in Grandma's room. Pops was "standing up" then he was "laying there" and she recalls all kinds of details. The sisters came in, but now it was not **Lacy** and **Carly**, but **Carly** and **Lettie** (the youngest girl). She does not recall **Lacy** coming in at all! In the police report, **Lacy** said she came in and saw Earnest with his [] out, etc....

Ms. Konchek passes the witness and the defense begins its cross:

He asks:

"Q. Why didn't you tell your daddy before last summer what was happening with Pops? A. (No response). Q. Can you tell us why? A. No."[155]

There follows a series of questions about the incident in "the dining room." It was the DA who first mentioned the **dining room** and asked Mamie questions about it.[156] Defense Attorney:

---

[154] Hutchins Trial, Vol. II, 104:25 to 116:9.

[155] Hutchins Trial, Vol. II, 119:4-8.

[156] Hutchins Trial, Vol. II, 96:3-4.

"Q. When you described this incident that happened in the dining room, do you remember telling us about that? Do you remember telling us about the incident in the dining room? A. (No response)."[157]

"Q. I am not going to ask you any more questions about that. I want to know if you know the period of time I am talking about. Do you know the time when you were sleeping in the dining room with your sisters? Did you sleep in the dining room or was it the den? A. The den. Q. So it was the den and not the dining room? A. Yes."[158]

Mr. Daly asks Mamie whether she knows the meaning of the expression []. Mamie says she does and he asks: "Q. Do you know if Paul Mosely is [] with your sister, Lacy? A. No. Q. Are you saying they have never had sex? A. I haven't seen it. Q. Does your sister talk to you sometimes about that? A. No. (II, 123:9-17)."

While exploring the relationship between Mamie and Lacy, Mr. Daly asks:

"Q. Do you trust your older sister, Lacy? A. Yeah. Q. Do you feel like you can tell her anything? A. Yeah. Q. Now, this other incident that you described that happened a long time ago during the daylight, Lacy called the police when you told her what happened? A. Yeah. [Actually Lacy had said that she had walked into the room and observed "the incident," then called the police. (See the "Investigative Report).] Q. Why didn't you tell Lacy what Pops was doing after that first time? A. (No response). Q. Can you answer that question? A. No."[159]

The next series of questions establishes that Mamie was never by herself with Pops. At times, however, she and her two younger sisters would be alone with him in the Violet Morse home. Mrs. Morse worked

---

[157] Hutchins Trial, Vol. II, 120:22-25, 121:1.

[158] Hutchins Trial, Vol. II, 121:2-11.

[159] Hutchins Trial, Vol. II, 125:1-16.

all the time . When the girls returned from school Mrs. Morse would be there, because she got off work in the afternoon.[160]

Mamie is asked about the children's relationship with Pops, whether Paul Mosely was there when the 1997 incident occurred, and whether he could have helped:

> "Q. Did Pops sometimes try to make you do things that you didn't want to do? A. Yeah. Q. What kind of things were those? A. Wash dishes. Q. On the occasions when you didn't do them, did you and Pops have some kind of confrontation? Did you and Pops get in a fight? A. No."[161]
>
> Q. No. When you were in the den with your sisters and Pops came in and started bothering you, why didn't you wake your sisters up? A. I woke my sister up one time. She woke up, she went to the bathroom and went back to sleep. I woke her up again. She kept on falling asleep. [All while Earnest is supposedly raping Mamie.] Q. Did you ever think about screaming? A. No."[162]
>
> Q. Was Paul Mosely not the kind of person that would help you if you were in trouble? A. Yeah, he would help. Q. He would help. Do you know why you didn't scream to have Paul Mosely come to help you? Do you want to answer that question? A. No."[163]
>
> Mr. Daly: Pass the witness, your Honor."[164]

In her re-cross, the DA has Mamie affirm that Paul Mosely never touched her in any inappropriate way. She then questions Mamie some more about how she told her dad about the molestation. Mamie says she does not know why it took her so long to tell her dad about the molestation. The DA then leads Mamie to testify that her grandma would hit her and throw boiling water on her, leaving a scar. Mamie

---

160   Hutchins Trial, Vol. II, 130-132.

161   Hutchins Trial, Vol. II, 136:4 to 137:3.

162   Hutchins Trial, Vol. II, 137:4-13.

163   Hutchins Trial, Vol. II, 137:14 to 138:11.

164   Hutchins Trial, Vol. II, 141:9-25 to 142:5.

adds that when Pops was drunk he would do nasty stuff and come around and sprinkle holy water on them, burning her sister's eyes.

The DA asks Mamie to help her clear up where the offense actually occurred, the dining room or the den. In this series of questions it appears that the DA is covering for her own earlier error when **she** was the first one to say that the offense occurred in the dining room.

The DA next attempts to elicit testimony about other assaults:

"Q. Was there [sic] any other times when he touched you nasty while you were in your granny's room? A. Yeah. Q. Is that where most of it happened or did it happen—you said it happened—you need to talk to me and tell me where it happened if it happened at all. A. In my granny's room. Q. In your granny's room? A. Yeah. [The DA is obviously prompting Mamie to say other assaults had happened and tells her where]. Q. Where was your granny when this would happen? A. At work. [Previously Mamie had testified that the girls were in school when the Grandmother was at work.] Q. Now, would you be there by yourself with Pops or who else was there in the house with you and Pops? A. My sisters. Q. Would he take you in there by yourself or would your sisters go in there, too? A. By myself. Q. Did it happen in the daytime or the nighttime? A. Both. [One wonders how this could be happening in Granny's room at night, when she was presumably asleep in her room.]

DA: Pass the witness."[165]

The defense attorney conducts a brief re-cross:

> "Mamie, when your grandmother burned you when you were in the kitchen, do you remember that? A. No, I don't remember. [Mamie had just testified that she had a scar on her back because she had been burned by hot water from the kitchen stove.] Q. You don't remember your grandmother— did your grandmother burn you with some hot water at one time? [Rather than challenging the witness by suggesting inconsistency in her testimony, Mr. Daly now helps her "remember" what happened.] A. Yeah. Q. Was that in the

---

[165] Hutchins Trial, Vol. II, 150:10-151:9.

kitchen? A. No. Q. Where was that? A. In my room. Q. That was in your room? A. Uh-huh."

Mr. Daly passes the witness and the trial is adjourned for the day.

Since this case is about sexual molestation by Earnest, what is the relevance of the extended questioning about Mamie's scar and how she got it? As we shall see, the purpose is to impugn the character and credibility of the grandmother, should she testify. The quality of Mamie's testimony about the alleged burn event may in itself cause some to question her story. The defense attorney did not see fit to challenge the relevance of the inquiry, instead asking questions that reinforced the episode in the mind of the jury.

Second Day of the Trial

The next day of the proceedings, February 18, 1998, begins with the Judge speaking to the two "minors. He gives them the "Instruction" that they were not to talk to each other or anyone else about their testimony. **The jury is not present for this or what immediately follows:**

The defense attorney began questioning the pediatrician, Dr. Nolan. She testified that she had examined Mamie on July 2, 1997 (the alleged offense was on June 1, 1997). She thought that she may have also examined Carly, but was not sure and did not have her records."[166]

The pediatrician explained to the defense attorney the remarks included on a green sheet that was among some notes she had brought with her:

She had examined Mamie's hymen. It was not "intact," but had a "cleft," i.e., a breach or healed tear, consistent with sexual abuse.

At this point the jury returns and the Assistant Prosecutor questions Dr. Nolan. She states her findings were consistent with the child's claim of vaginal penetration **but did not prove it** [emphasis added]. The cleft could have been caused by a finger.

---

[166]   Hutchins Trial, Vol. III, 7:24-8:2.

She adds that Mamie told her about abuse by her grandmother, including the burn and scar from boiling water. The remarks are almost identical to the story Mamie told on the stand. Nolan also found scars that seemed to support Mamie's testimony about her grandmother. [167]

Mr. Daly begins his cross-examination by asking Dr. Nolan how many times a year she testifies as an expert witness. She answers about twelve times a year, almost exclusively for the State. He asks whether masturbation, for example with the aid of a cucumber, could cause the type of damage to the hymen she had observed. She admits it is possible, but not likely.

Daly next asks if vaginal intercourse means penetration past the hymen? She responds that even if a child was subjected to vaginal intercourse for six years, one might not see more damage to the hymen than the slight "cleft" she has observed! In her exam she had not noted any redness or irritation around the cleft. This was attributed to the more than 30 days that had elapsed since the supposed offense.

The redirect by Mr. Elliott was brief and only served to establish that Mamie had not contracted any sexually transmitted diseases.

In his re-cross, Mr. Daly establishes that the scar from the curling iron was the result of an accident.

The State called the oldest sister, Lacy, who by then was nineteen. She confirmed that she was living with her grandmother, and her boyfriend, Paul Mosely, lived with them. Her mother, Connie Morse, had passed away in 1989. [At that time Mamie would have been four, and Carly three. She never knew her dad, or who he was. She believes that Claude Lyons was the father of her sisters, but is not certain.

The questioning turns to why the girls were living with their grandmother instead of the supposed father, Claude Lyons:

> "Q. Do you know why the girls lived with their Grandma instead of Mr. Lyons? A. Well, I know at one point in time my grandmother had a guardianship paper signed over to her from my mother, but later in the years when we went to go—me and Paul Mosely had went to go get married and we

---

[167] Hutchins Trial, Vol. III, 9:9 to 11:2; 31:18 to 34:23.

had the guardianship paper. It wasn't proof enough for the courts. I don't know if it was legally a guardianship. I don't know, but that's just who we lived with."

Lacy testifies about her close relationship with Paul Mosely, even though they were only in their teens, and how he would stay over wherever she was living at the time. In the years from 1991 onwards her relationship with Earnest was becoming quite bad. When Earnest Hutchins and Violet Morse moved to a new home around 1996, she did not go with them:

> "Q. Why did you move out of the house on 17th Ave.? Why didn't you want to live there? A. Because my grandmother and Pops were going in together on this house and so I didn't want to be any part of it because I knew he wouldn't welcome me there so I went my separate way.

> "Q. Why didn't you feel like he would welcome you there? A. Our relationship had got too bad. We argued constantly, constantly. It is no point in me being around there. Q. Why would y'all argue? A. Out of hate for each other, I guess. **We just really hated each other** (emphasis added). Q. Why did you hate him without going into details yet? What did it stem back to? A. From '91."[168] [The prosecutor is setting the witness up in order to bring in testimony about the alleged sexual abuse in 1991, which was dismissed as unfounded, but which can only be prejudicial to the defendant in the present context.]

Lacy testifies that after moving around, she moved back in with her grandmother in January of 1997. Then she said she moved out again in May of that year. She said she was certain of this timing because "they" had called her **grandma**[169] to see what the kids were doing on Juneteenth. The DA tries to be specific about the date of this move and

---

[168] Hutchins Trial, Vol. III, 62:10 to 63:7.
[169] Hutchins Trial, Vol. III, 65:20.

when Lacy found out about the alleged abuse of the children (which according to trial records happened on June 1, 1997):

> "Q. So you know you moved out pretty close to the time of Juneteenth or within a month of Juneteenth? A. Yes, it was before June. Q. We need to make this sure because it is important. A. It was around May, the middle of May we moved out. Q. Then you found out about what happened about Mamie telling Claude Lyons what happened when? A. When I called, it was maybe around June 11th I called to see what they were going to do on Juneteenth. That's when my grandmother told me Claude had taken them. [Although she said she was talking to her grandmother, she does not say who, at this time, told her about what Mamie told Claude Lyons. Since, as we shall see later, the grandmother says the molestation never happened, why would she have told Lacy anything along these lines?]
>
> "(Whereupon state's Exhibit No. 5 was marked for identification purposes.) MS. K: Offer state's 5 if there is no objection. Defense: I have no objection. THE COURT: It is admitted."[170] [Five exhibits have now been introduced, but their purpose is not yet clear and none was included with the transcript.]

Ms. Konchek then guides the testimony back to 1991:

> "Q. I do want to talk about why you [Lacy] don't like Pops. Okay? A. Okay. Q. I want you to think back to May 19, 1991. How old were you then?"[171]

Mr. Daly intervenes to request a "limited instruction on 3827. The Judge grants this request:

> "THE COURT: Ladies and gentlemen, about the subject that we may proceed into, I am not sure because I haven't

---

170   Hutchins Trial, Vol. III, 65:25 to 66:20.
171   Hutchins Trial, Vol. III, 68:24 to 69:3.

got an answer. However, I have an instruction for you. The defendant is on trial solely on the charges alleged in the indictment. In reference to evidence, if any, that the defendant previously participated in recent transactions or acts against the child, [Mamie] other than but similar to that which is charged in the indictment, you are instructed that you cannot consider such other transactions or acts, if any, for any purpose unless you find and believe beyond a reasonable doubt that the defendant participated in such transactions or committed such acts, if any. Even then, you may only consider them for the purpose of determining the state of mind of the defendant and the child and the previous and subsequent relationship between the defendant and the child."[172] [How could the jurors apply this instruction without prejudice to the defendant?.]

The DA questions Lacy about a lady named Polly Boone, a friend of her grandma:

"Q. Was she at your house last week? A. Yes. Q. What did she tell you? A. She was making accusations saying that Paul, that test results came back that Paul molested my little sisters, but she was speaking more rudely than that.

"….Q. Have you known Polly Boone for a long time? A. Yes. Q. What is your opinion about her character for truthfulness? A. Not good. She is very manipulating and she lies constantly. Q. Is she a good liar? A. A very good liar. Q. Are you aware of any tests that have come back about Paul? A. Paul hasn't took any tests, therefore no tests have came back. Q. Has he ever been a suspect in this case? A. No. Q. Have your sisters ever complained that Paul was hurting them or touching them in any way? A. No."[173]

The prosecution leaves this line of inquiry and delves in some depth into what supposedly happened in 1991:

---

172   Hutchins Trial, Vol. III, 79:4-23.
173   Hutchins Trial, Vol. III, 72:13 to 73:6.

"Q. Let's go back to 1991. Okay? A. Okay. Q. You said you were twelve years old at that point. Is that right? A. Yes. Q. Can you tell the jury how old Mamie was? She is twelve now. A. I believe she was five years old.

"….Q. What were you doing? A. I was outside at first. Q. Where were you outside? A. Across the street with a friend of mine. Q. What were y'all doing? A. Sitting outside talking. Q. Did you come back over to A Drive [this was the home where Violet Morse, Pops and the young children lived before moving to 17th. Ave. where the offenses being tried were said to have occurred] and sit on porch? A. Yes, at first I tried to go in the house and the door was locked. Q. Where was your granny? A. She had went to the grocery store. Q. Where was the grocery store? Was it far? A. Maybe a five to ten minute drive.

"Q. You said what was the deal with the door? A. It was locked. Q. Where was [sic] Mamie, Carly and Lettie? A. In the house. Q. What did you think when the door was locked? A. That they were trying to lock me out to play games. [Would it not have been more logical to think that the grandmother had locked the front door, since she would be away at the store? But that would not fit the scenario about to be developed.] Q. That was the door to the inside of house? A. Yes, the front door.

"….Q. What happened when you were sitting out on the porch? My two youngest sisters, Carly and Lettie came outside. Q. How old were Carly and Lettie? A. If Mamie was five, then they would be four and three. Q. They came outside and unlocked the door? A. Yes. Q. What did you say to them? A. 'Why did y'all lock me out?' Q. What did they say? A. 'I didn't.' Q. Who did? A. They said the reason why the door was locked is because Pops was in the house getting booty with Mamie. [A three and four-year old already know about 'booty'?.] Q. What did you take that to mean? A. Having sex or whatever, attempting.

"Q. What did you think when you heard that? A. I was shocked. I just jumped up to go see as soon as they said it. Q. So you went inside. Where did you go? Did they tell you where he was? A. Yes, I said, 'Where?' 'In grandma's room.' I told them to stay there. Q. Could you show the jury where grandma's room is on that diagram? A. Back here. Q. Was the door opened or was it closed? You can have a seat. A. Closed. It was closed? A. Yes. Q. What did you do? A. Opened it and walked in. Q. What did you see when you walked in? A. Mamie was laying on the bed on her back and so was Earnest. His pants were down, her pants were down. Q. Where were their pants down to? A. Their knees. I am not sure about Earnest, but I know Mamie's was down to her knees because I helped her pull them up when I got her up.

"Q. When you looked at, what did you see? A. His [male sexual organ] Q. Was he touching []? A. He had [] he was just talking and waving his hand, mumbling to himself. I just said, 'what are you doing?' Q. How did Mamie look when you saw her? What was her face like? A. Scared to death, disgusted. Q. When you said, 'What are you doing,' what did he say? A. 'Nothing.' I just grabbed Mamie and told her to come on, put her clothes on.

"Q. What did you do then? A. Pushed her on out of the house, took my other sisters, told them to get out, go across the street. I went across the street and dialed 911."[174]

Further questioning establishes that after the police came, Pops was taken away for about a week, according to Lacy. She says that the girls' father, Claude Lyons, did not come to know about this incident until 1997 [which seems rather incredulous, since he claims to be their dad and the young girls are allegedly being molested by Pops from 1991 to 1997.] Next, the videotaping is recalled:

"Q. Now, did you ever go down to a CPS [Child Protective Services] building and give a videotape regarding the '91 incident? A. Yes. Q. When you were twelve years old? A. Yes. Q. Did you tell them the same thing you told us here? A. Yes. Q. Did Mamie go down there, too? A. Yes. Q. Did you ever go to Court on that case? A. No. Q. What did you

<hr>

think about that? What did you think about what happened with the case? A. I thought well, they didn't do nothing so now all I can do is try to watch out for them. Q. Is that what you tried to do? A. Yes. [So, she watches for six years before finding something to report?]

"Q. Did Earnest come back to the house? A. Yes. Q After that, how did you feel about him? A. **I hated him** [emphasis added]. I had no respect for him. Q. How did your grandmother treat the situation? A. Like nothing. She didn't believe it, I guess."[175] [Every effort has been made to bring the grandmother's character into disrepute. She is said to have personally abused the girls and is indifferent to whether abuse has happened, either in 1991 or 1997.]

Lacy is questioned as to whether she and her step-father, Mr. Lyons, conspired against Pops:

"Q. Is this some type of conspiracy? [The question comes out of nowhere, yet the witness seems to know exactly what the DA is looking for.] A. No. Q. Six-year conspiracy that you and Claude Lyons and everybody has dreamed up in order to get Earnest out of the picture? A. No. Q. Is it a conspiracy so Claude can get the social security check that your grandma wants? A. No. Q. Have you always known Mr.Lyons to work and maintain a job? A. Yes."[176]

There is a break for lunch. Before the jury is brought back in, the defense attorney asks the Court to allow him to bring up the fact that the step-father, Claude Lyons, served time for aggravated robbery, on the basis that that crime indicates the man would "do anything for money." The DA tells the defense that it should not go into this, because she has not brought up the previous convictions of Earnest. For the time being, the Judge refuses to allow the previous conviction of the step-father to be mentioned. [Yet he had allowed extensive testimony about

---

[175] Hutchins Trial, Vol. III, 84:4 to 85:7.
[176] Hutchins Trial, Vol. III, 85:19 to 86:6.

events in 1991 that had been incredible in themselves and dismissed as "unfounded."]

The jury and Lacy return to the courtroom and Mr. Daly begins his cross-examination. From the time of the alleged offense in 1991, Lacy continued to live in the house with the girls until at least 1996, when Violet Morse and Pops moved to another house. Asked about how Pops treated the children during this time, Lacy replied:

> "Q. If anything had been happening with Pops, would your sisters have come and told you about it? A. Well, yes, if they felt like it. I mean yes, as far as I know."[177]

> "Q. From May 19, 1991 until mid-1995, they never came to you and told you anything? A. They would tell me little things. There wasn't nothing I could do but tell them to stay away from him, stay away from him. Q. What little things did they tell you? A. That he tried to grab them or tried to touch them or he kept telling them come here, come here, stuff like that. Q. So they did tell you whenever he tried to bother them? A. Yes. Q. When he tried to touch them and grab them and said come here, would they come to him or would they confront him or what would they do? A. They told me that they came to me. Q. Did you ever see him try to grab one of the children? A. Not really. He wouldn't do it when I was around. Q. But they didn't have any hesitation in telling Mr. Hutchins no, that they didn't want to be touched? A. Not as far as I know.[178]

> "…. Q. Lacy, what was your relationship with your sisters, Mamie and Carly and Lettie? A. Sisterly relationship. Q. Did you have a close relationship? A. Yes. Q. Did you feel like they would tell you everything? A. Yes."[179]

Prior to the trial the Court had made $500 available for an investigator to try to locate witnesses or evidence that might be helpful

---

177   Hutchins Trial, Vol. III, 101:20-24.

178   Hutchins Trial, Vol. III, 102:8 to 103:6.

179   Hutchins Trial, Vol. III, 109:17-25.

to Mr. Hutchins. Mr. FM, a long-time friend of Earnest, was chosen for this work. The defense now questions Lacy about her interview by FM:

> "Q. Do you remember talking to an investigator in this case? A. During what period of time? Q. Just within the past couple of weeks. A. Yes. Q. A man by the name of FM came out to see you? A. Yes. Q. Do you remember talking to him about this case? A. Yes. Q. Do you remember telling him that you didn't think anything happened between Mamie and Mr. Hutchins back in 1991? A. No, I didn't. Q. You didn't make that statement to him? A. No, I did not make that statement to him. Q. Did you make a statement to him that you didn't think anything happened because you were sure that Mamie would have called out if something had happened and you didn't hear call out? A. No, I did not make that statement either. Q. Did you make any statement similar to that? A. No, I told him the story that I told this Court earlier this morning."[180]

In 1996 Violet Morse and Mr. Hutchins had moved to a home on 17th Ave. It was purchased with the help of Mr. Hutchins's VA loan. Mr. Daly questions Lacy about her relationship with Earnest, her boyfriend, Paul Mosely, and her step-father, Claude Lyons, after she moved into this home:

> "Q. After you moved back into the house on 17th. Ave., at this time you and Earnest still not getting along? A. We had a hi and bye relationship, yes, but we didn't get along, no. Q. Why would you move back into the house on 17th. Ave. if you weren't getting along with Earnest A. Because I needed somewhere to stay and my grandmother and Earnest talked it over and they said it was okay if I stayed there. Q. Why did you need someplace to stay? You were working. Why couldn't you afford your own apartment? A. Because I was the only one working. Q. Why wasn't Paul working? A. Because his license had got suspended when he got on

---

[180] Hutchins Trial, Vol. III, 112:4 to 113:7.

probation [for marijuana found in his car.] Q. And he can't work without a driver's license? A. No.

"Q. What was your relationship with Claude Lyons? A. It was fairly close. Q. Do you know if Mr. Lyons ever paid Violet Morse regular child support? A. No. Q. You know that he didn't or you don't know? A. I don't know. Q. Did you ever see him give any money to Mrs. Morse? A. No. Q. Did he ever tell you he was paying child support to Mrs. Morse? A. We never discussed it. Q. Did Mr. Lyons ever give you money? A. Yes. Q. How much money did he give you? A. Whatever I asked for, $20 here, $20 there whenever I needed it, whenever I was broke or something. Q. But you are not Claude Lyons' blood daughter, I guess? A. No. No. Q. He is not your biological father? A. No.

"Q. In 1995 when you found out that Violet Morse and Earnest were going to buy the house together, why did you object to that? A. Because I don't think Earnest is the kind of person that she needs to be bonding with in legal matters....Q. Did you know that Earnest used his VA loan to help— A. Get the house? Q.—to finance that house? A. Yes. Q. Did Violet discuss that with you that they were doing that? A. Yes....Q. Now, did Earnest want you and Paul Mosely to live with him at the house on 17th. Ave.? A. We never discussed it, but I knew we wouldn't be welcome there.... Q. Now, when you left, why did you leave? A. Because my grandmother asked me to leave because she was tired of having arguments with Earnest about my dogs, about me being there, so we left....

"Q. It was about a month after you left the house that this report against Earnest Lyons [sic: the defense attorney uses the wrong last name for his client, then corrects himself] was made—against Earnest Hutchins was made by Claude Lyons? A. Yes. Q. Now, about how many times did you see Claude Lyons between May of 1991 and June of 1997? A. About how many times? Q. Uh-huh. A. A lot. Q. You would see him a lot? A. Yes. Q. Like every weekend. A. Not every single weekend, but at least a weekend out of the month he would come do something with my little sisters.

Q. Would he do something with you? A. If I wanted to go, I was welcome, but I never went. Q. Did Earnest Lyons [the defense attorney now mistakes the first name of his client for that of Claude Lyons] sometimes take your little sisters over to his house? A. Did Earnest Lyons? Q. I am sorry, Claude Lyons. A. Yes. Q. And they would stay over there for a few days? A. Yes....

"Q. (By Mr. Daly) So what was the reputation among the remembers [sic] of your household concerning the paternity of Carly and Lettie? A. That they weren't Claude's biological kids. Q. Did this fact, the fact that Mamie was sometimes jealous of Claude Lyons, would that cause any friction between Mamie and Carly and Lettie? A. No....

"Q. Concerning the situation that's going on in the family, did you ever see Violet Morse beat or abuse Carly or Letti or Mamie? A. Not abuse them, no. Q. What did you see her do? A. Discipline them. Q. Were the kids sometimes difficult to discipline? A. Well, no, not for her, no. They respected her. Q. She didn't have any trouble controlling the kids? A. No....

"Q. What is Mamie's reputation for truthfulness? A. Not very good to a certain extent. Q. Do you think that she is telling the truth when she says that your grandmother pored boiling water on her? A. I don't know. I don't know. Q. Did she ever mention to you that your grandmother had done that? A. No. Q. Did she ever tell anybody else about that story? A. As far as I know, it came up when all of this came up in '97. Q. That never came up until '97? A. No, not to me....

"Q. After you moved there [to 17th. Ave.], didn't Carly and Lettie and Mamie sleep in the den? A. Yes. Q. And you and Paul slept in the bedroom? A. Yes. Q. During that period of time did you ever—how close is your bedroom to the den? A. Across the hall. Q. Right across the hall from the den? A. Right across the hall....Q. The whole time you were there while the children were sleeping in the den, did you ever hear any unusual activity going on in the den? A. No. Q. Did you ever hear any of your sisters call out to you? A. No.

Q. Did any of your sisters ever tell you that Earnest was coming into the den and bothering them? A. They told me that he had threatened them to do it. Q. What do you mean had threatened to do it? A. That he came and said I am going to get you tonight if you don't behave or something to that nature. She told me that. Q. Okay, that he said I am going to get you tonight if you don't behave? A. Yeah. Q. They told you that while you were living in the house in 1997? A. Yes. Q. What did you do about that? A. I told them to stay away from him and if anything was to happen, to come get me wherever I was, no matter what time it was. Q. And you never thought to tell any of these incidents to Claude Lyons so that he could intervene? A. No. Q. Did you ever think to call the police? A. No."[181]

"Q. Now, I want to go back to the incident in 1991. When you went into the bedroom, did you state that you had seen some fluid that had come out of Mr. Hutchins's [male organ]? A. No, I didn't state that. Mamie stated that to the police and they questioned me about it. Q. Did you and Mamie clean up some of that fluid with paper towels? A. No. Q. Did Mamie clean up some of the fluid with paper towels? A. No. [According to the police report in 1991 Mamie said she saw [a fluid] coming out of Gramp's "thing", and wiped it up with a paper towel—which was collected by the police.]

"Q. Did she have any fluid on her when you went in there? A. I didn't see any, but I didn't wait around to look, either. Q. The underwear that she was wearing, did you help her pull up her underwear and pull up clothes? A. Yes. Q. After she got dressed, did the police later come and take those clothes off of Mamie? A. I don't remember. Defense Attorney: I pass the witness."[182]

Both the DA and defense have a few more questions for Lacy, without adding much of significance to the trial. The DA gets Lacy to testify that while Mamie would lie about "petty" things, she would tell the truth about important things.

---

[181]   Hutchins Trial, Vol. III, 119:23 to 132:15.
[182]   Hutchins Trial, Vol. III, 133:16 to 134:15.

We have arrived at page 141 of the Third Volume of the trial transcript, which runs 350 pages in all and ends with the state concluding its prosecution. Pages 142 through 350 cover the following: Testimony of Mamie's younger sister, Carly; a conversation between the attorneys and the Judge about potential offenses by Lacy's boyfriend, Paul Mosely, that could make him a suspect in the violation of the girls; testimony of Dr. DP, a psychologist in private practice, the testimony of the father/ step father, Claude Lyons; questioning of the grandmother, Violet Morse, outside the presence of the jury, with regard to whether she would testify or take the Fifth Amendment; a recall of Claude Lyons for another question; testimony of police Officer LD who on June 15, 1997, was called to the house on 17th. Ave., Violet Morse's home; and testimony of detective Grudge, who interviewed Mamie on June 23 1997.

Carly's testimony is much like the story told by Mamie. Her memory of details of something that is alleged to have occurred when she was four years old is surpisingly clear. She also claimed there were sexual assaults years later at the home on 17th. Her tale was not particularly convincing to a critical listener. For instance, she testified that her grandmother was always at home and she felt she could tell her if anything bad had happened. Carly said she would **always** yell when Earnest first came into the room and he would run down the hall.

She said she saw Earnest "get booty" from Mamie. He came into the den, got on top of Mamie, **with her clothes on**. Then she saw []. It was dark, she pretended to be asleep, but could not see much. Later she heard Mamie tell her grandma what had happened, but Violet Morse did not do anything about it.

She said in 1991 or 1992 she told Claude Lyons four or five times what was happening.. He did not call the police.

During the re-direct she is questioned about Paul Mosely and says he never touched Mamie in a nasty way.

Under re-cross, Carly says she told Lacy about what Earnest was doing and Lacy "tried to file." She told Paul Mosely and he tried to stop Earnest.

Much of this is inconsistent with testimony of other parties.

There is a break for lunch, then the jury returns and the Prosecution examines a witness from the Department of Protective Services who testifies for the State in criminal child abuse cases about three or four times a year. It is the strategy of the DA to have him tell why a child might delay an outcry for six years.

Dr. P says there could be several reasons: The abuse is "presented" as a loving relationship; the child is threatened by the perpetrator; or due to cognitive development the child comes to understand why an "outcry" is appropriate.

Although the witness has said it is not his purpose to give an opinion about the case, the DA presents all of the details that have been alleged in the case as a "hypothetical" case and asks for his opinion about those "facts." Not surprisingly, he agrees that under those circumstances, a delayed outcry could be expected

In the cross-exam, Mr. Daly is told by the Dr. that he has testified for [] County about twenty times in this type of case. If the information in the hypothetical was incorrect, he would adjust his opinion according to the true facts. It could be expected that a child would tell a loving father or caring older sibling about the abuse, but not necessarily.[183]

The father/foster-father, Claude Lyons, is next called to the stand. He had received two fifteen year sentences for various crimes, but by 1982 he had been released from prison, turned his life around (with only minor incidents), now was forty-nine years old and had a job.

Under direct exam by the DA he asserted that he and his wife had wanted to have the children:

> "Q. Since 1982, do you feel like you have pretty much turned
> your life around? A. I have. I goes to church and I have been
> working on a regular job. I enjoy being with my kids, what
> time I was allowed with them at the time. Now they are with
> me full-time. We have been working with them trying to get
> them. They have been through a lot and I hate to see them
> to go through like I went through a lot when I was a kid.
> I lost my mother and father at a young age, so that's why I
> got off track."[184]

---

183   Hutchins Trial, Vol. III, 189-217.
184   Hutchins Trial, Vol. III, 224:16-25, 225:1.

Everything had been fine until Earnest entered the picture. After 1991 it was hard to see the kids because of Mrs. Morse. Each week he would give Violet Morse $150, until the children said they were not getting any food or school clothes. So he stopped. [The testimony of Lacy did not support monetary support anything like this.] He had no idea how much the social security check for the girls was. CPS had transferred the check to his wife, Rita. The DA says it was $800.

He testified that he could always pay his bills in 1997, even if late at times. Mamie told him what Pops was doing to her in June 1997. Two or three weeks before the police were called, he got a phone call from Mamie saying Pops was "messing" with her again:

> "Q. What did you think "messing" meant at that point? A. He is an alcoholic. Once he gets drunk, he is liable to go to playing and wrestling with her. I told her don't play with grown-ups. I thought that's what she meant. She said no, he came into my room and [sexual molestation.] I said, "Are you sure?" She said, "Yeah." Q. Did you know what "nasty thing" meant by your conversations with Mamie or knowing her? What did nasty thing mean? A. She was talking about his [male organ]."[185]

At that time, Claude Lyons did nothing about what Mamie told him. He received a second phone call from Mamie two weeks later saying Pops was "messing" with her again. This time he went and got the girls. He got a "cursing message" from Violet Morse, telling him to bring the kids back. Mamie had not told him about what was going on earlier, because of threats:

> "Q. What did Mamie tell you? A. My sister said I need to talk to Mamie, so she called me. She told Mamie to tell me what she told her. She told me that Earnest Hutchins had been molesting her all along. She was scared to tell because her grandmother threatened if she say anything about it, she was going to put a gun up to her head and shoot her."[186]

---

185   Hutchins Trial, Vol. III, 236:14-22.
186   Hutchins Trial, Vol. III, 218-250.

Lyons did not call the police when the second call came in on Tuesday. On the following Sunday, he says he went to Violet Morse's home to get the kids' clothes for church. Mrs. Morse [about 70 at this time] hit Carly [ten years old] so hard in the chest she could hardly breathe as she came through the door. It was then the **grandmother** who called the police because of all the uproar. A police Officer came and talked to the kids.

The cross-exam of Claude Lyons by Mr. Daly follows

The Lyons family had lived in four or five places between 1991 and 1997. At the time he learned Violet and Earnest were buying a new home, he was not jealous but glad for his kids to have a good place to stay. He stopped making the $150 payments in 1995, or 1996, or 1997, then settled on 1996. (When he was giving the $150 weekly, that would have been $600 a month, out of a paycheck of $1,600 a month. In addition, he also gave money to Lacy.)

At first he says Carly told him Pops was coming into her room and bothering her on 5th. Street. Then, he reversed himself, and said he was sure it was on 17th Ave. (which would have put it after the move in 1996). [Carly testified that she had told Mr. Lyons about the abuse four or five times when they lived on 5th. Street, in 1991 or 1992.]

From 1991 on, no one had said anything to him about the 1991 incident. He did not know about the sexual abuse until June of 1997:

> Q. You found out the night before that night in June of 1997
> when the kids were removed from home. That's the first time
> that you found out that Earnest had allegedly sexually molested
> Mamie in 1991, about six years prior to that? A. Yeah."[187]

Lyons saw Lacy often and they were close, but for six years she never told him about the 1991 molestation, although she complained all the time [according to him] about Earnest's drinking and cussing. He thinks Lacy did not tell him because she knew he would jump all over her grandma [for whom she had so much affection?].

Lyons let them live with Violet Morse in spite of his dying wife's plea:

---

[187]   Hutchins Trial, Vol. III, 264:25-266:1.

"Q. You wouldn't let your kids stay in a house and let them be abused by a man repeatedly, would you? A. Oh, no…. Q. Yet these, your kids, your own flesh and blood, you let them go stay with Violet, you? A. Yes, I did….

"Q. (By Mr. Daly) So even though the mother of these children made you promise that you would not let them go live with Violet Morse, you let them live with Mrs. Morse and be abused for eight years. Is that correct? A. The reason I let them stay there because at first she was a good grandma to them [disregarding his own allegation that her daughter had said she was a terrible abuser], then all of a sudden Earnest Hutchins came into the picture and everything changed."[188]

As he nears the end of his cross-examination, Mr. Daly gets Lyons to admit that the actual call to the police on the Sunday of the fracas at the Morse home was by Earnest Hutchins, and not by Violet or Claude himself.

"Q. When you went over to Violet Morse's house and Earnest Hutchins's house, it was Earnest who called the police, wasn't it? A. Yes. Q. Not you? No. Q. Not Violet. It was Earnest that called the police. The alleged sexual molester called the police to come out there and investigate the situation."[189]

Mr. Daly closes by suggesting the reason Claude got in his truck and left the scene before the police arrived because he had a gun with which he had threatened Earnest and Violet.

In her redirect, the DA endeavors to establish the reason Mr. Lyons was not told about the 1991 incident until June, 1997:

"Q. For whatever reason, you didn't know about the 1991 incident, did you? A. No. Q. Tell you what, just to—I think we all want to know why didn't you know about the 1991 incident? Was it because you weren't— because they didn't

---

[188]   Hutchins Trial, Vol. III, 268:17-270:3.

[189]   Hutchins Trial, Vol. III, 273:23-274:4.

tell you or was it common knowledge or do you know why you weren't informed of that? A. Well, their grandma had threatened them and told them if they tell me anything, that she was going to—she always keeps a gun—that she was going to shoot them with the gun and that she had been beating them. They got scars in their head [since she was intimidated out of testifying, Mrs. Morse will never have a chance to deny any of this.]"[190]

The DA then "reformulates" Mr. Lyons' testimony to say that "they" (the girls) phoned him to say that "they" were being molested, first Mamie, then Carly. He has to correct the DA, saying that it was Mamie who told him. The DA suggests that Carly was also being molested, so he agrees that "they" told him that as well. But Carly would "fight him off." The DA clarifies that by "messing" with the girls, Lyons meant they told him Earnestwas coming into their room and sexually harassing them—to which he also agreed.[191]

In his re-cross, Mr. Daly determines that after the Sunday dispute, Violet Morse and Earnest Hutchins went to the Justice of the Peace in Precinct One and filed a formal complaint against Mr. Lyons for threatening them with a gun. Lyons says their story was a fabrication

The Court is about to take a 4:00 p.m. break and the jury leaves the room. Out of their presence the Judge and attorneys go into the issue of whether Violet Morse can take the Fifth Amendment. Mrs. Morse is present, but her attorney, Mr. BT, is not. Instead, another lady, Ms. BF, is taking his place. It is noted that Mrs. Morse has been indicted in district court for injury to a child.

Mrs. Morse is called, outside of the presence of the jury, and questioned by Mr. Daly. He repeatedly asks her if she wants to testify on behalf of Earnest Hutchins, but her attorney interrupts and prevents her from answering. Finally, Violet Morse says she does not wish to testify.

---

[190]   Hutchins Trial, Vol. III, 276:10-24.
[191]   Hutchins Trial, Vol. III, 277:3-278:8.

Violet's attorney continues to tell her not to answer questions, and after being told several times she has to actually say "I take the Fifth Amendment," she says the words: "I claim the Fifth."[192]

The Judge refuses to accept Mr. Daly's contention that Mrs. Morse has waived her Fifth Amendment rights, so she cannot be asked any other questions and the trial adjourns. **The jury will never know why Mrs. Morse does not appear as a witness.**

The next witness for the prosecution is Officer LD. He is questioned by the second assistant DA, Mr. Elliott. He is a patrolman, working for …PD. On June 15, 1997, about 9 a.m., he responded to a call from the Violet Morse/Earnest Hutchins home. Mr. Lyons had left the scene, with the girls, but phoned while the officer was interviewing Mrs. Morse. He quickly returned to the home to speak with LD.

The officer does not recall anything being said about a gun, but Mr. Lyons might have mentioned something about a rock. Lyons told him that the live-in boyfriend and Mrs. Morse had been "abusing" the girls. He then had Lyons walk a short distance away, so that he could speak to the three girls alone.

According to the officer, Mamie tells them about the "abuse":

> "A. The oldest, Mamie, spoke up and she stated that she had been—when they are spanked, they are hit on various parts of the body using various items such as extension cords, sticks, the hand. They are called names. Q. Was she able to show you any kind of scars or markings? A. Yes, she proceeded to show me on her body, arms and legs, various scars that ranged in length from a half inch to about four inches [the number and dimensions of the scars seems to have grown considerably since earlier testimony.]
>
> "Q. What about sexual abuse? Did they tell you anything about that? A. When the mention of sexual abuse arose, there wasn't really a whole lot of detail [much detail about beatings, etc., but not about sexual molestation?], but I had to stop at that point. Q. Is that what you are told to do in your training? A. Yes, sir, in the training. Q. What do

---

[192]   Hutchins Trial, Vol. III, 288-289.

they tell you to do when that issue comes up? A. When you receive this kind of information that there is a possibility of physical and sexual abuse, we contact Child Protective Services….Q. The call to CPS was made from the scene by …PD? A. Yes, sir. Q. You didn't actually talk to the girls about sexual abuse, you waited until they could see a counselor? A. Correct."[193]

CPS did not come out at that time, but gave instructions to have the girls pack some things for a night, return to Mr. Lyons' home, and stay there all day. In further questioning, the officer says he talked to all of the parties, and Mr. Earnest Hutchins was the most cooperative. But Mr. Lyons was more cooperative than Mrs. Morse—he was willing to follow instructions (those of CPS).

Mr. Daly begins his cross-examination and the officer concedes that he does not actually recall the details of his visit to the home, but is relying on a written report he prepared at the time. [A copy of this police report was not available in the Court file on Earnest Hutchins].

The Officer was asked if CPS had made an investigation of Lyons before giving their instructions, but he did not answer that question. Instead he said "they" were on the scene and felt comfortable with the decision.

In his redirect, the DA leads the witness to recall more information about the sexual abuse [which apparently the witness had forgotten to mention in the earlier questioning]:

> "Q. But he did subsequently tell you that the girls had made an outcry to him about physical and sexual abuse? A. Yes, he said that they had been telling him things during the course of the previous night's stay."

The defense has no additional questions and the witness is excused.

DA direct exam: The next state witness is Officer Grudge, an …PD detective in the child sex abuse section for seven years. He

---

[193]   Hutchins Trial, Vol. III, 302:18-304:2.

had investigated 167 cases in the year preceding this one and had been assigned to it June 17, 1997. A videotaped interview of the victim, Mamie, was conducted on June 23. It was Mr. Lyons who brought the three girls down for the videotaping. The officer was not present during the procedure.

After the videotaping, the detective met with Violet Morse and Earnest Hutchins, to get their side of the story. Mr. Hutchins said that he did not molest the girls and that was all he wanted to say. Officer Grudge says Mrs. Morse also did not want to talk about the abuse investigation, but said she would take a polygraph. He says he set up an appointment for this, but she did not come. With regard to the sexual abuse:

> "Q. What did she tell you, if anything, about the sexual abuse charges? A. Later I did talk to her in reference to Earnest's interview because he did not want to talk to me about the investigation. I asked her if this was possible, if this did happen. She basically said that he was a man and yes, it's possible. Q. She didn't admit that he did it, but she said anything is possible? A. Yes, sir."[194] **[In the Earnest Hutchins file there was an "Investigative Narrative" written by the detective dated August 13, 1997, with entries for eight different days, but not a single entry with regard to this alleged interaction with Mrs. Morse.]**

The DA goes in some depth into the events of 1991 and the evidence collected at that time. The detective has reopened that case because of the current incident and has had that evidence examined. Some semen was found on a bed sheet [there was never a test to determine whose it was], but "No semen was detected on the two paper towels. No semen was detected on Mamie Morse's blue cut-off jeans or panties." A stipulation agreed to by both sides, Exhibit 6, was entered to this effect.

The cross-exam by Mr. Daly evinces an admission by the detective that he does not actually recall the details, but is basing his testimony on the offense report of 1991 and the videotapes of 1997. He admits that

---

[194]   Hutchins Trial, Vol. III, 322:6-16.

the semen on the bed sheet could have an innocent explanation and does not question the fact that although there was testimony that Mamie was on top of Earnest, or the other way around, there was no evidence of semen on her clothing or the paper towels, even though ["pee", i.e. semen] had supposedly been seen coming from Earnest's [male organ].[195]

Because the victims had identified Earnest as the perpetrator, the police had not looked for any other abuser, and had not investigated Paul Mosely. In fact, he did not know who this person was. Daly then tries to implicate Mosely as a possible offender, but this approach proves ineffective. The witness states:

> "In 1997, it was clear who the suspects were in this case from the video, so the answer would be no, I did not investigation [sic] anyone other than Earnest Hutchins and Violet Morse."[196] [Although the trial establishes that the deceased mother of the girls had engaged in drugs and prostitution, the notion is never raised that any number of "visitors" to the home while the mother was alive could have molested the children.]

Mr. Daly asks the officer if after hearing earlier questioning in the courtroom he went to his computer to look up the offense record of Paul Mosely. He said he did. When asked what he found, the DA objects. The Judge rules that if anything was found, it could not be admitted unless it had to do with child abuse or sexual assault. The witness answered that he did not find that type of incident, and Mr. Daly passed the witness.

In the redirect, the detective said he had no evidence that Paul Mosely was having sex with Lacy. He had no reason to investigate him, or anyone else, as a possible violator of the girls. With regard to Lacy's claims, he testifies:

> "Q. Now, you testified earlier that you had taken a statement from Lacy about—I guess it was late June of '97? A. Yes,

---

[195]   Hutchins Trial, Vol. III, 333:6-10.
[196]   Hutchins Trial, Vol. III, 337:22-340:19.

sir. Q. In that statement did she also tell you about the '91 incident? A. Yes, sir, she did. Q. Did you have a chance to compare her version in '97 to what she had said on the videotape from the offense report from '91? [In fact there was no 1991 video of Lacy, only a "pre-video" interview, and there is nothing in the written report about what Lacy said at this point.]

"A. Based on the '91 offense report I read, it was pretty consistent in reference the two statements. Q. Even six years later? A. Yes, sir." [Not so surprising, since the State could easily have "refreshed" Lacy's memory or even shown her the earlier report.][197]

In his re-cross, Mr. Daly has the officer clarify that he does not have any information about whether or not Paul Mosely and Lacy were having sex. He does not know, one way or the other.[198]

The State rests its case, it is 5 p.m. on the second day of the trial, February. 18, 1998. The Judge informs the jury that the next morning the defense will present its case, "if it wishes to do so", and tells them there is a good chance they will begin their deliberations. This instruction is consistent with his penchant throughout the trial to rush things along.

Day Three, February 19, 1998

The defense attorney (outside the presence of the jury) renews his motion for a continuance and asked for a mistrial so that Violet Morse could be persuaded to testify. The Judge denies this request and also the jury will not be allowed to know that Mrs. Morse is taking the Fifth Amendment.

Although the claim was unfounded, the Judge allows the 1991 incident to be brought in to show an on-going "relationship" between Earnest Hutchins and the victim. In the process it appears both the Judge and DA are confused about details of the case.

---

[197]   Hutchins Trial, Vol. III, 345:3-17.
[198]   Hutchins Trial, Vol. III, 346:1-19.

The first witness Mr. Daly calls is the defendant, Earnest Hutchins. Outside of the hearing of the jury, Mr. Daly notes that he is going to introduce evidence about the 1991 incident, but only to show that there was reasonable doubt in its regard.

Earnest Hutchins testifies that he had known Violet Morse since between 1975 and 1978. They were real good friends. He had known all the children since before their mother passed away. After he moved into the house on 5th. Street in 1991, he was never alone with them. Either they were away at school, or when Violet left the house, he would also leave.[199]

Earnest Hutchins says his relationship with the children was pretty close, but after their mother passed they really did not want him in the house because they did not want anyone to come between them and their grandma.

Lacy would take advantage of her grandmother and Earnest Hutchins thinks this is why she did not want him around, since he would step in.

Mr. Daly asked Hutchins if there was trouble with some of the neighbors who lived in a duplex across the street. He replied that they were openly using drugs and Lacy would associate with the girls who lived there.

Mr. Hutchins was aware of the May, 1991, incident and had heard the testimony of Lacy and Mamie. He denied anything had happened at that time:

> "Q. Can you tell us what happened in that incident in 1991? A. Well, nothing actually happened. I don't know why she brought up all of this, made it up or something because nothing really happened.
>
> "Q. At some point the police came to your house, correct? A. Yeah, well—Q. Did anything happen before the police came to your house? A. Nothing happened, but.... next thing I know here come the police telling me to come out of the house, put the handcuffs on me and put me in

---

[199] Hutchins Trial, Vol. IV, 19:1-24.

the car. I didn't know nothing about all this report or of this. I didn't know nothing about it. They had made all of this into it. They released me from the city jail about two or three days later.

Q. Did you have a chance to explain your side of the story to the police? A. They didn't want to listen to me."[200]

Earnest admitted he did not have a very friendly relationship with the children. They did not want him to touch them and would curse him when he wanted them to do chores. Sometimes he would give them a whipping. They had no trouble hollering out when he did anything they did not like…. I would get me a belt and hit them two or three times. And every time, 'I am going to tell my daddy,' you know. 'Tell daddy you cursed me' or 'tell my daddy you whipped me.' And I would tell Violet, you know."[201]

Asked about Paul Mosely, Hutchins said he and Lacy got together around 1992 [when she was about thirteen], and after a while he began slipping in and out of the house on 5th. Street:

At times Lacy would spend the night or weekends elsewhere with Paul. At first, Paul would spend two nights a week at the house on 5th. Street, then he started staying regularly. During those times, Lacy and Paul would sleep in the den. Violet got tired of arguing with Paul, and finally just allowed him to stay. When Mrs. Morse tried to get Lacy to tell Paul not to come in to spend the night:

> "She tried and like I say, she [Lacy] would always bring up an argument that he wasn't staying there, you know. I would get up and catch him there and she would get mad at me, tell me it wasn't none of my business."

The children had their own room but also spent a lot of time in the den with Lacy and Paul, at times sleeping there or sometimes watching "R" rated and sexually explicit movies on the Cable.

---

[200]   Hutchins Trial, Vol. IV, 30:2-33:7.
[201]   Hutchins Trial, Vol. IV, 36:11-20.

The testimony of Hutchins is interrupted abruptly so the defense attorney can question another witness who has to return to work, a Mrs. Cole. Claude Lyons had worked for her and made about $1,600 a month. He had been a hard worker and was truthful, as far as she knew.

The direct exam of Mr. Hutchins by his attorney is resumed. He asks if Lacy and Paul were having sexual relations. Earnest replies that Violet would fuss with them because they were hugging and kissing in front of the children. Paul was spending the night there, but Earnest never saw them having sex.

All three of the girls slept on one bed in their room. Hutchins testified it would not be possible for him to crawl into that queen-sized bed and molest one of them without waking the other two. There was nothing unusual that police should find semen on the bed sheets from the bed he and Violet slept in, since they would have sex there.

Earnest and the kids saw Paul with marijuana in the house. It was more than a person would need for personal use, and he suspected Paul was selling drugs. Basically he depended on Lacy to support him. (She had quit school and worked at McDonald's to bring in some money).

While he was living with Violet, Hutchins did yard work—which consisted of four jobs. On days he did not work, he was not alone with the children:

> "Q. Where would the children go during the day? A. If the kids was out of school, wasn't no school going on, and if I was going to stay at home or leave home, like I say, the kids would go and stay with somebody else."

Earnest and Violet decided to buy the home on 17th. Ave. together, with both of their names appearing on the deed. At the time he told Lacy that if she and Paul wanted to stay with them on 17th, she would have to pay him rent. She resented that and did not want them to buy the home together because she knew she would not be able to have her way.

They moved into the house on 17th Ave. around Christmas, 1995. Lacy and Paul remained in the home on 5th, since Violet had about a month's rent left there

In 1997, Hutchins became ill and the family members wanted him to draw up a will. He consented to do this because, if something did happen to him, he wanted Violet and the grandchildren to have the house on 17th Ave. without any problems (e.g., from his children from a previous marriage).

Over the years, until he started getting the social security check, Violet would give him small amounts of money. He was unable to help with the rent. This was another reason the children resented his presence in the house.

He never knew Claude Lyons to give Violet $600 a month, although he did give her $50 or $60. Sometimes he would bring it every week, then he wouldn't be seen for a month or so. Lyons did not bring groceries to the family. He did buy school stuff for the kids, hamburgers and that kind of thing.

On 17th Ave., Mamie, Carly and Lettie all slept on the same bed they had on 5th Street. They had their own bedroom, but sometimes made a pallet in the den to sleep on, so they could use the phone there or fall asleep watching TV.

Earnest thought Lacy and Paul moved back into the house on 17th Ave. in the fall of 1996, Lacy being about sixteen and Paul nineteen. They were just supposed to stay for about a month, until Lacy had time to save some money.

> "I said it is all right with me as long as they are just going to stay here long enough to get them a place to stay. But after they moved back in, they didn't look for no other place to stay. On top of that, Lacy quit her job. Paul didn't have a job."[202]
>
> "Q. Between the time that you moved out of the house on 5th until Lacy moved back into the house, were there any complaints from the children that you had been molesting them or touching them in any inappropriate way? A. No, sir. Q. Did the children complain to Violet or anything else about you touching them? A. No, sir."[203]

---

202 Hutchins Trial, Vol. IV, 76:3-8.
203 Hutchins Trial, Vol. IV, 76:9-17.

After Lacy and Paul moved back in, several things happened that caused Earnest to ask them to move out.

Violet and Earnest went to church every Sunday. The pastor was a Rev. Badgett. The children had plenty of opportunity to talk to the pastor, since they were taken to Sunday school every week. The pastor also came by the home and visited. The pastor also tried to mediate the dispute between Claude Lyons and Violet.

The children went to Sunday school most Sundays, until Lacy returned to the home.

Mamie continued to go to school, but would pretend to be sick so she could stay home with Lacy. The children had to move out of their room and begin sleeping on the mattress in the dining room, so Lacy and Paul could sleep on the queen-size bed in their room.

Earnest admitted going into the den at night to turn off lights and the TV, but denied ever doing any of the things of which he had been accused. Just before June, or at the beginning of June, 1997, Earnest insisted that Lacy and Paul leave.

> "Q. And that was just a matter of weeks before or maybe days before these allegations were made against you? A. Lacy and Paul left one week, Claude come pick up the kids that Friday. He comes back that Sunday to get the kids' clothes and go to church and that's when all of this started."
>
> "Q. When Claude came over to get kids' clothes to take them to Sunday school, who called the police? A. I did. Q. Why did you call the police? A. I called the police because him and Violet was arguing and.... he had a pistol in his hands."[204]

After this incident, Violet and Earnest went to file a complaint against Mr. Lyons, and spoke with a Justice of the Peace, Mr. Stone.

The defense attorney asks Mr. Hutchins if he cooperated with the police and personnel from Protective Services when they came to the

---

[204] Hutchins Trial, Vol. IV, 88:9-24.

house in 1997. He said they did not arrest him at that time and he answered their questions.

Earnest describes another "incident" with Lacy:

> "She come back high and she come back cursing, and me and her got into an argument. She tells her grandma she is going to get rid of me. We keep lye, Drano, in the kitchen. She ran in the kitchen, grabbed her some hot water. She poured some lye and who knows whatever. She is going to come out, dash it in my face and get rid of me. She throwed it at my face but she hit me on my clothes. Then she got scared about that. I told her I was going to call the police....
>
> "Q. (By Mr. Daly) Did you call police after that happened? A. I called the police, but when the police came out, she had left.."[205]

Ms. Konchek takes up her cross-exam. She asks Hutchins if he remembers the night he had passed out, Lacy had called 911 for him and he was taken to the hospital for several days. He replied that he remembers waking up in the hospital, but there were three or four people in the house and he does not know who called 911.[206]

She reminds Mr. Hutchins he said he was never alone with the children, but says he was alone with them in 1991. He admits that Violet was gone, but thought that Lacy was around and might come in and out at any time. He also conceded that he was in fact alone with the kids from time to time.

The DA comments on how sad Mamie appeared on the stand and how it looked like she did not want to be there, and asks Hutchins what sense he could make of that. Mr. Daly objects to the question and Earnest says he cannot answer it:

> [A more pertinent question might be: Why would these girls, who everyone agreed were often out of control at home, yelling, cursing, fighting, disobeying, etc., suddenly be so

---

[205] Hutchins Trial, Vol. IV, 96:17-98:2.

[206] Hutchins Trial, Vol. IV, 101:8.

"sad" and submissive on the stand, even with the "comfort" of their foster mother right there taking notes?]

Konchek reviews another part of the 1991 incident:

"Q. Isn't it true that when they [the police] arrived, you were sitting in the living room drinking, drinking out of a big bottle, some alcohol? A. Yeah. [Other testimony[207] establishes that there was no "big bottle" of alcohol, Earnestwas simply drinking a beer Q. But you were able to tell them your side of the story, weren't you? A. I wouldn't call that a side of the story." [He means he was not allowed to directly address the accusations by the girls.]

The DA repeats in graphic detail all of these accusations and Hutchins says the girls are all lying in what they testified.[208] Ms. Konchek brings up an alleged incident not mentioned up to this time, even by Lacy:

"Q. Do you remember a time about a month before the incident in 1991 when you called Lacy in your room and she was twelve years old and you asked her to give you a kiss? Do you remember that? A. No. Q. Do you remember her turning her cheek and saying, 'Here, you can kiss me,' and you said, 'No, I want to kiss you on the lips.'? A No, I did not. Q. Do you remember her saying, 'That's not right. You don't kiss me on the lips.' Do you remember that happening? A. It never happened.[209] [There is no indication where this allegation came from, but the defense does not object.]

The DA mentions that Mrs. Morse did not believe the girls' story in 1991, and, knowing that Violet will not testify, proceeds to review the issue of the abuse of the children:

---

207   Hutchins Trial, Vol. IV, 106:17-21.

208   Hutchins Trial, Vol. IV, 104.

209   Hutchins Trial, Vol. IV, 106:22-107:10.

"Q. Did you ever see Violet throw water, hot, boiling water on Mamie's back? A. No. Q. Were you aware of that ten-inch scar that Dr. Nolan talked about? [The scar was not ten inches, but ten centimeters—about four inches.][210] That scar, do you remember her talking about that scar on Mamie's back? A. Yeah, I do. Could I finish answering the question? Q. Are you going to tell the jury where that scar came from now? A. I can't say whether Violet put it there or not because her and Mamie and Lacy had a fight and a scar come in on her back. And then Lacy used to get extension cords and whip those kids because she said she is going to whip those kids like her grandmother used to whip her."[211]

Finally, the DA gets around to questioning Earnest about the alleged offense for which he is actually being tried:

The DA "re-describes" the 1997 offense:

"Q. (By Ms. Konchek) When Mamie testified that you came into the den and that you pulled down her pants and you pulled down her pants and you got on top of her and [sexual assault] was she telling the truth or was she lying? A. She is lying."[212] [Mamie said nothing about who was on top in 1997, and did not remember about 1991; at first she did not feel Earnest's [male organ] in 1997, then she did. The testimony was much more convoluted than the DA makes it here. It was Carly who claimed that Mamie was on top, then Earnest was on top in 1991.]

Ms. Konchek asks Hutchins about the evidence of possible penetration to which Dr. Nolan had testified. He says he can't comment one way or another on what she found. If there was something there, Mamie's boyfriend should be questioned:

---

[210] Hutchins Trial, Vol. III, 34:13.
[211] Hutchins Trial, Vol. IV, 108:23-109:20.
[212] Hutchins Trial, Vol. IV, 112:4-10.

"A. I really don't know. Maybe you should take that up with Mamie. She had a boyfriend. Q. So Mamie had boyfriends she was having sex with. Is that what you are saying? A. I didn't say she was having sex. She had a boyfriend."

In his re-direct, Mr. Daly asks Earnest a bit more about Mamie's boyfriend. He is much larger than her and about a year older. He had seen the boy a number of times

Ms. Konchek begins her re-cross by asking Hutchins why he brought up the boyfriend. He replies:

"Q. Why did you bring it up? Why did you bring this twelve-year-old boy up that was giving her money? A. Well, like I say, when I took them out to my mother's, she wouldn't stop until she got to his house."[213]

The defense attorney begins his re-direct with the question:

"Q. You don't have any way of knowing whether Paul Mosely is or is not having sex with Mamie, do you? A. I don't have no reason—I don't know, but I know one thing that I saw while on 17th Ave. that I didn't like and I mentioned it to Violet and Violet got on Lacy about it and she [Violet] whipped Mamie about it."[214] [The incident involved Paul lying in the bedroom, with nothing but some shorts on and Mamie being there rubbing his chest.]

The trial adjourns for the noon break.

It is perhaps worth repeating that the preponderance of the cross-exam questions by the DA focused on the 1991 incident, which had been dismissed as "unfounded," rather than on the alleged 1997 offense for which Earnest Hutchins was being tried.

After an hour and fifteen minutes for lunch, the jury returns and Mr. Daly calls the neighbor and friend of Mrs. Morse, Polly Boone,

---

[213] Hutchins Trial, Vol. IV, 120:7-12.
[214] Hutchins Trial, Vol. IV, 120:25-121:4.

to the stand. She says Violet is her godmother. She was frequently in Violet's home. She would read her mail for her, because Mrs. Morse cannot read. She did not have a problem with any of the children, including Lacy. They trusted her and never told her anything about being molested by Hutchins. She never saw Violet abuse the children:

> "Q. Did you ever see Violet Morse abuse her children? A. No, I haven't. Q. Do you know if Lacy ever abused her sisters? A. I was told that. I didn't see it, but I was told that. Q. Who told you that? A. Their grandmother."[215]

Ms. Boone insists she never told the children to stay away from Earnest and—if anyone claimed that—it would be a lie.

In her cross-exam, the DA has Ms. Boone agree that she is close to both Mrs. Morse and Mr. Hutchins. Ms. Konchek begins to question about the conversation between Ms. Boone and Lacy by asking:

> "Q. Would you be surprised if Violet had asked Lacy if you had put her up to saying things about Earnest? Would you be surprised about that? A. I would be shocked."[216]

> "Q. Did you ever tell Lacy that she was going to be sadly surprised that the tests had come back that someone she loved very much, Paul, was the one who had molested these girls? A. I might have told her that. They used to be in the bed with them all the time. Q. What medical tests were you talking about? Is that something I don't know about? A. We had got a phone call saying that—he had called from the jail and said they gave him a blood test or whatever. They was testing him all kinds of ways. Q. You mean Earnest did? A. Yeah, that's what I was talking about. Q. But you don't know of any tests that say Paul Mosely did this, do you? A. No. I was telling her that. I just told her that. Q. You told Lacy that, right? A. Yeah, I did. I know it can't be him. That would be my suspect."[217] [The meaning of this testimony

---

215 Hutchins Trial, Vol. IV, 126:9-17.
216 Hutchins Trial, Vol. IV, 130:15-19.
217 Hutchins Trial, Vol. IV, 131:9-132:5.

remains unclear. Who was "him", Paul or Earnest? Who is her suspect, Paul? Neither the DA nor Mr. Daly attempt to clarify this important point.]

In his redirect, Mr. Daly is allowed to ask the witness if she had ever heard that Lacy had made all of this up in order to get rid of Earnest. She says that she had heard "they were mad" at Earnest because he did not want all their stuff in the yard and Mrs. Morse made them move out.

> "They got mad when grandma put them out of the house. She said— Lacy made the comment, said, 'Grandma, we was after Pops. We wasn't after you'."[218] Daly passes the witness.

There are no further questions from the State and the defense calls Paul Mosely back to the stand: He testifies that he worked at Sears for about eight months, sometime in 1995 or 1996, when he was about twenty years old. He was accused of rape by one of the employees and went down to the police department. The DA objects that Daly is leading the witness [he is questioning Mosely in exactly the way the DAs questioned the children, without objection] and the Judge instructs the attorney to question in a different way.

Mosely said he took a lie detector test and passed it. He also concedes he had sex with that employee, but it was consensual. He was arrested for having a handgun and was on probation for a year, but that was completed. He adds:

> "A. When they put me on probation for that, but I also had like a marijuana case, too, and evading arrest at the time I got the pistol case. They ran everything together and they made me go to the drug classes and everything and put me on one-year probation, but I got off. I didn't get revoked not once."[219]

---

218   Hutchins Trial, Vol. IV, 134:20-23.
219   Hutchins Trial, Vol. IV, 138:10-16.

In her recross, Ms. Konchek has Paul establish that the girl at Sears was twenty and she just made a complaint against him when she found out he would not be with her anymore. The gun just happened to be in the glove compartment of the car, and there was a very small amount of marijuana, for personal use.

He never slept in the room with the little girls, at either house. He loved them like little sisters, and had never touched them "in an inappropriate sexual way."

Under redirect, Mosely says he felt like the girls trusted him, but did not think they would have told him about being molested by Earnest. They might have told Lacy, but were "kind of shy kids" and would not have told him.

Mosely's testimony about living with Lacy at the 5th Street and 17th Ave. homes becomes somewhat self-contradictory but he agrees:

> "Q. Well, this was the first time [1995 on 5th Street] you were actually going to be living with Lacy, so to speak, as husband and wife, correct? A. Right. Q. You were going to be setting up house together, you were sleeping together over there? A. We slept for five days, just a week, it was temporary."[220]
>
> "Q. Do you remember when Lacy's birthday is? A. Yeah, January 31st. Q. How old would she have been in '95? A. '95, that would make her about—it's '98 now. She would have been fifteen or sixteen. Q. How old would you have been? A. I was about eighteen. Q. So it is undisputed that when you were eighteen or nineteen, you were living with this fifteen or sixteen-year-old girl and having sex with her? A. I was eighteen. I was in love with her. We fell in love. That's the way it happened [Is that a "Yes" or "No?"]."[221] The witness is passed by both attorneys.

Mr. Daly calls Amy Laverty to testify. She is sixteen years old and the niece of Mr. Hutchins. She lived close to the 5th Street home and knew the children well. (In 1991 she would have been about ten years

---

[220] Hutchins Trial, Vol. IV, 150:19-151:1.
[221] Hutchins Trial, Vol. IV, 151:7-19.

old). She would go over to their house almost every day after school. She believed they trusted her and would have told her anything. They never said a word about Earnest molesting or mistreating them in any way. She and Mamie talked about personal things, like her boyfriend. She saw them kissing once. Mamie was living on 5th Street and it was prior to 1995. This was the boyfriend she knew about when the family moved to 17th Ave. Amy said Mamie would have told her if Earnest was "mistreating her in some way."[222]

The defense passes the witness and Assistant DA, Shawn Elliott begins his cross-exam: He asks Amy whether Mamie was a slut and if she said anything about having sex with anyone. Amy denies both.[223] There are no more questions and the witness steps down.

The next witness is Georgia Hutchins, the mother of Earnest. She knows Violet and the children. She used to keep them, both at their home and hers. This happened on a regular basis and she had a good relationship with the children. They never complained about the way Earnest treated them. Lacy never mentioned anything about him trying to kiss her. The children never said anything about her son touching them in a way they didn't like. Mr. Daly has no more questions and the State does not cross-examine.[224]

The wife of Claude Lyons, Rita Lyons, is called as a witness by Mr. Daly. [In reality, Rita uses a different last name from Mr. Lyons, but to limit the confusion we will stick with "Lyons".] She met her husband while the mother of the children, Connie Morse, was still alive.

> "Q. So you met Claude Lyons while Connie Morse was still alive? A. Yeah. Q. And you began going out with Claude Lyons while Connie Morse was still alive? A. Yes, I did. Q. Were you going out with Claude when Carolyn Morse overdosed on drugs? A. No, sir, I was back with my husband and Claude was gone with another lady. Him and the other lady was staying in an apartment and Connie was staying

---

[222] Hutchins Trial, Vol. IV, 157:24-25.
[223] Hutchins Trial, Vol. IV, 158:11-14.
[224] Hutchins Trial, Vol. IV, 160-161.

back with her mom. Q. So when she committed suicide, Claude was with yet another woman at that time? A. Yes, he was. He was not with me."[225]

Whether or not the death of Connie Morse was a suicide was disputed by the DA. Mrs. Lyons said she did not know whether Connie was affected by her affair with Mr. Lyons. She and Lyons broke up, then got back together in 1990. She had been arrested one time for having a gun in her purse. Her son had been killed in 1991 and the gang had threatened to kill her.[226]

Ms. Konchek conducts the cross-exam: Mrs. Lyons and Claude have never had any money problems, because since 1982 she had been receiving oil money and they lease out land. The $800 social security she gets for the children only helped her to get a bigger house for them to live in. She also gets about $2,000 a month from her work at the health department.

According to Rita, CPS did a thorough investigation before placing the girls with her.

> "A. Well, they talked to the girls and what the caseworker told me, the girls said 'Please whatever happens, let us stay with Rita.' Now, I wasn't there. Q. Did CPS do an investigation? A. Yes, ma'am. Q. After their investigation, did they choose you to be the foster mother? A. Yes, ma'am." [227]

In the re-direct, Mr. Daly asks Mrs. Lyons about the way money was handled. She and Claude did not have a checking account, only a savings account. She told him to use money orders but he never did so (with regard to the $600 a month he claimed to give to Violet). After getting the children, they did not move to the bigger house for about six months—when they were "kicked out" of the place where they were

[225]   Hutchins Trial, Vol. IV, 163:6-20.
[226]   Hutchins Trial, Vol. IV, 166:12-22.
[227]   Hutchins Trial, Vol. IV, 170:9-17.

living because the landlord did not want so many children there. She had waited to move, so she could pay for it with her income tax refund.

In the re-cross, Mrs. Lyons tells Ms. Konchek that she and Claude did not devise a story so they could get the $800 in social security money [It is the contention of Earnest Hutchins that $800 was the amount for one child. The total amount could have been as much as $2,400.]

At this point both the defense and the State rest, and a discussion is held as to whether the jury will begin deliberations that afternoon.[228]

The DA (in this instance Mr. Elliott) addresses the jury:

> "I hope that that will help you reach a swift and sure verdict in this case. That's your job. That's the oath that you took to reach a verdict, to decide whether or not the State proved the elements of these crimes beyond a reasonable doubt."[229] He then reminds them of the evidence they have seen and heard:
>
> Mamie says she was [sexually assaulted] by Mr. Hutchins. Her sister, Carly, said she saw him do this to her. A psychologist testified that what the girls said was consistent with the experience of abused children. A medical doctor testified that Mamie's hymen was indeed damaged, showing that she was penetrated by someone who used force. The argument from the defense about a huge conspiracy to get $800 in social security money or they were scheming against a man who had kicked them out of the house has no credibility.

The DA attacks the notion that someone else might have violated the girl:

> "They brought you everybody and the kitchen sink. They mentioned her twelve-year-old boyfriend, Paul Mosely, anybody else that they could think of."[230] [In 1991, Paul

---

[228] Hutchins Trial, Vol. IV, 175.
[229] Hutchins Trial, Vol. IV, 191:11-16.
[230] Hutchins Trial, Vol. IV, 194.20-25.

> Mosely was sixteen, and in 1997 he was twenty-two; he
> was not the boyfriend of Mamie, but of Lacy. In a closing
> argument, an attorney's words are not subject to challenge.]

Elliott acknowledges the problem of the delayed outcry. Mamie did not tell anyone, until she told her father in 1997. But the two doctors and the detective testified this is to be expected in most cases. He brings up the 1991 incident and how nothing was done, which would make Mamie more reticent to speak out.

He doesn't know what to "do" about Violet Morse [whom the jury never saw or heard]:

> "You may be outraged at what you heard about her and
> her behavior, and that's okay."[231] "Violet Morse never did
> anything except beat those girls and yell at them and tell
> them they were liars (IV, 196: 7-9)."
>
> "What kind of affect [sic] do you think that had on
> Mamie in making her want to tell somebody about this? The
> important—Violet has charges against her. She will get hers.
> Don't worry about that. That will be for twelve other people
> to decide."[232] [Actually, after the trial was out of the way,
> all charges against Mrs. Morse were dropped. The purpose
> of the charges had been fulfilled. She was frightened out of
> testifying.]

Mr. Elliott comments that "reasonable doubt" means reason and common sense. It has nothing to do with Mr. Lyons sleeping with different women. There were inconsistencies between the stories of Mamie and the others, but if they all told exactly the thing, would that not have evidenced a conspiracy? The conspiracy theory is "half baked." No one has a motive for it. The DA reasons:

> "Claude Lyons has no motive. Their only motive is to see
> that that man stays away from those girls because of what he

---

[231]   Hutchins Trial, Vol. IV, 195:25-196:2.

[232]   Hutchins Trial, Vol. IV, 196:10-15.

was doing. Because of what he was doing, you should convict him of aggravated sexual assault of a child."[233]

It is Mr. Daly's turn for a closing argument: He tells the jury he cannot prove that Mr. Hutchins is innocent. He cannot prove a negative. He cannot prove that he is not guilty. He does not know the complete story of what happened in this case. To know that, Claude Lyons, Lacy and all the other people would have to tell the truth, and that was just not going to happen.

> "I think that you have seen their testimony over the past few days. You see there have been several inconsistencies in their testimony, that they lied about several things."[234] [The State has already admitted this; why does he not **specify** the inconsistencies/lies at this point, to demonstrate their importance and refute the State's "explanation?"]

The next part of his closing statement border on the bizarre, at least for a defense:

> "There was the evidence that Dr. Nolan presented. It was very compelling evidence." [Was it all that "compelling"?] "I want to apologize to you. I maybe asked a question I shouldn't have asked. I kind of made a stupid question about a cucumber." [If it was stupid, why remind the jury now?] "That was really kind of a stupid thing for me to do, but I am not perfect. Mr. Hutchins would probably want Johnnie Cochran to come in here and defend him, but he got stuck with me and I did the best I could. I do want to apologize to you for that because there was really no reason for doing that."[235]

They were told by the detective that Mr. Hutchins was the only suspect. No one else was investigated. There was Paul Mosely, who was

---

[233] Hutchins Trial, Vol. IV, 198:18-22.
[234] Hutchins Trial, Vol. IV, 200:6-9.
[235] Hutchins Trial, Vol. IV, 200:11-23.

sleeping with an underage girl. There was Claude Lyons, who had been an armed robber, who would do anything for money, who made an incredible claim to have given Mrs. Morse $600 a month for support of the children, he claimed he got an automatic raise—which his employer denied. He insists that the jury cannot convict Hutchins on the basis of what the State has presented.

The detective said he could not find anything about Paul Mosely on his computer, but Mosely later testified that he had been accused of raping a girl Sears employee. He explains why Mosely and Lyons could have been regarded as suspects:

> "He [Mosely] was living in the house at the time these incidents occurred, sleeping with an under-age girl. Does that sound like a suspect that you think should be worth an investigation? Do you think it is somebody who might have had something to do with it? When he took the stand, did you believe his testimony? And what about Claude Lyons? He is another potential person that I think should be investigated. Look at the relationships that he had with—I don't know if it's his wife, or who that person was. I guess he had some relationship with her over a period of time, but it has been a pretty sordid relationship. Is that the kind of person that you would want raising your kids?"[236]

The children testified in the case and Mr. Daly believes something did happen to them. But he also knows it is possible to manipulate and pressure children. Dr. Nolan testified that it is best to talk to children apart from their parents, but the foster mother, Rita Lyons, was right there through the entire trial.

> "Do you think these children would have told the truth in front of Rita Lyons, so they could come back to Earnest (sic) Lyons, the armed robber? [Mr. Daly has a worthwhile point here, but compromises it by using the first name of the man he is defending, instead of Claude Lyons.] Do you think he

---

[236] Hutchins Trial, Vol. IV, 205:11-206:1.

is a really good father? Why was she taking notes? What do you think she was doing? Hey, you had better stick to the story that we told because I am writing down everything that you say."[237]

Daly rehearses the unlikelihood of the State's story:

"I think if you look at the circumstances under which this crime occurred [which implies that a crime was committed], that they are absurd. Every transaction that was mentioned by the children on the stand took place in a room in which there were two other children sleeping on the bed, a queen-sized bed with two other children sleeping there. Not only that but the incidents that are the subject of this prosecution, the June 1997 incidents or whatever recent transactions occurred before then [again this wording seems to assume that such incidents did occur], all happened when Violet Morse was in the house, Lacy was in the house and her boyfriend, Paul, was in the house. Do you find it credible that Earnest Lyons (sic) [once more Mr. Daly sabotages his argument by confusing names, using the last name of the accuser, instead of the defendant, his own client!] would get up in the middle of the night when Lacy is over there sleeping with Paul Mosely and sneak into these girls' room and how he thought to molest one girl without waking the others up? If one would have made a cry out, Paul would have been in there in a heartbeat to protect them if they did that."[238] [Mr. Daly previously argued that Mosely should have been investigated as a possible perpetrator, but now he is suddenly the defender of the girls. How receptive would the jury be to this type of logic?]

Daly proposes that the State's explanation of why the children did not cry out (e.g., fear of Mr. Hutchins), was not convincing, since they had many options. There were many people whom they trusted

---

[237]   Hutchins Trial, Vol. IV, 207:2-9.
[238]   Hutchins Trial, Vol. IV, 208:2-22.

to whom they could have made an outcry at any time. He thinks the children want to see Mr. Hutchins go to prison, because they want him out of the house.

In 1991, Lacy tried this, but failed. She knew she had to come up with a better scheme, which she was able to manufacture in 1997.

> "In 1997 when it became clear that Earnest and the grandmother were going to live together, that he was going to be a fact of life, she was never going to be able to take over that house the way she wanted. She and Paul were not going to be able to live there without working, living off of her grandmother the way she wanted to. When that became clear, she decided that she had to get rid of Earnest and she knew just how to do it."[239]

With regard to the character of a molester, they normally do not want the police around, but Hutchins was constantly calling the police to come over to take care of a large variety of problems. They had the pastor come to the house. He [Earnest] called the police after Claude Lyons said, 'I am going to get you. You are the one who has been abusing and molesting my children.'"[240]

As for 1991, they can only consider that as to the defendant's "state of mind," and must believe beyond a reasonable doubt that the incident occurred. This was highly improbable. All kinds of people were around, Mrs. Morse was gone for only short time, the neighbor was just driving up.

> "If a child molester is going to do something, he's going to pick a time in which he is going to be pretty sure that he's not going to get caught. That wasn't the case here."[241] [This line of argumentation would have been much more persuasive if Earnest Hutchins had had the luxury of an **expert witness**, rather than having these remarks come only from his defense

---

239   Hutchins Trial, Vol. IV, 211:4-13.
240   Hutchins Trial, Vol. IV, 212:10-13.
241   Hutchins Trial, Vol. IV, 214:2-5.

attorney at the end of the trial. Unfortunately, in our system indigent defendants rarely are accorded expert witnesses.]

Mamie had said that she saw [a liquid] in 1991, which everyone agreed meant semen. While they collected clothing in 1991, they did not bother to examine it, but when the detective had them analyzed in 1997, the only semen found was on a sheet used by the couple. Nothing was found on the child's clothing.

> "There is physical evidence right there that contradicts the children's story. They said that they wiped up semen with a rag. There's no semen on the rag, no semen on her underpants. No semen on her clothes."[242]

The attorney professes:

> "As I said, I can't prove to you that Earnest Hutchins didn't do it. I don't have to prove to you that he didn't do it. That's why the burden is on the State. [Why not **begin** by saying: Ladies and Gentlemen of the jury, it is the burden of the State to prove beyond all reasonable doubt that the defendant is guilty, then follow with:] But I can say to you without hesitation that he is not guilty beyond a reasonable doubt. Thank you, ladies and gentlemen."[243]

The Judge gives Ms. Konchek fifteen minutes to complete the State's closing arguments. She begins by telling Mr. and Mrs. Lyons how bad she feels about being "up here", with all of them "barking" at them for the last forty-five minutes. To the jury she says, somewhat ingratiatingly:

> "I think that the twelve of you, we picked you because we thought you could use your reason and common sense and see through all this muck and all of this trash that has been

---

[242] Hutchins Trial, Vol. IV, 215:12-17.
[243] Hutchins Trial, Vol. IV, 216:8-14.

thrown into this case and focus on the elements of this case. That's what we are here for."[244]

They should not be concerned about when Lacy started sleeping with Paul [although a teenager engaging in statutory rape with a young girl, using drugs, being accused of rape by another girl, etc.—if one uses reason and common sense—might create just a small suspicion of the possibility he could have molested the girls—if they were molested at all—or at least impinge a bit on the credibility of his testimony.]

The jury is here to focus on the little girls. She agrees with Mr. Daly that this is a "hard case."

> "Because no matter how many times you read these types of offense reports, police reports and talk to these little kids, it is so hard to sit here and listen to little girls talk about their innocence being taken away by a sixty-eight-year-old man who snuck in their room at night and took away their childhood.[245] [In fact, in 1991 Earnest Hutchins was fifty-four and in 1997 he was sixty, not sixty-eight. The mistake once again demonstrates the State's indifference to accuracy with regard to factual information, or perhaps the DA wished to make the offense appear more disgusting by exaggerating the age.]

She ridicules the "conspiracy" theory that from the time they were five/four years old until Mamie was eleven, these girls were plotting to get Pops out of the house. [The defense had argued that the plot was on the part of the adults, who were quite capable of controlling the little girls, and especially Lacy, who was eighteen in 1997, and about to be ejected from the house on 17th Ave.]

She insists that the detectives conducted a good investigation. There was no manpower to look into anyone but Mr. Hutchins. The presence of Rita Lyons in the courtroom was fully justified. The girls had only met Ms. Konchek a week and a half ago. Mrs. Lyons was taking notes

---

[244]   Hutchins Trial, Vol. IV, 217:1-5.
[245]   Hutchins Trial, Vol. IV, 217:1-5.

so she could keep herself from breaking into a rage about all the terrible things she was hearing [although supposedly she had known about them since at least June, over seven months earlier.]

She has no regrets about sending Pops to prison, for all the things he had put these little girls through for the past six years [although the 1991 accusation was "unfounded" and there had been no complaints by any of the girls until 1997.]

Mamie's story about 1997 was fully credible:

> "If she was in here concocting a story, she would have said yeah, then he touched me on my [], then he touched me here and then he touched me there and then he jumped over and got Lettie, then he jumped over and got Carly. She said no, I didn't see his []. It was dark. If she was trying to make up some story to lie about this guy, she would have gone all out."[246] [According to Claude Lyons, Mamie told him: "Pops, which is Earnest Hutchins, came into her room and woke her up and [very graphic description of the act][247] So, according to Lyons, Mamie clearly saw the ["nasty thing"]. When questioned about the 1991 incident, Mamie had testified that she did see Pops' [], and it had white stuff on it [for which no evidence was ever found]."[248]

[It could equally be argued that if the accusations were being designed and refined with the help of the State or the adults, they would have been presented just as found in the trial testimony, with inconsistencies caused by the inability of the "victims" and witnesses to keep their stories straight.]

Ms. Konchek recalls how Mamie testified how much it hurt to be [] by this sixty-eight year-old man [error repeated as to age]:

> "The most telling thing that she said was she said it hurts. Children talk about from their senses and that hurt having a

---

[246] Hutchins Trial, Vol. IV, 220:9-17.
[247] Hutchins Trial, Vol. II, 41:10-14.
[248] Hutchins Trial, Vol. IV, 107:21-24.

sixty-eight-year-old man's [] in her tiny little [] she probably
didn't even know that she had at time [this awkward wording
is just as it appears in the transcript]."[249]

Actually, Mamie could not make up her mind whether what Earnest
allegedly did hurt or did not hurt. Recall the testimony:

"Q. How did it feel when he had his [] with your []? A. Nasty.
Q. Did it feel good or did it hurt? [Leading question, since
the first response was not good enough; no objection from
the defense.] A. Hurt. Q. Did you feel if it was inside of your
[] or outside of your []? A. I don't remember. [Unsatisfactory
answer to another leading question.] Q. Do you remember if
it hurt or it didn't hurt? [The State tries again]. A. It didn't
hurt. [Really bad answer]. Q. It did hurt or didn't hurt? A.
It did [Mamie finally gets it right]."[250]

The DA points out how Carly supported everything in Mamie's
story:

"Usually we don't have an eyewitness. We had Carly. She
corroborated everything Mamie said, at 17th Ave., on a
mattress, in dining room, living room area." [Again the DA
misstates that the alleged offense took place in the dining
room, not the den—then expands her statement to the
"living room area."]

Carly (eleven at the time of the trial) did not speak out in 1991,
but now remembers that when she was four, in the middle of the day,
when Mrs. Morse was gone for a few minutes, she walked into her
Granny's room and saw Mamie on top of Pops, but she could see his []
anyway.[251] . After six years she has a clear recollection that the bedroom
door was closed and the front door was locked. Carly says her Granny

---

[249] Hutchins Trial, Vol. IV, 220:18-23.
[250] Hutchins Trial, Vol. IV, 101:3-15.
[251] Hutchins Trial, Vol. III, 146:19 and 149:1-2.

was gone at the time, but does not remember where she was. A few seconds later she says Lacy was not there, because she had gone to the store with Granny.

Carly did testify that on 17th Ave. when Pops came into the den she pretended to be asleep, but peeked out and saw the molestation. The DA emphasizes this. However, neither she nor the defense ever recall that under cross-exam Carly testified:

> "Q. When Pops came into your room, did you ever yell at Pops to get out? A. Yes. Q. What happened when you yelled at him to get out? A. He would run down the hall. Q. He would run down the hall? A. (Nodded head up and down). Q. So he would leave when you yelled? A. (Nodded head up and down). Q. Was there any time that you didn't yell out when he came into the room? A. I always yelled."[252] [One wonders how she could pretend to be asleep, not interfere with what Pops was doing to her sister, but "always" yell and have him run down the hall at the same time! Yet, this conundrum does not seem to perplex anyone.]

Although Mrs. Morse was intimidated from testifying because of her fear of prosecution as a child abuser, this did not prevent Ms. Konchek from stating:

> "You heard what Violet said. You heard what Violet told Detective Grudge…. Even Violet said, 'Yes, it's possible. He's a man.' That is the kind of woman that they were trying to outcry and tell about this abuse. That is the kind of woman she is. Yes, it's possible. He is a man."[253] [In fact the jury has no idea what kind of woman Mrs. Morse is; they have never seen her; they do not know why she was unable to testify; **they do not know if she ever said these words or not**, because she could not be asked; all they have is what the detective claimed she said. They do not know the context: she did not believe the allegations against Hutchins were true,

---

[252] Hutchins Trial, Vol. III, 166:5-17.
[253] Hutchins Trial, Vol. IV, 221:17-22.

but when compelled to say something she acknowledged, as anyone would have to do, that anything is possible.]

The DA claims that the child told her grandmother what was going on, and was called a liar:

> "Mamie, which [sic] is five, six, seven, eight years old, every time she tells her grandma what is going on, she calls her a liar, what is she supposed to do."[254] [**One might counter that it is Ms. Konchek who is the deceitful one.** In testimony it was reported by others that Mrs. Morse said Lacy, not Mamie, was a liar; further testimony was that the children did not tell anyone anything about the molestation until 1997. The State even spent a lot of effort trying to explain why there was no outcry to anyone.]

The DA recalls that "they" [it was only Mamie] "tend to tell someone they trust outside. Who she told was Earnest Lyons (sic)."[255] [Once more, the attorney is unable to correctly name Claude Lyons, using the first name of the defendant.] Ms. Konchek reviews what Mr. Lyons says he was told by Mamie: "…this is what Earnest does to me, he puts his [graphic sexual details repeated to re-enforce them in the jury's consciousness] in my []. He puts his—same story, exactly same story exactly as she told you on the witness stand—puts his finger—he licks his finger, puts it []. Why do you think he does that? A kid wouldn't know to say that he does that to make it easier to [] little girl's []. That's why he does that."[256] [We might ask why a little child would mention this detail at all, unless prompted to do so by an adult who knew the significance of the act.]

The testimony of Dr. Nolan is emphasized:

> "She said that there was a break, a split. Those were her exact words, 'a split in the hymen that was **consistent** [emphasis

---

254   Hutchins Trial, Vol. IV, 222:3-6.

255   Hutchins Trial, Vol. IV, 222:13-15.

256   Hutchins Trial, Vol. IV, 222:22-223:5.

added] with vaginal penetration.' You don't get it from childhood injuries (IV, 223:18-23)." [The doctor had said there was a "cleft", a tear that had healed. Yet the claim was that Mr. Hutchins had been molesting this girl for at least six years on a regular basis, and as recently as a month before the examination by Dr. Nolan. Would not "reason and common sense" suggest that if this were true there ought to be more than a healed cleft not necessarily caused by penetration, but merely "consistent" with it? Why did the State present as an exhibit only a drawing by the witness, who could be expected to say what the State had hired her for? In child abuse cases, especially one as egregious as this, should not pictures be taken of the damage? Even if there was injury to the hymen, there are possible alternative explanations. Until she was almost five years old, Mamie's mother was a drug addict and likely prostitute. Who knows who may have entered the home and molested the girl when Mrs. Morse was away at work? Who else in this very dysfunctional family setting could conceivably have done it? Is there "reasonable doubt", i.e., probable certitude, leading to the inevitable conclusion that it might not have been Mr. Hutchins? Why were these questions not asked more assertively by the defense?]

The DA is grateful for the improved circumstances of Mamie:

"Thank God that little girl is now living with her real dad. She is coming out of it. She is starting to sing in the church choir. She is starting to be a little bit better."[257] [The truth is the "real dad" had no interest in keeping the girls at all. Not long after the trial was over and Earnest was out of the way, they returned to live with the supposedly horrible grandmother and the eventual outcome was that the girls became very troubled.]

The DA tells the jury that she cannot sleep at night when she awakes and thinks of the terrible things that have happened in this case.

---

[257] Hutchins Trial, Vol. IV, 224:18-22.

She gets to thinking about the meaning of Earnest Hutchins' actual nickname, "Cootie":

> "I couldn't stop thinking about that name. Do you know what the irony of that name is? It means a human louse, a body louse. You go a little bit further, do you know what that means? A louse means? A louse is a parasite that habitually exploits others and contributes nothing. He has lived up to his name. That's exactly what he has done with Violet Morse. He has lived off of her, hasn't worked, stayed drunk all the time. And he has really, really done that to Mamie. He has sucked the life out of a little girl. He has sucked the childhood that she deserves and that we all deserve."[258] [The State is favored by a format in which they are allowed to make two closing statements; Mr. Elliott goes first, to preempt the defense's closing arguments; then Ms. Konchek is able to indulge in this kind of unproven character assassination, with no fear of a rebuttal by the defense. The nickname can have the meaning given to it by the DA, but an almost identical word can mean "an aquatic bird". In any case, it is clear from many uses of the word by the family, it appeared to be more of a term of affection for an elderly man—used in that way before all the turmoil started.]

The DA concludes and the jury is sent to the jury room to begin deliberations. It is about 4:15 p.m. The jury sent out a question to the Court and the Judge decided that the subject area was too broad.

> "I have given them the standard instruction that says specify the witness and the dispute you have and then we will have the Court reporter search it."[259]

Both sides find this instruction acceptable and it is sent to the jury, rather than having them come out to receive it. The jury submits a more specific question and they are brought back in. It is now 5:20 p.m., so

---

258   Hutchins Trial, Vol. IV, 225:13-226:1.
259   Hutchins Trial, Vol. IV, 227:3-6.

they have been deliberating for about an hour (probably reduced by at least fifteen minutes for addressing their question, researching it, etc.).

The question did not bear on innocence or guilt, but on the exact nature of part of the offense:

"The statement in dispute is what did Mamie testify that Earnest [] penetrated her []. None of us remember specific testimony on [] by his finger."[260] [What difference does this make, since there was clear testimony of [] by the []? The question seems to go to heaping one charge upon another, since the indictment covered several charges. The jury is sent back to its deliberations and the Judge reminds them that, while they do not have to finish that evening, the Court will adjourn by 6 p.m.

The jury quickly reached its verdict and returned to the courtroom at 5:50 p.m.:

> "Count I, aggravated sexual assault of a child, []. We, the jury, find the defendant, Earnest Hutchins, guilty of the offense of aggravated sexual assault of a child as alleged in Count I of the indictment….Count II, aggravated sexual assault of a child, []. We, the jury, find the defendant, Earnest Hutchins, not guilty of the offense aggravated sexual assault of a child as alleged in Count II of the indictment….(So, he put his [] in, but not his finger.] Count III, indecency with a child by contact, genitals. We, the jury, find the defendant, Earnest Hutchins, guilty of the offense of indecency with a child by contact as alleged in Count III of the indictment…. Verdict of the jury. Count IV, indecency with a child by contact, breasts. We the jury find the defendant, Earnest Hutchins, not guilty of the offense of indecency with a child by contact as alleged in Count IV of the indictment….[there had been some testimony about "titties", but apparently not enough to satisfy the jury]….Count V, indecency with a child by exposure. We, the jury, find the defendant, Earnest Hutchins, guilty of the offense of indecency with a child by

---

[260] Hutchins Trial, Vol. IV, 229:14-18.

exposure as alleged in Count V of the indictment."[261] [Thus, within the space of less than one hour and thirty minutes, on this "hard case", with its abundance of conflicting testimony and details, the jury is able to conform to the DA's wishes, cut through the "muck", assess all five charges and find the defendant guilty on the three that really matter.]

Both the State and defense waive a poll of the jury. Mr. Hutchins, not wishing to assign his fate to the decision of the Judge, elected to have the punishment determined by the jury. The Judge instructs the jury to return at 9:00 a.m. the following morning to complete this task. After the jury left, Mr. Daly told the Judge that Mr. Hutchins had changed his mind and wanted him to decide the punishment. Ms. Konchek would not agree to this, Mr. Daly said he thought his client would agree to the "enhancement" charge [useful in obtaining the maximum sentence], and procedures were adjourned.

Assessment of Punishment

The punishment phase of the trial is much like what preceded it, with the assistant prosecuting attorney providing distorted and misleading information, and the defense attorney mounting only a feeble attempt to mitigate Earnest Hutchins' punishment.

In order to lay a basis for a Life sentence, molestation of Carly by Earnest is now emphasized. (Because the evidence of this claim was quite weak, Carly was not included as a victim in the first part of the trial.) To add to the argument supporting a Life sentence it is revealed that Earnest had a previous criminal record. This consisted of taking a vehicle without permission when he was twenty-three years old, an offence for which he served less than a year.

A sentence of fifteen years could have been rendered. There was some going back and forth between the jury and the Judge as to the appropriate sentence. The final verdict was Life, with the possibility of

---

[261] Hutchins Trial, Vol. IV, 232:17-233:25.

parole in thirty years, at which time Hutchins would be about 89 years old. (Earnest once conveyed to me that his attorney told him that the jury originally came back with a sentence of fifteen years, but this was rejected by the Judge.)

There was an Appeal after the trial, but it was a farce, with totally inadequate legal representation for Hutchins.

To sum up, in the case of Earnest Hutchins we witness a totally dysfunctional extended family unit. Given all the conflicting testimony and circumstances of the social setting how could an objective rational jury obtain moral certitude of guilt? Even the prosecution acknowledged the many inconsistencies, while explaining them away with the disingenuous proposition that if the accusers had been lying, there would not have been such inconsistency! This comment alone might engender a modicum of "reasonable doubt."

CHAPTER SIX

BEYOND THE FIVE TALES

The stories of Carlos Rojas, Ned Parker, Curtis Hutchins, Charlie Gilmore, Jr. and Earnest Hutchins shed some light on the nature of the court system in Texas, as well as treatment of the incarcerated by TDCJ. Yet, their stories are only the proverbial "tip of the iceberg" with regard to justice system deficiencies not only in TDCJ, but throughout the United States.

In the original version of *The Mysterious Story of Gitano Cervantes* a number of studies, articles and TDCJ episodes were cited documenting some of these deficiencies. They are briefly summarized in what follows:

March 28, 2012, Brian Tolj reported in *The Williamson County Sun* on the particularly egregious case of Michael Morton, a story also covered on *60 Minutes*.[262] He was wrongly found guilty of murdering his wife. Twenty-five years later DNA testing of a bloody bandanna found near the crime scene proved Mr. Morton's innocence and linked another man to the murder. Misconduct has been alleged against the prosecutor.

John Thompson, an African American, was wrongfully convicted of murder and spent fourteen years on death row. He was exonerated when evidence concealed by the prosecution proved that the actual murderer had acted alone.[263]

---

[262] www.cbsnews.com/evidence of innocence, 3/15/2012.

[263] Brian Tolj, *The Williamson County Sun*, April 1, 2012, 1, 9a.

The Northern California Innocence Project has brought out the fact that with ninety-one prosecutorial misconduct cases in Texas from 2004 to 2008, only one prosecutor has been disciplined by the Texas bar. Notwithstanding this record, a Supreme Court decision limits civil liability claims against prosecutorial misconduct. This leaves us with the question, in states such as Texas, how bad does the misconduct have to be before accountability comes into play?[264]

Brandi Grissom, Managing Editor of *The Texas Tribune*, has written frequently on criminal justice matters in Texas. In July of 2012, concerned with accountability, she headed up a team writing a multi-series report: "Errors in Judgment: The Consequences of Prosecutorial Mistakes." An analysis was made of eighty-six overturned convictions in Texas. In almost twenty-five percent of the cases, the prosecution made mistakes that contributed to the wrongful outcome.[265]

In 2003 the Catholic Bishops of Texas issued a statement regarding "Indigent Defense Reform in Texas." They wrote

> "We are gravely concerned about certain Texas trials where defense counsel grossly failed to diligently represent individuals facing the death penalty either because of their incompetence or for not receiving adequate funds to investigate and prepare for trials." The highest criminal court in Texas had ruled that an indigent defendant has a right to a court-appointed attorney, but **does not have a right to be represented competently** (emphasis added).[266]

The bishops noted that in 2001, the 77th Texas Legislature passed the Texas Fair Defense Act to guarantee access to adequate defense, but also expressed a concern that future legislatures might weaken rather than strengthen the Act.

---

[264] http://www.innocenceproject.org/Content/New_Research_Illustrates lack_of_Accountability_for_Prosecutors_in_Texas.php. Austin, TX, March 29, 2012.

[265] Brandi Grissom, "Errors in Judgment: The Consequences of Prosecutorial Mistakes," *The Texas Tribune*, July 5, 2012. http://www.texastribune.org/library/multimedia/ errors-in judgment/.

[266] *Statement by the Catholic Bishops of Texas Regarding Indigent Defense Reform in Texas*, 2003.

The case of Michael Morton is not particularly singular. The *Texas Star-Telegram* of June 20, 2012, carried on its *Opinion* page an article by Bob Ray Sanders detailing how Larry Sims, after serving twenty-four years, died at the age of sixty-two without being exonerated. One year before his twenty-five year sentence was completed, DNA evidence proved that the "victim" had sex with another man the night she claimed she was raped. Sims' cousin even testified that he and the woman smoked crack cocaine and had consensual sex that evening. In October of 2011 Sims' conviction was vacated and his case was dismissed, but he died without being declared innocent.

The experience of Conrad Black illustrates that not only poor minorities but the wealthy and powerful can also be caught up in the throes of the justice system, whether State or Federal.[267] Black, a Canadian, was identified in the interview as a member of the British House of Lords. He was prosecuted in the U.S. in 2005 for allegedly defrauding his company, Hollinger, of $60 million.

In 2007 he was sentenced to seventy-eight months. He appealed his case to the Supreme Court and won a sizable reduction of sentence when its 2010 ruling limited the scope of the "honest services" fraud statute. After serving just thirty-six months, he was released from Federal prison in 2012, and has written numerous articles in addition to a memoir *A Matter of Principle*. He was a victim of injustice in the system, but because he was wealthy he was able to greatly reduce its impact.

When he was released on bail after twenty-nine months, he had to have extensive dental work. He did not go to a prison dentist "because all they did was extract teeth." Extensive testing on the outside revealed that he had a malignant, undiagnosed, melanoma on his face.

> "It was a very small biopsie and it was removed with no danger. But if I had served my full sentence, I would have had a serious problem, and in my opinion, there is no chance that those nincompoops would have recognized it, or if they did, they wouldn't have cared."[268]

---

[267] Paul Wright, "Interview with Conrad Black, Former Federal Prisoner and Millionaire Media Magnate," *Prison Legal News*, September 2012, pp1-14.

[268] Wright, "Interview with Conrad Black...," 5.

> "A friend complained of blood in his stools, and he was repeatedly told, 'oh it's just hemorrhoids,' and he said, 'I don't have hemorrhoids.' And they said, 'of course you do,' and told him to go away. And finally, he was diagnosed with rectal cancer and it was too late."[269]

As for public defenders [who generally are much better than "court-appointed" attorneys], he observes,

> "If it's a murder case, and the accused is not a well-to-do person, he gets into the hands of the public defenders and they're stooges of the prosecutors, and their objective is not to provide a defense but to provide a fig leaf [which brings to mind Mr. Somoza, court-appointed attorney for Carlos Rojas.]"[270]

May 21, 2012, *The Dallas Morning News* reported on a project being carried out by the National Registry of Exonerations that, as of that date, had catalogued 891 cases of miscarriages of justice. Only Illinois and New York had more than Texas' eighty-seven cases.

> "Texas has two of the most spectacular examples of [railroading by lawmen] that in the nation—the Tulia scandal out of the Panhandle, which led to a mass pardon of thirty-five defendants by Gov. Rick Perry, and Dallas' own 'Sheetrock' scandal, in which Dallas narcotics defendants planted fake drugs on immigrants." [271]
>
> Texas leads the nation in its more than forty DNA exonerations. Other problems include bad eyewitness identifications, official misconduct, faulty forensic evidence, false accusation, perjury, and false confessions.

---

269   Wright, "Interview with Conrad Black…," 5.

270   Wright, "Interview with Conrad Black…," 10.

271   "Editorial: Hard truths about injustice," *The Dallas Morning News*, 5/21/2012, http://dallasnews.com/opinion/editorials/. See also "New National Database Reveals Nearly 900 Exonerations," *The Innocence Blog*, (a project of The Innocence Project founded by Barry Scheck and Peter Neufield, 5/21/2012, http://www.innocenceproject.org/Content/New_National_Database_Reveals_Nearly_900_Exonerations.php.

Of course, the justice system deficiencies stretch far beyond Texas or TDCJ. In December, 2012, a Judge in North Carolina ruled that race played a significant role in death sentences imposed on three convicted murderers and changed their sentences to life in prison without parole. Proof was presented that race influenced both the sentencing process and jury selection.[272]

In recent years North Carolina courts found Greg Taylor (seventeen years) and Willie Grimes (twenty-four years) innocent. Taylor and another man, Floyd Brown, were paid $12 million as compensation for "the years they spent incarcerated because of false evidence concocted by the State".[273] Brown had been held for fourteen years without even going to trial. Three men who had served over ten years to avoid the death penalty were also found innocent, as were three men on death row.

According to the *National Coalition to Abolish the Death Penalty*, September 28, 2012, Damon Thibodeaux had just been exonerated and freed after fifteen years on death row in solitary confinement in Louisiana. In 1997 he had confessed to a crime he did not commit, after a nine-hour police interrogation. Extensive DNA testing excluded Thibodeaux as the perpetrator. He had confessed because he thought it might keep him from being executed. He was the 141st person freed from death row in the U.S., and the ninth from Louisiana. Only eighteen of the exonerations were based on DNA technology.[274]

August 22, 2011 the web-site *Digest@DemocracyNow.org* carried the story of the release of three men who had been imprisoned since 1993 for the alleged slaying of three eight-year old boys in West Memphis, Arkansas. The story included an interview conducted by Amy Goodman. The young men released were Damien Echols, Jason

---

[272] Campbell Robertson, "Judge in North Carolina Voids 3 Death Sentences," *The New ork Times*, 12/14/2012, A19.

[273] Julie Lineman, "Justice system, back to business as usual," *The News & Observer*, 8/31/2013, 2A.

[274] Diann Rust-Tierney, "BREAKING: New Exoneration From Death Row! *National Coalition to Abolish the Death Penalty*, 9/28/2012, abe@ncadp.org.

Baldwin and Jessie Misskelley, Jr. Two of them had Life sentences and one was on death row.[275]

They were released because they agreed to take an "Alford Plea" in which they pled guilty in exchange for eighteen-year sentences and time served. Recent DNA evidence supported the claim they were not at the crime scene, while evidence of the presence of others was found. Goodman commented that the "move was a complicated legal proceeding that protects Arkansas from a potential lawsuit, should the men win a new trial, get acquitted, and seek to sue the State for wrongful imprisonment."

The men did not want to risk a new trial because they had no trust in the judicial system. They were ultimately released only because Joe Berlinger, a film maker, and a group of associates, worked for almost two decades to demonstrate their innocence.

Brad Heath, in *USA Today* article of September 26, 2012, tells the story of "former inmates abruptly freed after spending up to six years in Federal prison even though they were 'legally innocent'." They come home "with less help than the government typically provides the guilty after they are released."[276]

The National Coalition Against The Death Penalty, in a news release of September 6, 2012, noted the exoneration of Michael Keenan from Ohio's death row, after twenty-four years of imprisonment. This was the second exoneration within nine months. Keenan was the seventh man freed from Ohio's death row. At the same time, Justin Wolfe is waiting for the state of Virginia to free him, since the Fourth Circuit Court of Appeals declared that his conviction and death sentence were unjustified.[277]

Pamela Colloff, in her *Texas Monthly* article, January, 2011, details the case of the wrongful conviction of Anthony Davis, an African American imprisoned in Texas for eighteen years, twelve of them on death row.[278]

---

275 Amy Goodman, *West Memphis 3*, February 6, 2012, http://www.democracy-now.org.

276 Brad Heath, "For wrongly convicted, only a ticket home," *USA Today*, 9/26/2012, 1A.

277 Diann Rust-Tierney, "BREAKING: Another Man Walking Free from Death Row!" *National Coalition to Abolish the Death Penalty*, 9/6/2012, abe@ncadp.org.

278 Pamela Colloff, "Innocence Found," *The Texas Monthly*, January, 2011. http://www. texasmonthly.com/story/innocence-found.

According to Colloff, Graves was found guilty in spite of the fact that three witnesses placed him with his mother at the time of the crime, there was no physical evidence linking him to the murders, and the entire case was supported only by Carter's testimony.

Later it was discovered that Charles Sebesta, the lead DA, had withheld from the defense the fact that Carter had confessed to committing the crime by himself, resulting in a new trial. Before the new trial could take place all charges were dismissed, based on the determination that the state had found no credible evidence inculpating the defendant.

Because of his exoneration, Graves was entitled to as much as $1.4 million from the State of Texas. However, *The Houston Chronicle* (February 14, 2011) reported that the Comptroller had ruled that he was ineligible for compensation because the words "actual innocence" didn't appear in the document ordering his release.

According to the *Texas Tribune*, May 11, 2011, the State Senate passed a bill that would make Graves eligible for compensation. The *Window on State Government*, June 30, 2011, reported

> "Today Texas Comptroller Susan Combs paid Anthony Graves $1.45 million for the eighteen years in which he was wrongfully imprisoned. The payment was made after the passage and signing of House Bill 417...."[279]

Not only are there numerous cases where the innocent are dispatched to death row, only later to be exonerated, more tragically it is certain that some are executed. One instance of such a miscarriage of justice is found in the case of Todd Willingham. In 1992 he was convicted of burning to death his three children. He was condemned to death and only two years later, in 1994, executed by lethal injection, in spite of numerous

---

[279] Susan Combs, "Texas Comptroller Pleased to Announce $1.45 Million Payment to Anthony Graves," *Window on State Government*, http://www.window.state.tx.us/news2011/110630-graves.html.

concerns suggesting his innocence. A short time later scientific evidence established that the fire was not arson, but indisputably an accident.[280]

Rev. Carol Pickett, who served as the death house Chaplain for fifteen years in the Walls unit, Huntsville, Texas, ministered to ninety-five men as they were being executed at the unit. He has frequently testified that he was personally certain that a number of these men were innocent.[281]

The summer, 2012, *Texas Coalition to Abolish the Death Penalty* newsletter reported that since 1982 the state of Texas has carried out 482 executions, four times as many as the next most frequent state. Since 1973, 140 people, including twelve in Texas, have been exonerated from death rows nationwide. Serious questions have been raised about the executions not only of Todd Willingham, but Claude Jones, Gary Graham, and Ruben Constanza in Texas.

The TCADP article focuses especially on the execution of Carlos DeLuna in 1989. It reports that in *Los Tocayos Carlos: An Anatomy of a Wrongful Execution*, Professor James Liebman and a student team in an eighteen-month investigation catalogue

> "in minute detail all the failures of the system that wrongfully executed DeLuna [a young, poor Hispanic with diminished intelligence.] Everything that could possibly go wrong in a death penalty case did so here, including faulty eyewitness testimony, grossly inadequate legal representation, and prosecutorial misconduct."[282]

DeLuna was executed just six and one-half years after his arrest.

In a letter to its membership dated August 28, 2012, the TCADP declaimed the Texas execution of Marvin Wilson, who had been

---

[280] "Cameron Todd Willingham Wrongfully Convicted and Executed in Texas," *The Innocence Project*, October 2011, http://www.innocenceproject.org/Content/Cameron_Todd_Willingham_Wrongfully_Convicted_and_Executed_in_Texas.php.

[281] "At The Death House Door," a film (dvd) by Steve James and Peter Gilbert, Kartemquin Films, 2009, ISBN 1-56580-849-5.

[282] "Carlos DeLuna was executed nearly 25 years ago ---Why his case still matters," *Texas Coalition to Abolish the Death Penalty*, Summer 2012, 1, 5.

diagnosed with mild mental retardation, a violation of a 2002 U.S. Supreme Court ruling prohibiting this practice.

> "Texas officials took advantage of a loophole in the Court's decision that allowed states to develop their own criteria for determining intellectual disabilities and crafted a set of unscientific guidelines…which rely on gross stereotypes about mental retardation to exclude all but the most severely incapacitated from their constitutional protection against execution."[283]

Alex Knapp, on the staff of *Forbes* Magazine wrote on September 22, 2011, that the previous day the State of Georgia had executed Troy Anthony Davis, after he had been denied a stay of execution by the U.S. Supreme Court.

> "Seven of the witnesses against Mr. Davis have since recanted their testimony. Several have testified that the police applied intense pressure for them to name Mr. Davis as the killer of police Officer Mark MacPhail. There was no forensic evidence linking him to the crime."[284]

There were multiple doubts about the guilt of Davis, and international pleas for forbearance. Still, another man who most likely was innocent, was put to death.

The media is replete with stories of the mistreatment of the incarcerated and other systemic deficiencies not only in states such as Texas, but throughout the country

Texas Department of Criminal Justice failures are vividly exposed in *A Texas Civil Rights Project, Human Rights Support 2011, "A THIN LINE," The Texas Prison Healthcare Crisis and the Secret Death Penalty.* The report argues that if the medical care provided by TDCJ is constitutional, it is only marginally so. "Prisoners are killed and maimed

---

[283] Kristin Houle, Texas Coalition Against the Death Penalty, 4/28/2012.

[284] Alex Knapp, "Anthony Davis and the Truth," *Forbes*, 9/22/2013. http://www.forbes.com/sites/alexknapp/2011/09/22/troy-anthony-davis-and-the-truth/.

in Texas by appalling medical care (p. 1)."[285] In California, the state pays $28.55 per day for health care, yet it has been ordered to release 40,000 prisoners so that the others can receive constitutional care. In Texas, the amount expended for health care per prisoner is $9.99 per prisoner per day.

The "quality" of this care is perhaps best grasped by examining six specific instances of TDCJ maltreatment of offenders. Aged thirty-four, David West was serving a four year sentence in the McConnell unit, Beeville, Texas, for larceny and assault. At 8:40 a.m., May 11, 2003, he was escorted to the shower. An officer left him in a cloud of steam, only to return an hour later and observe him slouched on the shower floor. No one entered the shower to attempt to rouse him. He was left, unconscious, on the floor with hot water pouring over his body. At 10:30 a.m. the Sgt. on duty entered the shower and found that West was not breathing. At 10:45 a.m. he was pronounced dead.

> "An autopsy later revealed Mr. West had been literally cooked alive— the two-hour long exposure to water temperatures in excess of 150 degrees Fahrenheit had devastated his internal organs and caused heart failure

At a Huntsville unit on January 23, 2007, Larry Louis Cox, it is asserted by authorities, refused to leave his cell when the block was being evacuated, and kicked a guard. Another guard and Sgt. forced him to the floor. In the process it is claimed he hit his head on his metal bunk and began to bleed profusely. Complaining of neck pain, he was transferred to Huntsville Memorial Hospital. A CT scan showed "no sign of a fracture."

Back in his cell, he was unable to get up or move. He continued lying paralyzed on the floor in his own blood and waste for three days, calling for help. Eventually Cox was taken to UTMB's John Sealy Hospital in Galveston, where he died eleven days later.

---

[285] "A THIN LINE, The Texas Prison Healthcare Crisis and the Secret Death Penalty," *A Texas Civil Rights Project, Human Rights Support* 2011, 1.

> "The Galveston County medical examiner ruled his death a homicide as a result of blunt force trauma and medical negligence—a homicide in which no one was held responsible. The real killer: the appalling low quality of medical care provided in TDCJ."[286]

The *"Thin Line"* report argues that inmates like Cox continue to die because of the lack of accountability for such deaths. A "thick veil of secrecy" enshrouds inmate deaths. State law enforces the secrecy and even family members are not permitted to see all the documents related to the death of their relative

Poor medical care under TDCJ does not always end in death. Prior to incarceration, Alan Whitford injured his ankle in 2004. He did not receive his antibiotics as needed and his foot had to be amputated. At the time of the Human Rights report in 2011, it was hoped Whitford's leg might be saved.[287]

Josh Dillard had a long history of mental illness. (TCRP represented his mother in litigation after his death). After being confined in TDCJ his mental-state worsened. By 2002 he had attempted suicide four times. By 2003 he was diagnosed with major depressive and psychotic disorders.

These diagnoses should have resulted in increased mental care and supervision. Upon transfer, the new unit psychiatrist—without interviewing Dillard personally—changed his status to "no diagnosis", removing his designation as an inmate with "current psychiatric illness."[288]

On December 27, 2006, Dillard was placed in the solitary confinement conditions of Ad Seg, the penalty for violating prison rules. TDCJ policy in theory prohibits housing suicidal or mentally ill inmates in segregation, but the screening nurse was not made aware of Dillard's psychiatric condition. The next day he was found hanging in his cell, while also bleeding from a self-inflicted wound. He was taken to the hospital, where he died shortly later.

---

[286]   A THIN LINE, 15.

[287]   A THIN LINE, 20.

[288]   A THIN LINE, 30.

The TCRP's report includes in its Appendices what it calls three more "horror" stories:

Micah Burrell, age twenty-four, died from an asthma attack when guards ignored him in his Ad Seg cell because they judged he was faking.

Two days after being released and shortly before completing his entire sentence, Donald Novel (name changed), a Cystic Fibrosis patient, died from a heart attack due primarily to denial of effective medication and substitution of a medication banned by doctors of the Cystic Fibrosis Foundation.[289]

On November 14, 2005, TDCJ employees, including a physician's assistant, stood by while Juan Palote (name changed to protect privacy) committed suicide. While he was attempting to bring about death by hanging himself with a bootlace, a guard told him to stop or he would be pepper sprayed (a chemical that induces choking). Palote continued his efforts. When the Officers finally entered the cell, Palote was dead.[290]

If some innocent citizens are wrongly convicted and dispatched to Death Row, where at times they are executed before they can be exonerated, and if others suffer what *A Thin Line* has called "The Silent Death Penalty,"—what kind of treatment can we expect to find for other offenders, such as those confined within the walls of units run by TDCJ?

The treatment of Carlos Rojas and Earnest Hutchins within the court system, as well as Ned Parker and Charlie Gilmore, Jr. within several TDCJ units, at the very least raises serious questions. Yet these are only four cases. Are they rare exceptions? Personal experience with a large number of offenders in various units suggests that such failures are more systemic than "rare." Consider the following examples:

February 9, 2012, I received a letter from an inmate I shall call Jerome: He is a relatively young, generally cheerful and helpful African American man housed at Allred. During a "shakedown" a notebook of reflections written in a Kairos retreat and his Bible were taken and

---

[289] A THIN LINE, 44.

[290] A THIN LINE, 44.

never returned. The officer behind this subsequently had him "locked up" without justification and other officers collaborated in "destroying whatever they wanted to."

Jerome submitted a Grievance, but it was dismissed. In the year since this occurred, he continued to be the subject of various kinds of tormenting. Retaliation is prohibited under TDCJ policy, but nevertheless occurs systemically.

About this time a $100 medical fee was imposed on TDCJ prisoners by the legislature. The funds are deducted from offenders' Trust accounts they use for commissary, to be applied toward the cost of the medications, etc. Jerome wrote that this "crazy" policy resulted in inmates not seeking medical attention and becoming quite sick and a hazard to other inmates in order to avoid the fee. This happened to an ex-cellmate who developed a serous respiratory illness and spread it to those around him.

Jerome's letter culminated with a story detailing an incident that happened to another Allred offender ("Fred") on February 28, 2012 and days following. It involved "the unit Major of Corrections, Tim Wintry, [the same officer who made so much trouble for Ned Parker], Capt. of Corrections, Ernie Stepton and Lt. Don Thompson.

On February 18, 2012, a Sgt. and Correctional Officer were assaulted in Building 7. Lockdown status was imposed immediately. "About an hour or so later, Capt. Stepton, Lt. Thompson and some other officers came to my cell....then Capt. Stepton told me to 'strip' out of my clothes. They handcuffed me, took me down the run, stripped my cellmate and took him to the opposite end of the run. He was taken to Building 11 for pre-hearing detenton and

> "A few hours later a Sgt. came to my cell and asked 'What is your statement on this case for possession of a 10 ½ inch metal rod inside of a brown legal correspondence envelope?' I replied, 'you've got the wrong person, I came from G-Pod #11B. I slept on cold hard steel with no mattress, or blankets in the cold. Then days later they fed me three food loafs a day, for the following six days after.

"I lost ninety percent of my personal property including my family photos, greeting cards, addresses, etc. that Capt. Stepton threw away during the cell search."

Fred wrote that he had filed Step I and Step II Grievances and was preparing a Writ of Habeas Corpus under Disciplinary Proceedings. He insists

"These individuals must be addressed to the public under any and all circumstances for what has been done to me. This must not be allowed by any employee or ranking official in any institutions what-so-ever! Prison abuse is an everyday on-going issue that only very few outside of these fences know of!"

The experiences of Jerome and Fred underline once more the fact that offenders within TDCJ are regularly treated by staff as though they have no rights and can be subjected to whatever arbitrary "discipline" both high ranking and ordinary correctional officers wish to enforce.

Moving on with our stories, Leroy is a small man, a white inmate in his sixties, quite frail with poor hearing and eyesight, yet assigned to work hours before dawn in TDCJ's Walls Unit. On December 21, 2011, he suffered a hypoglycemic reaction also known as insulin shock, his second one in about twelve years. It was brought on because

"I was trying to eat less peanut butter sandwiches (in seventeen years I've eaten at least 6,000 of these sandwiches), and they have cut down on our food too, and that combination is not good for us. Also, when using insulin we must eat at the <u>same</u> times every day—no way that's possible in here

"As the time before, I was misdiagnosed, causing me to remain in a seizure state for almost two days while they sent me to [] Memorial Hospital and then on to [] Hospital in [], thinking I had a stroke or heart attack. These misdiagnoses are very dangerous. A diabetic (a <u>known</u> diabetic) should instantly be given an injection of glucagon, which is glucose, to get him out of a comatose state ASAP, to prevent any lasting harm.

Now I've become a chronic insomniac. Sometimes I'll sleep only two hours in a twenty-four hour period. I'm trying to get Medical straightened out on their care of diabetics, and it's now in the process of, I hope, change. They have tubes of a product called Glutose 15 which is for diabetics to carry on them <u>constantly</u> so when we feel we are going out we <u>immediately</u> take the entire tube. A so-called medical 'professional' refuses to let us carry these tubes—they do not even require a prescription. I'm going through the Grievance process to get these tubes dispensed to us. That medically ignorant person's failure to properly diagnose and treat me not only jeopardized my life, but cost TDCJ <u>quite a bit of money</u> they never needed to spend."

While suffering from colon cancer in the Allred infirmary, an offender in the cell across from Ned Parker, Brandon Horn, printed in pencil with a shaky, barely legible hand a twenty-one page statement describing some of the highlights of his stay in prison, as well as how he was treated as one of TDCJ's dying patients. In the early ninety's he was assigned to the Beto unit and worked in the kitchen. One day he witnessed an officer named Bulger apparently trying to rape an eighteen year-old named Johnny. The two were later called to testify against Bulger. He was disciplined and let it be widely known that one day he would set Brandon up.

Sometime later several officers came to his cell. Upon searching it they almost instantly "found" part of a hacksaw blade, painted red. Brandon pointed out that he worked in the craft shop and had ready access to black hacksaw blades, if he wanted to use one, whereas the red blade was the type used in maintenance. Nevertheless, he was found guilty of trying to escape and severely punished. Subsequently, higher ranking officers assured him they were going to get to the bottom of the case. Brandon's story suggests that he was treated fairly by at least a few of the ranking officers.

His ability in repairing prison equipment helped him gain favor with some prison personnel and Brandon wrote

> "I'm telling this to show I was trustworthy and the word
> going around that I would soon be up for S-2 or even 5-1
> [an improvement in security grade] before long." Instead of
> this happening, one day he was abruptly put on a bus and
> transferred to the nearby Michael unit.

There he was told by the Assistant Warden:

> "Plano and Black [Assistant Wardens at the Beto unit] had
> both been over there and told them what a shitty deal I had
> got because of Judy Dockman [Beto unit Warden]. He said,
> 'I'm going to put you on our best building (3A) and put you
> in the laundry.'" The Warden offered to put him back in the
> craft shop, but he declined.

When Brandon was moved out of the Beto unit, he was forced to
leave behind eleven desktop stereo radios that he had built in the craft
shop and loaned to various officers. Some of them eventually paid in
full for the radios, which was proper craft shop protocol. When he sent
an I-60 requesting return of the other radios, he was told they did not
exist. At this, he had his family hire a lawyer to intervene. Brandon
received a visit from the attorney and impressed upon him that "they
were committing theft by conversion—a felony." The unit received a
visit from the lawyer and the sheriff, the upshot being that the radios
were returned to Brandon at his new unit. He had them sent to an
orphans' home with which he had become familiar several years earlier.
This was in 1992.

One day a Capt. Canton told Brandon

> "'Horn, I've got some really good news and some really bad
> news.' He said 'I'm going to give you the good news first.
> I.A.D, has been working on this mess ever since it started.'
> A black woman officer named Mrs. Burns went to I.A.D.
> and said she looked at that piece of red hacksaw blade and it
> is the same piece of blade she found in J-Wing's pipe chase
> where the plumbers had been working and turned it in to her
> Lt. who was the one that charged Deron and I with escape.

"Judy Dockman [the Warden] called the three goons that had shook our house down, fired all three of them with no rehire on their records. Bulger had gone to the Warden… before all this started and stated that his wife and I were having sex on G-Wing. (She worked the eleven to seven shift). The Warden…then pulled Mrs. Bulger in and bluffed her and said they had proof that she was having sex with an inmate on G-Wing. She broke completely down and named the inmate. The Warden asked here 'What about Horn?' She told them she had never had anything to do with me, that she only knew me from the laundry.

"She fired Mrs. Bulger and Jim Bulger the same day, with no rehire. Capt. Friendly then picked up the story and said that he had heard that the Lt. that had charged me with escape was known to drink heavily and sometimes came to work reeking of alcohol. So, Capt. Friendly went to the unit on a weekend night and waited for the Lt. to come to work. When he came in, Capt. Friendly said 'Come here, need to tell you something.' He got the Lt. talking and could smell alcohol. So Friendly grabbed two officers and they escorted the Lt. off of the property and the next day he was fired for being drunk—no rehire."

"Capt. Canton said, 'Now for the bad news. About a week before all of this broke open, Capt. Nestor called and said, 'Canton, are you ready to go to [TDCJ headquarters] with me, I have the whole story on why they did Horn like they did and I'm going to get a bunch of people fired.' That night they found Capt. Nestor's truck parked on the road to his house and he had his driver side window down, and had been shot in the left temple. The gun was a …Smith and Wessen that was thrown over to the passenger floor board. The gun's serial number had been obliterated and Capt. Nestor was right handed. I asked if the Sheriff's dept. had run paraffin tests on Capt. Nestor's hand for G.S.R. (gunshot residue) or latent prints on the gun or on the shells. He said they just ruled it suicide, had a service and cremated him. I shed a lot of tears over his death. Capt. Nestor was my friend."

"I have written all of this out to show the perfidity that pervades this system. It only takes one liar to create a conflagration that can cause irreparable harm to people....
The biggest loser was TDCJ, when they lost Capt. Nestor. He was a decorated Airborne Ranger who did two tours in Vietnam....TDCJ can look high and low, they can hire many and promote many, but they will never find another man with the integrity and sensibility of Captain Nestor. OooRah Captain Nestor, OohRah!"

Horn concludes:
"Unfortunately, I have colon cancer, two strokes, diabetes and high blood pressure, and I can't fight back like I used to."

Another issue of great concern not only within TDCJ, but throughout the country's prison sysem is the use of "solitary confinement,"[291] which brings to mind the mistreatment alleged by Charlie Gilmore, Jr., who was kept in isolation for years. Gilmore was confined in these conditions, year after year, without an iota of psychological treatment or medication for mental illness. When his mental state was reviewed, he was found to be normal by health personnel [notwithstanding an avalanche of Grievances that would appear paranoid to some.]

The Allred infirmary has a small number of "psych" cells. Inmates who manifest severe mental problems are brought there, where they are stripped naked and given only a blanket, on the basis that suicide is being prevented. They could be kept there for up to forty-eight hours. Then they are moved to other arrangements or shipped to a psychiatric hospital. On one visit to the infirmary I heard an offender in one of the cells, which had no visible window, beating on the door and screaming. This went on continuously while I was in the building without anyone paying the least attention. As a volunteer I could say nothing.

---

[291] Neil Conan, "The Grim Realities of Life In Supermax Prisons," *Talk of the Nation*, National Public Radio, June 21, 2012, http://www.npr.org/templates/rundowns/rundown.php?prgId=5&prgDate=6-21-2012.

EPILOGUE

Having been apprised of what seems to have been a horrendous kidnapping/sex operation in Houston and possibly other large cities throughout the U.S, run by certain members of the "power elite", I felt obliged to bring to the attention of various authorities what I had been told.

In March of 2013 I communicated my information to Stephen L. Morris, the FBI's "Special Agent in Charge" in the Houston office, with copies of the letter to Greg Abbott, Attorney General of Texas at the time, Eric Holder, Jr., A.G. of the U.S., John Boehner, Speaker of the House that year, and the U.S. Commission on Civil Rights. On a later occasion I also spoke on the phone about the matter with another top FBI agent. The only response was from the Civil Rights Commission on April 11, 2013: "After carefully reviewing your correspondence, we find that it does not contain allegations that may be forwarded to an enforcement agency."

I had not asked them to forward anything. My purpose was to inform them about what the FBI was doing, or not doing. The Civil Rights Commission not only returned my original letter, they sent it back along with the envelope I used to mail it to them! Perhaps they did not wish to retain evidence of the correspondence in their files?

CARLOS ROJAS

When we last examined the correspondence of Carlos, it was February 27, 2012, over eight years from the present. In the interim, subsequent letters and events added substantially to his story and his fate.

In the letter of August 6, 2012, Carlos provides curious details about the circumstances of his arrest. After arriving in Texas in 1999, he made a friend named Enrique.

He eventually became a close friend of Enrique and gained his trust. Enrique confided in him that at the age of thirteen he was kidnapped and brought to Houston, where he was kept with other young boys. He was taken to a sex club in a seventy story office building located near Travis & Lamar—whose significance will become clear.

Carlos states that after he became friends with Enrique he started receiving phone calls in the middle of the night. When he answered, there was no one there. It was as if someone wanted to know where he was. The day he was arrested in August, 2000, was right after one of these calls. The police who arrested him did not even use his correct name. At the county jail someone else was used to provide finger prints to match the name they were using for his arrest.

He was taken to court every week "for nothing". They finally used a boy to accuse him, but his testimony at the Grand Jury was bungled and self-contradictory, and this time he was not indicted.

In his letter of April 8, 2020 Carlos provide insights into the two court-apppointed attorneys who represented him. He only talked to the first attoney (a Mr. Valdez who was only appointed five months after his arrest) three times. This man was useless and was replaced by Mr. Somoza.

Carlos **"told him many times that that was impossible to have met these persons in 1997, because I was not even in this country"** [emphasis added]. Carlos said he could prove this, if Somoza would help him. This help was not given. After his incarceration it took Carlos several years to assemble the nine documents demonstrating he was teaching in Cuba in 1997 and 1998.

Rojas filed a formal complaint against Mr. Somoza. August 16, 2005, Somoza replied to the charges against him. He claims he and Carlos did get along. His response consisted of a series of lies: He said he did the best he could, yet insisted Rojas never mentioned an alibi; he said Carlos never offered a list of witnesses, completely untrue; he asserted the State made an offer of eight years, yet the best offer was twenty years. Somoza did not acknowledge the fact that the State did not present a single witness to place Carlos in the United States, much less in Houston in 1997, other than the boy accusers and their mothers,. He did not bother to depose the witnesses for the State because he "already knew what they were going to say." He does not admit that after the prosecution signed off on its case, his entire argument for the defense consisted of the five words: "The defense rests, Your Honor."[292] It turned out that his "best" amounted to almost nothing.

Somaza's license to practice law was actually suspended at the time of the trial for non-payment of his student loan and was lifted only after the trial when he actually paid off the loan.

The concluding statement in Somoza's letter is the most problematic of all: "At the conclusion of this trial, Mr. Rojas was pleased with my effort [resulting in a Life sentence] and thanked me numerous times."

Carlos' complaint was dismissed and his appeal was futile. August 9, 2012 he received the reply: "the Board has determined that your appeal should not be granted as the conduct described therein does not allege a violation of the Texas Disciplinary Rules of Professional Conduct."

In his letter of May 16, 2012, Carlos mentioned for the first time the existence in downtown Houston of "a private night club exclusive for politicians, judges, and people from the high society; all they do there are orgies with minors of both sexes brought from many countries all over the world."

---

[292]   Rojas trial, Vol. IV, 114:13.

I asked Carlos for more information about this. His letter of July 1, 2012, began with an account of his troubles due to a cellmate transferred in from death row. Having killed his wife and two kids and mutilated their bodies, he had escaped the death penalty on the basis of insanity. This was the person the system placed in the cell with Carlos for thirteen months!

One day he returned from a meeting in the chapel to find that his psychotic "cellie had destroyed everything, broke my radio and hot pot into pieces and flushed all the commissary and cut the clothes, boots and shower shoes with a razor blade."

It was against this background that Carlos began to write about the activity in Houston. He came to know of the club through Enrique (mentioned above), who told him he had been kidnapped in Costa Rica and brought to Houston in a private plane with fourteen other kids. The others were moved to different cities, while he was placed in a big house on the outskirts of Houston with ten more kids from different countries like Russia, Romania, Albania, Bulgaria—even China.

Enrique told Carlos that these children "were compelled to a series of tortures and doses of drugs to erase the memory. He said that of all the kids who had been brought to that place, no one has ever escaped, all of them after two or three years die and are cremated."

Enrique was helped by a friendly guard in exchange for sexual favors. He was taught how to fake taking the drugs that would erase his memory of the sexual orgies. When he did this, there was a " man of renown and honor in Houston who ordered him to be murdered after he found out that he was not brainwashed and knew everything what he had seen in that place, even his name and what kind of depravation he has."

While he was being driven in June of 1999 to be executed, the SUV in which he was tied up was hit by an 18-wheeler. His captors were killed and he was rescued by two Colombians with whom he became friends. With regard to this incident that saved Enrique, Carlos added "I remember there was a report about the tornado which threw away several roofs of the houses of Channelview (that's the name of the place) and suspended into the air an eighteen wheeler. But it was by the Hispanic channel UNIVISION."

> "Enrique told me all these things on Mother's Day, 2000 [about three months before Carlos's arrest] in Houston. We spent there the whole day together and when we came back to Houston…showed me the building [near Travis and Lamar]."

Enrique confided to Carlos the name of the "man of renown" who ordered that he be killed. It seems plausible that, if the sex club did in fact exist, because of his knowledge of the club and the role of this individual, Carlos was arrested, falsely convicted and condemned to life in prison. All the other events that followed in his life flow from these circumstances.

August 28, 2012: I had asked Carlos if I should use a fictitious name in the narrative of the Houston operation. He replied, "I don't mind if you use my name on these stories. They can't do anything to me."

Carlos then supplied information supplied by a second source: "When I was in the Houston county jail I met a twenty-four-year-old young man….He also liked poetry and we became very close friends. His name was Johnny Johnson III. He was accused of a sex crime and he was waiting his trial's day."

After having known Carlos for eight months, Johnson revealed to him that he also had attended the sex club on many occasions. He described in detail what Enrique had disclosed. Through his contacts in the sex club he knew someone who would preside at his trial. This person had the charges dimissed for lack of evidence and Johnson was released.

"It was December, 2001. Jimmy had a wonderful Christmas; two months later he wrote me a card and gave me an address where I could always reach him, but when they moved us from the county to the Allred unit they took everything."

September 16, 2012: More information was provided about Johnson and the sex club:

> "Johnny Johnson finally told me that during three years that he had visited that place with his friend he had mess it up

with more than a hundred men there and also his friend, the [official]. Jimmy never met Enrique there, or if he did he couldn't recognize him because there were almost a hundred kids and they changed every two nights. They only have about twenty every night, but Johnny never was counted as one of them because he was the lover of one of the richest members....

"At that time in Houston County was [the official] who was feared by his cruelty. [He had] accused his own wife and son of conspiracy against himself. [His son was sent to prison where he was murdered and his wife received ten years' probation]. That is the man who fell in love with Enrique and when he discovered that the boy was completely aware of everything he was doing to him—he ordered his death.

"I was shocked to hear that the same man who has done so much evil to humankind....That man more corrupt than Tiberius Claudio-Nero.

"My ex-cellie psychopath came back to the same section, but they housed him in Cell 52....He tried to commit suicide on August 30, he tried to jump from the third floor, but someone who was close to him grabbed him and others came to help, including the guard and managed to slide him to the second floor and from there they took it to the hospital.... But I will file the Step I Grievance. They knew that man was crazy and they housed with me to put my life in danger."

In a letter of March 4, 2013, Carlos included a brief remark about the Houston official:

> "I didn't want to mention that name because that man is still powerful. Enrique told me he's a **psychopath** and **paranoid**, but a genius in wickedness and depravation."

Through July of 2016, Carlos continued to correspond. He had heard from an Innocence Project that they still had him on their waiting list, but there was no follow-up. On Sept. 17, 2015 he wrote to the Actual Innocence Clinic at the University of Texas:

"I have new evidence to prove my innocence beyond any doubt, but I do not dare to challenge the machine from inside prison. I have seen they have the power to overrule anything….They hate the word "INNOCENCE", that is why I am requesting your help. The courts want all of us to die in these diabolic dens of torment, abuse and mischief…. What hope is there?...What chance is there to survive the machine…?"

He did not receive any help. In the **Final Chapter** we will review several additional comments from his letters and document two critical developments.

NED PARKER

After September of 2011, Ned continued to write frequently. He sent approximately seventy letters after that date, in addition to a huge volume of copies of I-60s, Grievances, letters to TDCJ and other state officials, and documents preparing for a civil lawsuit. He continued to be tormented by the system:

He was given a major case for having the eye-glasses with which he came to prison. A lens had somehow disappeared and he was accused of having a weapon. Because of this, he was not allowed to phone his sister for ninety days.

Because of his need to have his "oxygen machine" with him, it was made difficult to use the Law Library.

At one point the warden unilaterally decided no infirmary patient could attend church.

He was not permitted to exercise by walking in a way that would be therapeutic.

No priest came to the infirmary to bring him the Eucharist.

He had to endure a continual campaign of harassment, inability to obtain items he needed from the commissary, lack of response to his identification of TDCJ policy violations.

He lived in fear because of the retirement of a Major and his replacement by an officer who had threatened his life.

He was confined in his cell at least twenty hours a day, but more often twenty-four hours, which meant that he could not even go down the hall to the dayroom.

There was a "hearing" for his case, but he was not allowed to attend to defend himself. When he was permitted to listen to a tape of the hearing, he discovered it was filled with lies told by the officers involved.

The prison infirmary doctor refused to order meds he had previously been able to obtain for years.

His body began to be covered by "scab looking protrusions" birthed from eczema red spots that looked like measles and itched terribly. He was told to treat them with a lotion that he would have to purchase for himself, but it was not available from the commissary.

March 1, 2012 he sent a packet including a three page letter to the Civil Rights Division of the U.S. Dept. of Justice, with copies or similar material to the TDCJ Office of the Inspector General, the TDCJ Attorney General, the TDCJ Civil Rights Project, a special TDCJ Commission, and the American Correctional Association. None of these submissions ever received a response.

> May 17, 2012: Ned expressed his excitement over the approaching TDCJ Sunset Commission Hearing and his desire to have input. Based on his personal experience he identified a number of areas TDCJ needed to address (1) Classification: "highly successful in isolating gang members and other dangerous inmates…but has left elderly population mixed in—with no way of monitoring failing ability to function and has yet to develop housing of medical inmates with similar diseases." (2) Disciplinary: "has perfected 'Cruel and Unusual Punishment' by violating every fundamental tenet of due process of law'. DSP is accountable to NO ONE and is confident they have nothing to fear from Federal Courts." (3) Grievance: "…functions blatantly/primarily to 'Watergate'/cover-up: policy features; prisoner abuse; TDCJ personnel rule violations; departmental failures; abuse of disabled prisoners; violations of religious freedom; violations of Federal & TDCJ codes, etc., etc." (4) Medical: "The standards and quality of care are imploding because 'Prevailing Standards of Medical Care' are ignored under the guise of 'safety and security.'"

Sadly, none of these deficiencies were recognized or acted upon by the Commission.

From this point on the treatment of Ned and quality of his life continue much as before. He was tormented by TDCJ practices, which he persisted in protesting, his health deteriorated and he was moved to the Montford Unit in Lubbock, Texas, where there was no improvement. As things got worse he was transferred to the Estelle hospital unit near Huntsville.

From this location on January 25, 2017 Parker mailed a letter to the American Prison Writers Archives in Clinton, NY, asking them to accept his story. The letter was accompanied by a "Staff Complaint" regarding security violations dated Feb. 21, 2016, a "Patient Abuse/Harrassment" declaration, May 2, 2016, a detailed list of harassment incidents, May 4, 2016, and a declaration of "Psychological Abuse of ADA Disabled Elderly Patient," May 15, 2016. Copies of all these documents were also sent to Texas Representative Toni Rose.

About the same I received copies of these documents from Ned. His letter was accompanied by his picture with two prison dogs. He was smiling, looked happy and as healthy as I had ever seen him.

On February 15, 2017 Ned wrote requesting an IRS form allowing him to check certain tax records, and he also needed the names of certain Executive Medical Directors and a "Super-Nurse" officer from the University of Texas Medical Branch/Correctional Managed Health Care system. His letter concluded: "Valentine's over and it's time to face the real world of the kingdom of Trump. Pray, pray, pray."

On March 6, 2017, I received an email from Ned's sister, telling me that on February 23 Ned had been taken to the hospital in Galveston, and had passed away on February 24, only eight days after requesting the information about the Medical Directors and Nurse. The death certificate showed the causes of his death as: COPD, pneumonia, renal failure, and Sepsis. He was 75 years old.

His sister was not able to ascertain whether he had even been given an antibiotic.

EARNEST HUTCHINS

For several years Earnest continued to serve his Life sentence, still believing that one day the Lord would find a way to bring about his release, so that he would not die in prison.

On one occasion a friend of Earnest's and I arranged a visit with his common law wife, Violet. On the morning of our visit, in addition to Violet, her sister (who is somewhat younger), Paul Mosely (the boyfriend of Earnest's accuser, Lacy, who is now her husband), and a baby just a few months old, were present.

When questioned about the alleged offenses, Violet confirmed what I had heard previously, that the two girls supposedly abused by Earnest had told her that nothing ever happened. I asked how the "victims" were doing now and Paul offered that they were not doing well. Mamie, in particular, was really messed up. He theorized that her present condition was the result of what had been done to her as a child. When I suggested that if a person was manipulated into telling lies that sent a man to prison for his entire life, and had to live with that, it might also mess with her mind a bit. He was silent but almost seemed to nod in a kind of unwilling agreement.

Throughout the years Earnest continued to hope that the Innocence Clinic connected with the Texas School of Law would take up his case. They did assign a student to look into it, but the effort was dropped when the student left for a summer vacation. December 4, 2017, Hutchins received notice from the Clinic that his case was being closed. He was told their decision had nothing to do with his possible guilt or innocence. They were simply unable to help. Earnest's last hope was that one day the girls would recant their false testimony.

Earnest would write several times a year. On March 5, 2018, he drew and decorated a Christmas/New Year's card, which my wife and

I received on March 12. On the outside of the envelope he had written "Amazing grace! I once was lost, but now am found."

When a number of months passed and I did not hear from him again, I phoned the records department at the Allred Unit. After some effort, they finally revealed to me that Earnest had passed away. He was 79 and had endured his final twenty years in prison. He loved to sing "This little light of mine" during prison services. I like to remember him that way, now singing his favorite hymn for the God whom he so trusted and loved.

CHARLIE GILMORE, JR.

Between April and September 2012, I heard from Charlie about five times:

May 6, 2012:

> "In every way as I been going through ongoing **abuse** and **torture**....Now I'm feeling real bad. Please keep me on the list for much Prayers.

May 7, 2012:

> "I was trying to get some good news to tell you. O.K., it's not.... No, the Dr. have not gave me nothing when my AFP test as high like this two times!...Yes, I'm sick like I got the pneumonia, in pain all over!... They are just letting it get <u>worse</u>. So it will be nothing they can do to help me."

May 29, 2012: Charlie wrote that—since not receiving the MRI in April—he had not been back to the hospital.

> "I have took too much of this ongoing torture.... You all please know it's a big need for you all to pray and write someone for me, the Ombudsman....

I did not have another letter from Charlie until August 8, 2012:

> "And the Dr. came on the run **two times** and told me, the officer and inmates that I have cirrhosis of the liver & Hepatitis C and that No I don't have cancer. He know that's not right letting everyone know all my diseases."

Charlie's letter of August 22, 2012 indicated that all of his customary problems continued unabated and he was more confused than ever about the true status of his health:

> "Oh, the Hepatitis C Dr. is a New One and now she is saying she don't think it's a good thing for me to do by taking the medication because I have cirrhosis real bad and the Med's can kill me! You know, every time it's something different. I don't believe nothing these people say, so I don't know what to do…? Our Love Always, Please take good care, You and Your Loving Wife!

October 25, 2012 I received a letter from Charlie's sister, Teresa, letting me know that Charlie had died. She had been told by prison officials that Charlie had been found unconscious in his cell, frothing at the mouth. Somehow he had suffered a serious injury to his head. Prison officials speculated he must have fallen accidentally. He was taken to the hospital in a coma. He died about two weeks later. The coroner judged that he had "died from natural causes." (Shortly before his death, I received a letter from another inmate at the unit who knew him well telling me that everyone on the wing "hated him." This observation might cause some to wonder how "natural" his death – related to a blow to the head – really was).

I wrote to the Office of the Inspector General and asked for information about Charlie's death available to the public. The reply indicated only that he had died due to "complications from a stroke." For several years Charlie had been writing of his fears of having a stroke, connected to his medical treatment. If this indeed was the cause of his death, his fears were not misdirected.

In almost his last words, Charlie wrote to his sister: "My death will count for nothing."

Goodbye, Charlie. Rest in peace.

CARLOS ROJAS:
THE FINAL CHAPTER

Carlos wrote a number of times between 2013 and 2016. His letters typically contained his reflections on the state of the world, how things are done in the U.S., and in prisons such as Allred. Excerpts from a few of his letters during this period follow, along with details of certain key events.

January 6, 2014: "If all those cheaters of the courts would fear the Divine judgment of God and would practice this rule, many of people wouldn't be here today. The judges and DA's have the power of life and death of the poor who are brought to them and they are cruel, merciless because they think that nothing can happen to them for the injustice they do….There are more people incarcerated for false accusation of sexual assault than anything else here in TDC."

February 24, 2014: "On January 28 a young man hanged himself on the fence behind 4-Building and the next day other was beaten and stabbed on the hallway. We are even worse than wild animals who don't kill themselves if they are of the same kind or species, but I can see an evil living inside of every human being, but how can we suppress the evil and vindicate the most noble instincts in human beings?" Because we humans are half gods and half beasts and some people are undecided if they would like to be gods or beasts.

"Many people who came to this prison with long sentences and knowing almost nothing about the System ended like shadows with human appearance leading to Hell in agonizing pain, where there is no help….No hope arises on the horizon, no light has shown for us in the other side of the tunnel of death….Our pleas are lost in the emptiness and no response is given; from the sky rises no echo, the echo is in our heart….We are wandering like shadows in the darkness of an interminable night, still I am singing at the gate of Heaven, waiting for the dawn."

May 5, 2014: Carlos commented on his court appointed attorney: "I don't think that Mr. Salazar (Joel E. Salazar was his actual full name) would ever answer my letter and if he one day would have to face the truth he will say he never has received any mail from me."

This letter was accompanied by a letter to the National Child Abuse Defense & Resource Center, asking for their assistance. He reported how he had been given two court appointed lawyers, neither of whom wanted to help him, but only urged him to plead guilty. In addition he explained how he was deceived by Salazar into not testifying: "At trial, my Attorney to stop me from testify told me if I did testify, the court will not allow my witness to testify on my behalf and I agreed because I did not know this stratagem. My witness came and swore but then was taken somewhere never to be seen again in court,…they never called to testify."

July 6, 2014: "I have not heard anything from NCADRC…I neither have heard from Actual Innocence from Austin, TX; a year ago they wrote me saying that I was on their waiting list."

On this same day Carlos wrote to Salazar, asking for his entire case file. He did not receive a response. When Rojas did not get the help he needed from Salazar, I contacted his office. I was told he had suffered a stroke, was taken to El Paso, and it would not be possible to obtain any documents (such as a police arrest report) related to the case.

Nov. 24, 2014: Carlos heard from Actual Innocence, only to be told that their backlog was two years. He added: "On November 2nd my friend committed suicide. He was barely twenty years old. That deeply affected me because I loved that kid, and I feel embarrassingly because I couldn't do nothing to avoid the terrible end of a beautiful human being who was my friend." This letter ended: "Today is Thanksgiving Day."

March 22, 2015: Carlos had tried to get us on his visitors' list, but had heard nothing. He also commented on issues at Allred: "There is many problems here because of personnel, people from the nearby towns don't want to come to work here lately they have hired a bunch of guards from Africa but due to that lack of personnel many times we don't have neither supper nor breakfast only sandwiches but they are not good."

June 28, 2015: A seven page letter written in his very neat form of cursive that mainly lamented the terrible state of things in the U.S. and many other countries. It ended with the sad reflection: "Those kids who I see it everyday [many sentenced to life without parole] they were disregarded, outcasted and predestined not by a god but for the *ELITE* to be criminals even before they were born and they are here to fulfill their fate to die in prison. I feel unconsciously a sadness and frustration when I hear that a baby is born, especially a boy,___I feel that they have to add another bed in prison."

August 19, 2015: "I am actually preparing all the evidence because this is the month they supposedly would begin to review my case. They have not contacted me yet but if they don't do it, I will write to them."

Carlos then expresses his concern about Ned Parker: "I fear for him because he is doing something very dangerous, suing the machine which is the devil itself. I can't believe he with experience and all the time he has spent here he still does not know the machine can get along with murder; I think he believed that Hart Wilson died by natural kidney failure. I am afraid that the same thing could happen to him." [Wilson was an inmate at Allred who also fought the "system." He was moved to another Unit where he soon died under suspicious circumstances].

Between this letter and the one following, my wife and I were able to visit Carlos at Allred. He was in good spirits and at this time had gained some weight and looked in the best of health. I believe it was at this time he told us when he was released from prison he was going to write a 500 page book revealing many things he could not disclose while in prison – too dangerous even to talk about them.

September 17, 2015:
Rojas wrote to the Actual Innocence Clinic asking about the status of his case and reminding them that he had been on the waiting list for two years. He concluded his letter "**I have new evidence to prove my innocence beyond any doubt** [emphasis added], but I do not dare to challenge the machine from inside of prison. I have seen they have the power to overrule anything….What hope is there? Dear Ladies and Genlemen…? What chance is there to survive the machine…?"

Undated, but after Thanksgiving, 2015: Carlos was informed by Actual Innocence in Austin that his case was under review and he would hear from them when the process was completed.

Nevertheless, his view of world affairs and his life in prison as expressed in his letters had become more and more pessimistic: "To where are we heading to as human species…? I don't see any future in the long term….We are doomed to the utter extinction and after millions of years life will emerge again….That is the ugly reality which many people don't want to think about it, people want hope,___but hope in what? I don't need hope, I want to live the reality___that is deepest than reason and right. We need to appreciate and care what we have because one day the things we have now they will be no more."

"On Nov. 24, a little past 11:00 a.m. another man hanged himself and died in E Pod, four bldg.. Is astonishing to see the coldness and indifference for human life in all these people." "When I see the prison's guards to come to replace the shift, most of them look like a bunch of demons who are coming to HELL to bring us fear and evil because they have been trained to be mean and cruel. Then in the middle of the night I try to see into the future and I cannot see---only darkness…darkness that envelops the whole planet."

"The System thought they could use me as rat of experiment. They checked me and after saying that everything was OK then the doctor told me that it was necessary for me to take a kind of pill in case that something wrong was in my system. I wanted to follow their game, I said yes but I never took any and after they tested my blood during three months I sent to see the doctor again and [he] told me that the pills were working good."

In light of what will happen in the following year, these observations of Carlos about his "treatment" and the state of his health are critically significant.

February 14, 2016: Carlos commented that things were getting worse at Allred. The prison population was overflowing capacity and inmates who did not have a job could be sent to solitary confinement, simply because there was room in that building "where there is an insane screaming all night long…some people have come back very scared after two weeks [spent in that building]."

March 22, 2016: "In the last three years has been a great affluence of youngster who come to prison with long sentences. That's something new. When I came to this prison in 2002 we could count the youngsters of medium custody with the fingers of one hand; now is quite the reverse."

"Like in other places, there are bad elements who come to work in prison because they like to abuse others and they find prison a good place to abuse of the inmates without being caught;…I have known guards who really hate the prisoners but there are many who are good persons, they do their job and never abuse to nobody."

Again with regard to the youth: "Most of these young men look like us though they are destroyed inside and they don't care anymore what they do it to them, when they get out they go full of anger, bitterness and hopelessness; how they can restart a new way of life in such conditions?... They were pushed into crime; the judges who most of them are sexual maniacs, psychopaths they don't hesitate to give at anybody the maximum of time." [Here we see Carlos generalizing from what he had been told about a corrupt Judge]. "About the forced labor, we are forced here to work for nothing and they don't care if we are sick or starving, what is that? Slavery? Forced labor? It's not the same?"

"My friend who is seventy six year old is sad that none of the Innocence Projects we wrote asking for help has answered. The only one was the one in Lubbock saying they can't help."

"About the poems [the forty he had written}, I have read some of them and the majority are no good, some only two lines I liked of them. I will rewrite all again. I send you one."

[The date of this letter is near the end of March. It is only eight months until the start of December. It hardly seems this is written by a man whose health is badly deteriorating.]

July 10, 2016: Carlos had heard from contacts in El Salvador that his victim was willing to provide an affidavit stating that the Court had told him everything to say at trial, under threat of being separated from his family if he refused. His accuser also revealed the name of the teacher who was having a sexual affair with him at the time he accused Carlos. This man (in 2016) was in prison in Florida. He also said he recalled the name of the person who trained him in the Court.

Carlos continued with comments on the candidate Trump that now seem surprisingly insightful:

"He is a malignant narcissistic spoiled of too much good [treatment] and he thinks he can reshape the planet, but he knows how to inflame the emotions of the people, appealing to their prejudices and foolish pride. He often says he would make the U.S. great again and everybody know that it's for the Whites because he's openly a racist."

"I hope that recantation will help because they said it is a requisite of Texas law to have a recantation. They say a phone call, e-mail, or a simple letter from the victim would be enough, they only want to fulfill a law requisite."

"One day we will sing at the gate of heaven again." [A remarkable aspiration from a man who often wrote that he no longer believed anything and claimed to be an atheist!]

July 27, 2016: In the first part of the letter, Carlos tells of how he had become friends with two of the "kids" in Allred, providing a few stamps to one of them and sharing some of his commissary with the other, assuring both of them that he did not want anything in return. They both liked poetry and inspired him to rewrite all of his poems.

He goes on to mention that he had received a letter from a former Allred co-worker, Gregorio, who had been released and was now in Santa Rosa de Lima, El Salvador, and had met the boy (fictional name of Antonio in the original version of this story - now a 28 year-old man) who had testified against him. Antonio told Gregorio the entire story of how his Sunday school teacher had asked for his help to frame Carlos to divert attention from his sexual molestation of the school boys. He also explained how the teacher had stolen Carlos's picture to give to the police to match to a driver's license and identify him. It was the teacher who had identified Carlos to Antonio's mother, getting her to testify against him in Court as the rapist against her son. As Carlos writes:

"Now I remember Antonio says the teacher told his mother he had saw Antonio with me twice in my truck [Carlos never had a truck] and she believed. Once in the court they instead of investigate if it was true, the court started to prepare Antonio and his mother, telling them what to say in court.

> "What concerning me more is that he says he will say in the recantation that ***the accusation he made against me in the 184th. District Court in Harris County Houston on February 9, 2002, was false and made up with the knowledge and assistance of the court and everything which they told him to say were lies.***"

Apparently by this time Antonio had already executed the affidavit recanting his testimony, since the above words were almost exactly those of the document and must have been shared with Carlos by Gregorio in his letter.

The letter of Carlos ends

"I wish everything continue good for you both. My greetings to K… (my wife). Sincerely, Carlos Rojas."

Although this was July, and Carlos always wrote every few months, this was my last correspondence from him. Possibly he wrote, but his letters were not allowed to come to me.

On December 8, 2016, I received the following letter from an Allred inmate to whom we had ministered:

> "Mr. and Mrs. [names redacted]: With the utmost love and respect, peace be with you. Thank you for the holiday cards. You are very good and caring people.
>
> "I am sorry to inform you that something terrible here happened to Senor Rojas, 12/2/16, 18-Dorm, S-Pod, between 10 a.m. and 3 p.m.. He was found unresponsive on his cubicle floor. He had been complaining to the infirmary about pains, but they would take it lightly, give him gas pills, and blow him off. Last Friday he went in again in desperation and they still turned him down. An injustice was done to our friend. Do you have any way of contacting his sister? I strongly believe they should have it investigated. The doctor didn't give him proper attention and Senor Rojas must have been laying there for a while, so the guards were not doing their proper check up either.…Peace be with you."

About the same day, I received letters from three other Allred inmates who lived in the dorm with Carlos, none of whom I knew, giving me similar information about his death. One gave the name of the Physician's Assistant who denied medical attention and the inmate stated he would be willing to testify about what had happened. Another said that Carlos was told he merely had a stomach ache, although he continued to suffer for two days. The final letter reported Carlos had gone to the infirmary three times and was turned away, being told there was nothing wrong with him.

It was clear from all of the letters that the inmates strongly believed the cause of Carlos' death ought to be investigated.

Just as these letters were arriving, I received a voice-mail from the Allred Unit asking me to phone Greg Burt, Department of Law Enforcement, Office of the Inspector General, TDCJ. When I returned the phone call, I was told by the Operator that there was no one at the Unit by that name. When I told her that he had just left a voice mail, she immediately put me through to him.

Mr. Burt denied everything that the inmates had reported. He said Carlos had refused treatment at the infirmary and that he was a liar. He claimed that he had previously passed Carlos working as a janitor in one of the corridors and he looked terrible, like a man much older than his actual age. He added that Carlos was a very ignorant, uneducated man.

After the call, I forwarded documents to Mr. Burt proving that Carlos had received a degree in Humanities in Cuba, and had taught in their schools at the very time he was accused of committing sexual offenses in Houston. The documents were sent certified mail and received at Allred. I never heard from Mr. Burt or the OIG again.

He never explained why Carlos, who his friends said was in great pain, would walk almost a quarter-mile from the dorm to the infirmary, only to refuse treatment three separate times. One must also wonder about the pills he was supposedly given for gas, considering the pills Carlos refused to take months earlier because of his suspicions.

December 21, 2017: I received a letter from Carlos's sister in New Sparta, El Salvador. Attached was the affidavit of "Antonio" in Spanish, with an English translation. The entire text follows:

"SWORN DECLARATION"

TO WHOM IT MAY CONCERN:

I, Antonio (true name replaced), 28 years old, bilingual public accountant, employee of the bank trade of this city with personal identification…and with address…[omitted here to safeguard his identity and location] REPUBLIC OF EL SALVADOR Central America. OVERY JURAMENTO DECLARO: Before the witnesses [two names of the witnesses of the affidavit omitted here] 'That the accusation I made in court #184 of Houston, Texas on February 9, 2002, is false and fabricated with knowledge and assistance of the court'

The Sunday School teacher of the Cristo Rey church located on Main Street, Pasadena, Texas. Jose Aleman, he had been the intermediate teacher for many years and had sexual relations with many even with me in the name of God, but when he realized that some brothers in the church were following him and accusing him he decided to make a scandal, a photo of [mistranslation of the word "de" for "from"] a house was stolen. A neighbor told my mom that she had seen me with that man in the photo and my mother believed her because she thought that man was a saint, I took the photo to school, the police and finally to the court we ended up memorizing a compilation of lies to accuse a man that I had never seen. When I was going to identify him, I asked how I would know who he is? do not worry, said the PROSECUTOR, in the whole room there is only one that we have dressed in black and white, he is CARLOS ROJAS: I gave his name to them to believe that you know him.

"I was used to commit an act of cruelty, vileness and shame, to send an innocent man."

THE NOTARY SUBJECT, GIVES FAITH: that the signatures that appear below the document are authentic because they have been placed in my presence in handwriting."

The names of the two witnesses follow, but the document does not include the name or a seal of the Notary, or any signatures, which would have been added on a second page.

After receiving this copy of the affidavit, I wrote to "Antonio" at the address given in the document, asking that he mail me a copy of the affidavit page with the signatures. I included a check to cover the cost of postage, but there was never a response and the check was never cashed.

In early 2021, I again wrote to Antonio telling him I was revising my book about Carlos and that I intended to use his actual name unless he objected. I have not heard from him.

CONCLUSION

W e have seen stories of possible false imprisonment (Carlos Rojas and Earnest Hutchins), neglect of cancer (Curtis Hutchins), medical mistreatment (Ned Parker), misrepresentation of self due to life's humiliations (Curtis Hutchins), and mental harassment, medical bungling, and betrayal (Charlie Gilmore, Jr.). Yet, as we see day after day in our times, we must be wary of what we do to our prisoners, for our society in one way or another may do it to any one of us.

Recommendations for Change

The stories presented here have documented in detail the pressing need for changes in our justice (prison) system. Because of the size of its prison population, the state of Texas provides an excellent subject for evaluation of the present status of reform of the correctional system. Texas has established a body known as the *Sunset Advisory Commission*. The Speaker of the Texas House appoints five legislators and one member from the public, while the Lt. Governor does the same for the Senate. A staff is hired to carry out the Commission's responsibilities. On June 5, 2012, it met to conduct its periodic hearing on TDCJ and the Correctional Managed Health Care Committee. In theory, if an agency does not pass muster, it would be abolished.

In the course of the June meeting 268 recommendations were submitted by various "interest groups" or members of the public.[293]

---

[293] Final Report with Legislative Action, *Sunset Advisory Commission*, July, 2013, http://www.sunset.state.tx.us/83.htm.

Under Item sixteen was included a suggestion to create an independent Task Force that would:

1. Investigate the various ways in which TDCJ is not complying with the Ruiz settlement.

2. Investigate the failures of TDCJ Health Services and Correctional Managed Health Care to provide the required standard of medical care for all offenders, and especially the elderly.

3. Revamp the I-60 and Grievance system to enable offenders to be able effectively to appeal TDCJ neglect of its own policies and procedures, in relation to health care, areas of retaliation, abuse of inmate property, and physical abuse, using a process outside of TDCJ [to ensure a modicum of independence. There is so much dissatisfaction with handling of Grievances within TDCJ, that even a TDCJ correctional Officer appeared at the hearing to plead for improvement of the system's treatment of complaints filed by officers.]

4. The Task Force should make every effort to identify and conduct in-depth, confidential interviews with inmates who have long-time experience in TDCJ and who are well known to volunteers.[294]

Also submitted were a multitude of well-thought-out recommendations coming from criminal justice advocates intervening on behalf of the many offenders and families, both of inmates and of their victims, who have pleaded for assistance from their agencies. Only a few can be mentioned here:

1. Institute an **independent** criminal justice Ombudsman's Office.[295] During the hearing proceedings, Senator Whitmire questioned TDCJ's Brad Livingston (the Executive Director

---

[294] "Final Report…," 82, item 16.

[295] "Final Report…," 83, item 20. Ana Yáñez-Correa Ph.D., Executive Director of the Texas Criminal Justice Coalition, Austin.

at the time) about the independence of his Ombudsman's Office, since it reports to him. He assured the Senator there was independence between that office and individual units. (It has been reported that this has not been the experience of offenders/families who have taken their concerns to the TDCJ Ombudsman's Office).

2. Require TDCJ to train correctional officers on how to model appropriate behavior for offenders, and instruct correctional officers in leadership, supervision, and management practices necessary to instill discipline in the offender population

3. Require TDCJ to review its Administrative Segregation policies, rely on a frontloaded program to ensure offenders are not gang-affiliated when released from Administrative Segregation, and place offenders back in the general population.[296]

4. Require TDCJ to administer regular mental health assessments and treatments to individuals in isolation for long periods of time.[297]

5. Create an independent Grievance Board, appointed by the Governor, and composed at least in part by members who were never employed by TDCJ. Members' credentials, expertise and decision patterns should be made public to constituents.[298]

6. Appropriate dramatically more money for offender health care.[299]

7. Require TDCJ to reduce reliance on the use of Administrative Segregation and increase opportunities for rehabilitation. Require TDCJ to reexamine classification policies that automatically assign security threat [gang] members to Administrative Segregation; undergo a thorough review of other states' Administrative Segregation policies, especially Mississippi's; and

---

[296] "Final Report…," 93, item 132. Matt Simpson, ACLU, Austin.

[297] Final Report…," Sunset Advisory Commission, 94, item 135. Ana Yáñez-Correa Ph.D.

[298] Final Report…," Sunset Advisory Commission, 94, item 145. Ana Yáñez-Correa Ph.D.

[299] Final Report…," Sunset Advisory Commission, 101, item 208. Brian McGiverin, Texas Civil Rights Project, Austin.

> assess individuals in Administrative Segregation for likelihood of violence.[300]
>
> 8. Release Texas' most medically expensive and least dangerous offenders.[301]
>
> 9. Reduce the prison population by increasing parole releases, reducing sentences for nonviolent crimes, or both.[302]

One might wonder how seriously the Commission would take the plethora of recommendations arising under "New Issues." Of the 268 suggestions, approximately 123 were submitted by Ana Yáñez-Correa Ph.D., Executive Director of the Texas Criminal Justice Coalition, Austin, ranging across the entire spectrum of TDCJ operations, from Administrative Segregation, to parole policy, to health care and food. While some of these were incorporated by the legislature, at least in a modified form, only one recommendation was accepted by the Commission without reserve, item 76: This proposal requested that the legislature study the impact of the current method of providing health insurance for CSCD staff and retirees (Community Supervision and Corrections Departments). It came from Chair of the Sunset Commission, Representative Dennis Bonnen.

While this no doubt is an important consideration, the fact that **not a single one of the recommendations coming from the public merited adoption by the Advisory Commission** casts a shadow over the effectiveness of the Sunset review process and the likelihood of future corrections reform in the state.

The 83rd regular session of the Legislature concluded in May of 2013. While some of the legislation was consistent with a few of the above recommendations, many areas needing reform were left untouched. There was little to reform internal performance: e.g., nothing was done

---

[300] Final Report…," Sunset Advisory Commission, 93-94, igtems 129-140. Ana Yáñez-Correa Ph.D.

[301] Final Report…," Sunset Advisory Commission, 104, item 235. Brian McGiverin and Michelle Smith, Texas Civil Rights Project.

[302] Final Report…," Sunset Advisory Commission, 104, item 236. Brian McGiverin and Michelle Smith.

about the deficient Grievance system, nor were any substantial steps taken to ensure appropriate medical care on individual units.

Notwithstanding modest contributions by the legislature, the pressing need in Texas (and similar states) for more intensive efforts to transform the system is exemplified by the following:

"Today the American Bar Association's Texas Capital Punishment Assessment Team released the <u>results of its more than two-year study</u> of the fairness and accuracy of the death penalty system in Texas."[303] The report finds that the Lone Star State is significantly out of step with better practices implemented in other states that allow the death penalty.

Notwithstanding all of the excellent recommendations for reform made to the Commission, the experiences of Carlos Rojas and the other subjects of this study point imperatively to several priorities for change:

- Dependence on Court appointed attorneys or public defenders must be radically revised. Funding should be sufficient to afford "equal justice" to all defenders.
- The "Grievance" system must be reformed so that legitimate complaints are actually heard and the appeal system is real, not perfunctory.
- The Medical system should be reviewed from top to bottom and adequalely financed, so that inmates in fact receive the "standard" quality of health care to which they are entitled by law.
- An independent commission should be established to investigate in depth the deaths that occur within TDCJ. There are too many "suicides" that are not actually suicides. There are other medical deaths that are the result of one form or another of malpractice.
- Finally, perhaps the foremost enemy of the American penal system is mass incarceration itself. There are far too many

---

[303] "American Bar Association Releases Texas Capital Punishment Assessment," *Texas Coalition for Abolition of the Death Penalty* Newsletter, September 18, 2013, 1, http://tcadp.org/2013/09/18/american-bar-association-releases-texas-capital-punishment-assessment/.

"offenders" unnecessarily in prison, and too few qualified, adequately paid correctional officers to supervise their care. Vastly reducing the prison population would liberate funds for other uses, including better medical and supervisory care.

The Ultimate Question

Of all of the issues raised in the histories of these men, what are we to conclude is true in the narrative of Carlos Rojas? Certain facts seem indisputable: He was in Cuba in 1997 when the offenses were alleged to have been committed; he was arrested in August of 2000 and not charged until over five months later, in January of 2001; transcripts reveal that both of his Court appointed attorneys were incompetent; the attorney during the trial was performing with his license suspended; after receiving a Life sentence he was placed in a cell for thirteen months with a psychotic inmate who had recently been released from death row because of his mental condition; this cellie obtained a razor; fortunately, instead of using it on Carlos, he merely applied it to cutting all of their property to pieces; in 2016, after more than sixteen years in Texas custody, in agony with stomach pain, he walked a considerable distance to the Allred infirmary three days in a row and was not treated but given only a pill – supposedly for "gas", as attested by four different offenders; as a result, he was found lying dead in his cubicle, after not having been checked on by guards at the customary interval; about the same time as his death, in El Salvador his main accuser executed an Affidavit recanting his testimony, saying he had never even met Carlos prior to the trial. (In the unlikely event that this admission were pursued, resulting in a new trial in which Rojas was found innocent, under Texas law it is possible that he would have been entitled to $1.6 million, the penalty for false imprisonment – another conceivable motive to ensure that there would never be such a trial).

Thus, it seems incontrovertible that an innocent man was imprisoned by the Texas system of justice for over sixteen years and ultimately died due either to intentional malfeasance, or deliberate neglect. Which raises the final question: did the story he had been told by two very different individuals (a victim and a participant) about a sex club of the elite in Houston lead to his incarceration and premature death – because it was true and had to be covered up?

On the face of it, the tale of the sex club strikes one as beyond incredible. Children snatched off the streets in foreign countries? Taken to sex clubs run by the rich and powerful in major U.S. cities? Drugged and used up in sex orgies, then disposed of who knows how? One of these clubs having an important Judge as a key member? Attempted murder of one of the young boys when he evaded the drugs and became capable of understanding what was going on?

Some years ago I had lunch with a retired executive who had held a government position at quite a high level in Oklahoma. In our conversation I briefly described the alleged activities of an important Judge in Houston. My lunch partner immediately guessed the name of the Judge and adamantly protested that this was a very fine man whom he knew very well and who could not under any circumstances have participated in the enterprise of the elite which Rojas had learned of from his friends.

Upon reading biographies of the Judge, one receives the same impression. He supported legislation on behalf of victims of trafficking, was a member of groups combating child abuse, and received prestigious awards for such work.

As improbable as association of such an individual with the sex club may seem, the existence of such an operation itself is not beyond doubt. When psychopathic individuals wish to hide evil behavior, they typically practice exactly the opposite kind of behavior in their public lives. Furthermore, in this age of absurd "conspiracy" theories, they are especially astute at destroying the credibility of anyone who might expose them. How better achieve this than have one who has discovered the sexual exploitation convicted of pedofilia and sentenced to Life in prison?

In recent years, sex trafficking has received extensive attention and an astounding number of individuals believed to be of unquestionable character have been identified as involved in a variety of sex offenses:

the notorious Jeffrey Epstein and Harvey Weinstein, James Divine and Placido Domingo in opera and TV commentators or executives such as Bill O'Reilly and Roger Ailes, well known football coaches), entertainers like Michael Jackson and Bill Cosby, highly trusted physicians assigned to take care of young girls preparing for gymnastic events in the Olympics, thousands of Catholic priests, some bishops, numerous Boy Scout leaders, and possibly certain politicians (such as Donald Trump and Andrew Cuomo – accused but not convicted, and most recently Congressman Matt Gaetz, close associate of Trump, alleged to have indulged in sex parties and have had sex with at least one minor) . Often the sex offenses continued unrecognized for years, if not decades.

The sex club of the elite that Carlos Rojas was told functioned in Houston in the year 2000 actually may never have existed. If it did, it probably has long been dissolved. If it did exist and had been exposed, it would have been one of the most egregious sex scandals in American history: involvement of individuals in the judiciary, the CIA, the District Attorney's office, the police, and TDCJ (OIGs office, correctionals officials and medical personnel). Kidnapping of children from foreign countries, sexual orgies with drugging of the victims, cremation of those who died, false imprisonment and eventual liquidation of the one who knew. Unimaginable!

Yet strange things have happened in our times. A mob of "patriots" marching on the Capitol, rioting, breaking in, searching through offices to find and hang the Vice President. Never in 200 years! Unimaginable!

But what of TDCJ? Perhaps it has introduced needed reforms in recent years? Inmates with whom I regularly correspond have given no indication of such improvements. Just last week I received a letter from a Texas inmate asking that I contact the Ombudsman Office on his behalf. While doing his SSI work he was assaulted by a "close custody" inmate who should have been confined in his cell. He had to be hospitalized with serious injuries. If the Texas Sunset Commission had been able to meet as originally planned, perhaps some light would have been shed on recent advances, but Covid-19 prevented such a possibility. On the other hand, one significant negative development has surfaced recently.

Keri Blakinger is a reporter for *The Marshall Project*. She testified as part of a panel at the Texas Coalition to Abolish the Death Penalty on February 27, 2021, that she had been trying to obtain data from TDCJ on the effect of Covid within the institution. Not only was she not given the data, she said she was lied to and sued to prevent her from obtaining the data. If TDCJ cannot tell the truth with regard to a matter as basic as this, why should it be believed when it "investigates" the death of Carlos Rojas?

Thus, we are left where we began. Very little seems certain; most allegations cannot be proved. However, two facts have been established: the accuser has recanted his testimony, and it did not happen in a way that saved Carlos Rojas. Possibly it may have precipitated his death. May you who read his story and that of others in this work be so astute as to perceive the truth and discern what is false, so that in your own world you may begin, or continue, to do what needs to be done.

In his last months Carlos had his hopes. But they expired in illusion. Perhaps resignation to this outcome was reflected in the darkness of a final poem:

Welcome to Hell!

Eternal light forever shines, upon this cruel world unfair.
The reign of Lucifer, where the poor fade and pine.
Thunder may moan far away, yet light comes never again
For those in everlasting pain, every night and every day.
A living Hell with rising towers, cruelty and corruption alone are seen.
Perversion, Queen of the night, where rules alone the tyrant's power.
For those who from man's grace have fallen, their world teems with monsters all around.
Glory honors only the most ugly and unsound,
While the vilest worms proclaim, "Welcome to Hell!"

Carlos Ismael Rojas

"'A THIN LINE,' The Texas Prison Healthcare Crisis and the Secret Death Penalty," *A Texas Civil Rights Project, Human Rights Support 2011*, 1. www.**texas**civilrightsproject.org/docs/***thinline***/tcrp_***thinline_2011***. pdf · PDF file.

Beecher, Henry Ward. "Peace be Still," 651, *American Sermons: The Pilgrims to Martin Luther King, Jr.,* copyright © 1999 by Library Classics of the UnitedStates, New York, N.Y. All rights reserved.

Bond, Bill/with Adler, Max. "Second Sight," *Golf Digest*, May, 2013, p. 57.

Colloff, Pamela. "Innocence Found," *The Texas Monthly,* January, 2011, http://www.texasmonthly.com/story/innocence-found.

Tietz, Jeff. "Slow Motion Torture," *Rolling Stone* Issue No. 1171, December 6, 2012.